Portraits

A Novel

By

Sharon Teresa

Here I Am Publishing

Portraits

ISBN 978-1-937429-00-3

Portraits

The Greatest Mystery Can Be Life Itself

Luis, this book is for you.
Without you, it would
not exist.

You once told me, in a dark hour of mine,
to *Look to the Light.*
I'm doing my best, Sweetheart.

We'll see you in the
5th Dimension.

Acknowledgments

I would first like to thank my husband and kids, who offered encouragement and support through all the ups and downs of writing this book. Thank you, my darlings. And thanks to Tom Bird for guiding me through the process of getting my book from "there" in the ethers, to "here" in this reality. Thanks, Tom. And thank you, Joannara Fox, Animal Communicator extraordinaire, who personally helped me "talk" with my four-legged kids on a level previously never experienced. Amazing. Any misrepresentations in this book, concerning her fine craft, are mine, not hers. And thanks to a well known medium for relaying the message from my departed father to "Write that book! You're not getting any younger, you know!" And gee, thanks, Dad—for the sentiment and all....

Thank you Alli, Nate, and Jazzie, for allowing me to share in your lives. And last, but not least, thank you Infinite Universe because, with your endless number of possible realities, this story is true—somewhere.

Foreword

Luis, a feline companion who was teacher, comedian, and guardian angel, was with me for almost every word I wrote of this book. He was there beside me when I finished the first draft (which remains largely intact) as we listened to one of his favorite CD's—Kamal's *Reiki Whale Song*. Soon after, Luis passed over.

For months after that I couldn't pick up my manuscript. Finally, one day, the pain had lessened enough to at least take a look. Since I had written the entire book using Tom Bird's method (which involves connecting to your Higher Self and channeling a book you assume is already written, since time is an illusion) I had little recollection of details. Upon reading it I realized that much of the journey experienced by Alli was the same journey I was taking—guilt, recriminations, loss (although cloaked in different circumstances)—then, finally, redemption and growth.

I suppose a critic might say that this book can't make up its mind. And perhaps they would be right. But neither does life make up its mind. It's sometimes mundane, sometimes beautiful, and sometimes scary. It's part comedy, and part tragedy—with love and loss and mystery thrown in. But, in the end, we've learned something.

May this story entertain you, touch you, and help to ease your journey—and may someday we meet, as friends, in the coming New Dimension.

Chapter 1

Walking away should be easy, shouldn't it? I mean you just put one foot in front of the other and keep moving. Yet it had taken me two years to walk away from my marriage, mincing along one little cramped, agonized step at a time. And no, the agonizing isn't something I'm proud of. But the leaving is. And in the end I'd loved it! When I finally drove away for good (my ex watching from our front door, disbelief lining his face), and when I'd finally cleared the towering red rocks of Sedona, and the vistas opened before me — I'd cried like a baby. With relief. I'd returned to the Valley of the Sun, to friends, to laughter, to freedom, and I could breathe again. It was, in a word, glorious. Now the bastard I'd put safely away in my past was here. Right here in my kitchen. Right here on my newly tiled kitchen floor. Lying right here, dead, in a big pool of blood. Blood which will, I fume, probably stain my new grout. My expensive, custom-colored, drive-my-tile-contractor-crazy-with-my-anality, grout. God! Do you have any idea how many paintings I had to sell to pay for this kitchen remodel?

The man is dirt.

"Hi, Rico," I murmur as my little buddy saunters in. "What do you make of this?"

Rico sits and calmly surveys the gruesome scene before him. He looks up and beams at me, then starts purring his brains out, all happy-happy, joy-joy boy. Which somehow does make me feel better.

"Yeah, I know," I laugh. "But look at my floor!"

Rico gets off his ass and stretches languidly, first his front legs, then his back. He sashays over to my dead ex and stares in earnest for several seconds, frowning at the bloody mess around him. With all the sincerity he can muster, Rico then lifts his beautiful face. His solemn eyes meet mine, searching their depths, soul to soul. Then with a snicker he starts purring again. Big, wet, trilling purrs.

"Yeah, yeah," I sigh. "You didn't like him either. And you're right. It's worth the price of having to have the grout cleaned to see him dead. But shit, Rico! I really didn't need this right now."

Rico just keeps beaming and purring and saunters off. Probably to find Bonnie and give her the good news.

Pacing the kitchen, carefully avoiding the blood, I wonder what to do now. What pisses me off most is that I also paid for a security system when I had the kitchen redone. A security system which had somehow failed, since dead-man is here cluttering my floor and the security panel is all pleased as punch with whatever went down. So, on that note, I call Christian, the guy who sold to me and installed the system. The guy who may or may *not* be my friend anymore.

"Hey, Christian," I sneer into the phone. "How're you doin'?"

"Oh hi, Alli!" he sings back, all chummy-chummy good mood. "I'm great! How 'bout you?"

"Well," I say, "I have a little problem."

"Problem?"

"Yeah. With my new system."

"Really? What's wrong?"

"I'd prefer you come see for yourself," I tell him. Then I add, "Yes. You really *should* come see for yourself."

By now Christian perceives that maybe I'm not in the best of moods, so he says he'll be right over. Perhaps with just a *touch* of suck-up in his voice.

"Good," I say. And punch the off button, wishing I had an old-fashioned phone I could slam down. It's hard to make the same statement with current technology.

I move to my newly installed wood-framed window and stare out at the ancient, desert landscape. The utter peace of it calms me a bit. Involuntarily I take a big breath and slowly release it. Then another. My breathing slows altogether as I soak in the lengthening shadows and the first hints of heart-stopping gold outlining the maverick clouds. I realize it's shaping up to be a beautiful sunset. Not that those are particularly rare around here. As a matter of fact, they aren't rare at all. But I treasure each and every one. Time to pour a glass of wine and step out.

Choosing a full bodied Cabernet with a kick-ass 14.5% alcohol content because, after all, there is a dead guy in my kitchen, I pour a generous amount into my biggest wine glass. I call for Rico and Bonnie, who come trotting out from the front room, and we all step outside together. Rico, in particular, likes sunsets. Always has. He takes an easy leap to the top of the patio table and plops down, sprawling to face the west. Bonnie hears the rustle of a lizard in a sage bush and bounds off to show it who's boss. She's not really that much into sunsets. And, fortunately, she's hardly ever the "boss". But we take our fun where we can, right? I swirl and twirl the wine in my glass, then fish out a gnat. Before I can acquire another little beastie I take a sip. It's really, really good. Yes it is. Before long I may just forget the asshole in my kitchen.

Okay. I'm dreaming.

In the quiet of the growing dusk I hear Christian's car pull up my drive. As the door slams I call out that we're in the back and the gate's unlocked. Christian appears, carrying his satchel of tools. As though *they* are going to solve my problem! But then, I remind myself, I didn't let poor Christian know exactly what the problem was, now did I? By now the few sips of wine I've had have gone to my head, and I actually feel bad about the way I treated Christian earlier. Oh well. I'll make it up to him by inviting him and his partner, Ben, to dinner soon. They are the only gay couple I know where neither one cooks, so they always appreciate my invitations. Not that I'm a great cook or anything. But, you know — everything's relative.

"Hey, Allison," Christian almost whispers. Uh-oh. He's called me Allison. Guess I really did make an impression!

"Hi, Christian. Look, I'm sorry about the way I acted earlier..."

"No, no! If there's something wrong with the system then I expect you to be upset!" Very tactful, I think.

"Well, nice of you to say so, but I still apologize," I murmur, head down, watching my gnat-filled wine.

"Okay, well, that's all out of the way. Can we go see what the problem is now?"

"Sure," I say, then start giggling as I lead the way to the sliding glass door.

Floating like a dream, I open the door, step through with Christian right behind and, as he blurts out "Oh my God!" my giggling dissolves to tears.

"What the hell happened here?!" Christian screams, sounding even more panicked than I.

"I don't know!" I retort. Somewhat testily. Which is a good thing, because it means I'm not going to get hysterical. "I just came home and found him here like this! God, Christian! I don't know what happened!"

"Do you have any idea who he is?" Christian asks, gulping back what appears to be an oncoming fit of nausea.

"Ummm...," I hedge, "well, yeah. That part isn't a mystery," I finish. Christian just looks at me, eyes round, brows raised in a knit. Kind of like he's never seen me before, and I'm the two-headed boogie monster who used to hide under his bed as a boy. "Ummm...," oh jeez. "He's my ex-husband," I finally exhale in a rush.

Christian just continues to stare at me and I realize, when he's giving me *that* look, I don't think he's quite as attractive as I usually find him. At just over six-foot, all muscle, slim hips and long legs stuffed into tight, designer jeans, he usually makes both sexes sigh. And if you're into green-eyed blondes with long necks, chiseled chins, and cheekbones worth paying a fortune for, then you really appreciate the hunk he is. Actually, I wonder how Ben got hold of him. I mean, Ben *is* a very talented sculptor, and a super nice guy, but he's also a tad on the frumpy side. Okay. Let's be real. He's a total frump. A mushy lump. A whining grump. Okay, okay. I made up the last one. But suddenly I'm feeling very poetic! Frump! Lump! Grump!

Okay. Here comes the hysteria.

As though Christian realizes the screaming meanies are beginning their assault, he rushes over and pulls me into a reassuring embrace.

"I'm sorry, Alli," he croons. "I'm so, so, sorry." He strokes my hair like I'm a little girl, and, I admit, it helps. "Did you care a lot for him?" he whispers into the top of my head. Which, of course, brings giggles. Then snickers, then out and out snorting which turns quickly into a full, howling belly laugh. By now Christian has, obviously, released me, and I double up with laughter, holding my sides which are starting to hurt. Christian spreads his feet and firmly places both fists on his hips, glowering me into submission.

"Okay, okay," I hiccup. Breathe, Allison, breathe. That's it, I tell myself. Okay. You've got it together. Okay. One more deeeeeeep breath, then let it go. Yeah. Okay. I turn pleading little puppy dog eyes to him. He continues glowering. "Actually, I hated his guts." There. Said it. Something passes through Christian's eyes that I can't exactly read, but I blink it away. Now it's his turn for a big breath, which I notice makes his tee shirt nice and tight around his pecs.

Good. I'm coming back around.

"Okay. Well. Are the cops on their way?" he asks. "I'd have thought they'd be here by now."

Oh. Cops.

You see, that's the funny thing about left brain, right brain. For most of my life I was a total left brain person. No one did better in school. No one was better at debate. I earned my living keeping books, running offices, creating bids for high-end custom homes. Once, in a Sedona office where I worked, I met a woman who turned out to be a writer. Curious as to how a writer handled a certain something (which something escapes me now) as far as income taxes went, I asked her about it. In a very friendly way, I might add. And to my smiling face she returned one of the most snippy, whiny scowls I've ever experienced and said, "*I don't know anything about doing taxes. I'm a writer!*"

Of course I figured she was the biggest ding-dong I'd ever met, and for days after I found myself muttering with a sneer, *I don't know...I'm a writer! Give me some shoulder pads so I don't hurt my head!*

But, the funny thing is, when I quit all that 9 to 5 stuff and started to paint, yep. The left brain started taking vacations. Like now. Cops? Wow. What a concept!

Hadn't even crossed my mind.

As I stand here, contemplating the merits of shoulder pads, the phone rings.

Chapter 2

From somewhere down a deep dark well, my dizzy mind struggles to grasp from where the annoying sound emanates. Then I realize my eyes are closed. So I open them and am rewarded with the sight of my bedroom aglow with the first rays of sunrise. The phone is on my nightstand, and won't shut up, so I reach for the tiny beast to answer it. But just as I do, the ringing stops. Somewhat dazed I replace it on the stand. Then I struggle to a sitting position, pulling my blanket tight around me. Even though it's summer I'm chilled. And confused. Wasn't I just in the kitchen with Christian? Wasn't I just about to explain why I hadn't yet called the cops concerning my dead ex, who was lying about my floor in a bloody muddle?

And, another mystery. Who the hell was calling me at this hour of the morning?

Snatching the phone I press the button for caller ID. Last call listed punches me in the stomach. It's my ex's number. Crap. Crap, crap, crap. What the hell is going on?

Then, as the light of dawn brightens, so does the light bulb in my head.

It was one of my famous dreams.

Or should I say infamous dreams? My startlingly real dreams had been one of the things my ex bitched about. At least twice a week I had to ask if I had actually done or discussed something with him — or had I only dreamed it? He grew to find it very annoying. Toward the end of our marriage he wouldn't even let me finish the question before he'd cut me off with, "You dreamed it, stupid."

So, it was all only a dream? I lie back down and start going over the details in my head. Find the body—check. Rico saunters in—check. Rico examines the body—check. Ohhhhh jeez. Okay. Definitely a dream. Rico doesn't snicker. At least not out loud. And Christian—Christian knows who my ex is, which he didn't in the kitchen. So, yes, it was only a dream.

Feeling a mixture of relief and regret I spring from bed and sprint to the kitchen. Sure enough, it's perfect. But just for future reference, I think I'll research whether or not blood comes out of grout.

Even though it's a good hour and a half before my usual time to rise and shine I decide to stay up. I put the coffee on and scoop out some food for the kids. Rico and Bonnie will be up soon, and I've selected their favorite breakfast to help diminish the disappointment of denying them their morning game. You know the one—the "what can we knock over (that won't actually break) to get mom mad enough she can't go back to sleep, so she'll get up and feed us" game. That one. I have to smile to myself. I honestly don't know what I would do without them.

As I'm wiping out the cat food can for recycling, the phone rings. Jeez. Good thing I didn't bother with trying to get more sleep! I grab it and check the number showing on the display. Cool! I punch the on button and sing, "Good morning, Jazzie! What's up?"

Her weary voice replies, "Glad to hear *you* are in such a good mood. But I guess that's because *you* didn't answer the phone when Don-the-Con called."

"Oh my god. He just called you?"

"Yepper," she sighs. "Said he had tried your house and you didn't answer. Said he was *worried* about you."

"Oh, crap," I mutter. "I'm so sorry Jazzie." I know how much she hates my ex—as any fine friend would. She has stood beside me through it all, lending support of every kind, including financial when I needed it. She's proud of the way I've come back into myself, rescued myself, from the cowering, dithering, puddle of goop I'd become, married to Don. And she's proud of her role in my transformation back to someone who can sparkle again. "Did he say what he wanted with me in the first place?" I ask.

"No. He didn't," she snaps. "And I advise you to think twice before you have *any* contact with him, for *any* reason," she finishes. Good advice, I think to myself.

"I'll take good care," I say, as reassuringly as I can. "And I'm sorry you had to awaken today to his slimebag voice," I add.

She sighs her thanks and tells me she has several appointments today for readings, so maybe it's a good thing to get an early start. We exchange our goodbyes and disconnect. As I pour my coffee I wonder—just what the hell is Don up to now?

Then something tells me, I don't really want to know.

Chapter 3

I have two commissions I'm working on at the moment. When I don't have commissions I paint whatever I want. But my specialty is that, what I paint, comes true. Therefore people hire me to paint for them what they wish to manifest. I first noticed this gift of mine a few years ago. I had just started painting for fun, and was very stylistic in my art. I painted several things that don't actually exist in "reality", but as the months went on I was suddenly finding these "unreality" things here, on this plane! Leaves were variegated that weren't supposed to be variegated. Grasshoppers were golden. Things like that. So, I tried it out for real. I painted what I wanted to see. And lo and behold, everything came true! I painted an inheritance for my ex. I painted laughter for myself. I painted a new home for a friend. All came true. So that is what I now do. I paint new hopes for people.

One of my present projects concerns a woman who wants the perfect, new, dog companion. She lost her great dog love a few months ago and contacted Jazzie for one of her consultations. Jazzie is an animal communicator who can telepathically tune into animals, both living and those who've passed over. In her consultation with the woman she learned that her deceased dog very much wished for his mistress to find another dog to take care of her. The woman, however, was reluctant. Then one night the woman had a dream of what her new dog would look like. However it was a very unusual dog, and she didn't think she would actually find the dog she dreamed of—the dog she was sure her loving companion wanted her to find. So Jazzie told her about me, about my art. And the woman commissioned me to paint her new dog. She felt more confident that it would manifest into her life that way.

My second commission is of a more esoteric nature. A gentleman wants me to paint him a new consciousness, so to speak. He wants to see himself as "enlightened". I'm doing my best on that one. If I didn't have so much faith in my work I might not be able to accomplish the task, as, though I know it's not for me to judge, I think the guy's a real jerk. But I've been given this gift, and a commission is a commission, after all.

I take my coffee and wander into my studio, Yes, it is a wander— I'm still not fully awake. At my large north window I stand and gaze at the serene morning landscape. The mocking birds, doves, and woodpeckers are all loudly singing, so as to drown out the others. The hummingbirds are at battle over the two feeders hanging from my mesquite tree, and the quails are calling, calling. From the black bands across their chests I can see they are males, young, smaller than the hunks that usually strut through my yard. *Don't worry, guys*, I think to them. *Next year you'll find fine mates, and raise many strong children to grace my landscape.*

I sit at my easel and stare at the portrait of the man I'm painting. I decide I'm not taking him seriously enough. I mean, who am I to say what the proper route to enlightenment is? Jeez! I need to repaint the whole thing. I've painted him with a smug sneer for chrissake. What was I thinking?

Not ready to paint just yet I get back up and return to the kitchen. Rico and Bonita (that's Bonnie's formal name) are just finishing their breakfast.

"Hi, kids!" I call with more cheer than I feel. Rico answers with a thrppp. Bonnie doesn't say anything, just licks her lips and moves to her water dish. She's a woman of many, many words when she has something to say. But when she doesn't, conversation bores her.

The events of the night or, rather, the non-events, have left me feeling ill at ease. I'm disjointed in my thoughts, totally unable to concentrate on anything. Okay, I tell myself. Maybe a swim will help. Cool water on my skin, velvet ripples caressing me. Moving quickly to my bedroom, in a hurry to shed my nightgown and my mood, I decide that skinny-dipping is in order. That's the nice thing about living out of town like I do. Privacy is not at a premium. I toss my gown ingloriously to the floor, sure that I at *least* need to wash the sweat of the previous night's illusions from the fabric — not sure if I even want to keep it at all. I open the slider that leads from my bedroom straight to the pool area, and dive headfirst into the still, cool water. In a month it will feel more like a spa, but for now the water is refreshing and perfect. Coming to the surface I begin a slow stroke, languid almost. I turn on my back and let my arms be loose at my sides, propelling myself with only my legs and feet. My long hair brushes against my shoulders and back, feeling like seaweed in the water. I approach the other side of the pool and latch onto the ledge. The sun has risen enough to kiss my face with its still gentle warmth. Later, like say in an hour, it will feel fierce and powerful. It will be king. It will rule with the power of life and death if one is not careful. But at this early hour, it is a beautiful friend. A consort.

Feeling the need to quicken my blood I start some serious laps, stroking hard, kicking hard, reaching as far as I can with each pull of the water through my arms and hands. I become the one with power. I become the ruler of the moment. I bring into my body the essence of the desert air — clean, dry, magical. The oxygen awakens me, rejuvenates me, exhilarates me.

I pull up to the shallow end of the pool and lift myself up and out in one smooth move, depositing myself on the deck, letting the water run from my hair to puddle around me. It cools the already warming deck to body temperature, creating a feeling of floating indifference.

Only my legs, which still dangle in the water, seem to be in touch with anything concrete. But the air of power remains.

I will not let my ex take from me that which I've so worked to gain. I have a beautiful and meaningful life. It's mine, and I'll guard it jealously.

Rising to my feet I stroll confidently back to my bedroom, leaving the slider open to the call of the birds. I rifle through my closet until I find the garb that sings to me—a colorful tee shirt in the shades of a desert sunset, and a pair of comfortable white jeans. I step into the bathroom to brush my teeth and fix my hair, but decide that clean teeth is enough. I leave my hair to dry naturally, combed, but on its own after that. Besides, wet hair is very cooling, and the heat of the day has begun exerting its control.

Back in the kitchen I reach for cherries and homemade kefir. What the heck, I think, and add a large, gooey muffin to the plate. Striding to my little wrought iron breakfast table I plop down my morning selection and start on the muffin with gusto. Crumbs fall to my plate, and some to the floor. I don't even care. There's something about this morning that has given me an almost sadistic impetuousness. Inner power surges through me uncontrolled, and I grant it full freedom. My aura expands to fill the room.

I charge through the cherries and kefir, thanking them for their sustenance, yet aware that I ate with less grace than I should have. Apologizing to them I promise to do better next time. I take the dishes and place them unceremoniously into the sink. I'll load the dishwasher later. Then I grab my purse, holler goodbye to the kids, and head for the garage.

Where I'm going, I have no idea. I only know I must get out of the house for awhile. The morning is fully awake now and the heat bears down on me, as I've decided to leave the top down on my convertible. In the summer, in the desert, top-down riding is usually reserved for nighttime, when the air is warm but silky. However, today I am brazen. Today nothing can beat me up or make me hide. Today I am alive.

But I'm also fighting for my life.

Don-the-Con has made sure of that.

The bastard.

I drive through the desert roads north of Carefree, dipping into arroyos that are impassable in the onslaught of a summer thunderstorm, and cresting hills that give forbidden peeks at the towns of Carefree and Cave Creek in the diminishing distance. I think I'm going to visit Christian.

As I hit Cave Creek Rd., and my car automatically turns right, I'm sure of it. I'm going to visit Christian.

Cruising down the road, being careful not to exceed the limit-over-the-speed-limit that will reward you with a ticket, I see the locals opening shop. The last few days have seen some wind, so many are washing dust from their windows while others are sweeping the walks in front of the shop. Some have no walks, only dirt leading right to the door. They don't bother with the windows or anything else. It just is what it is. This is, after all, the West.

I turn left into the heart of downtown Carefree, and continue to the intersection of Ho and Hum Roads. I cruise past the giant sundial, continue to Easy Street, then wend my way to Christian's office. He is in an old Spanish style building with vigas, bougainvilleas, and rustic wooden columns holding up the porch overhang that runs the long length of the building. His shop used to be an art gallery, but it went out of business with the last recession. As did many others. And while several still remain, and do a very brisk trade, a lot of the storefronts now house more mundane aspects of civilized life, such as Christian's security business.

Parking in front I put my top up because, yes, it is getting too hot for the nonsense of having it down. And besides, one good dust devil could wreak havoc on my pretty interior. In the desert, dusty cars are a fact of life. But only on the outside. One doesn't want to be spitting dust on the inside. Top up, windows up, sunshade placed in the expansive front windshield, I exit the car, beep it secure, and march into Christian's freshly opened shop.

"Hey! How're you doin', Alli?" he greets me with the sexy lilt that matches his eyes — all green and cool like a highland meadow.

"I'm good," I return. "How 'bout you?"

"Great, great," he assures. Okay. So why do I doubt that? "Whatcha need?" he asks, not even looking at me. Something flits through his eyes, and the corners of his sensuous mouth are turned down, hosting a slight frown that is entirely out of character for the impossibly upbeat Christian.

"I want to discuss my security system," I tell him, and I see his eyes cloud for the briefest of seconds.

"Why?" he asks in a voice that sounds a cross between a croak and a whisper. Okay. This is weird. I approach him slowly, gently. I find my hand going to his face and lifting his chin so I can meet his eyes. They are worried, but evasive.

"Tell me," I say.

"Tell you what?" he counters. I hold his shielded gaze for several seconds, searching first one eye, then the other.

"Tell me," I repeat, and his visage crumbles. He draws a huge breath, then releases it in a slow, submissive, almost sad sigh.

"Your ex called."

"What?" I scream at him, making him jerk back, no longer guarded, but highly surprised. I clutch my purse to my stomach, and regain control. "Sorry, Christian. Didn't mean to yell like that. Let me start over," I say, and make little clearing noises in my throat. Then I look at him, all lady-like, flutter my eyelashes a few time and calmly ask, "What?"

"Your ex called," he repeats.

"Why?!" I yell again. This time Christian remains cool.

"He wanted info on your system."

"Oh, my God! Why did he say he wanted that?"

"He said he was considering getting a system himself, and was curious what system you had, and if you liked it and all. You know, was it a good one, how sophisticated, was it easily overridden—that sort of thing."

By now my heart is beginning to pound and bile is creeping up my throat. Son-of-a-bitch, I spit in my mind. Son-of-a-fucking-bitch.

"I didn't tell him anything, Alli," Christian assures me. "I told him that wasn't the sort of information any security company in its right mind would release to someone."

"What did he say to that?" I ask, already knowing.

Christian looks apologetic, sorry even. He takes my hands and slowly rubs the tops of my fingers, then lifts his kind eyes to mine. Mustering comfort, assurance.

"He said he would find out—one way or the other."

"And what do you think, Christian? Will he?"

"Not from me, Alli. That's all I can say." I gently but firmly pull my hands from his, and turn my profile to him, to hide the spate of tears.

All of my life I've ridden a rollercoaster. Up, down. Up, down. Until recently, that is. Until these past two years—the years after I freed myself from my marriage. I freed myself from bonds of all sorts. Emotional submission. Mental anguish. Physical fear. But now those prisons threaten me again. The emotions swirl through me like a whirlpool, laughing with insidious evil. *You are going to drown*, they sneer. *We are going to drown you.*

In that instant I rocket from the depths of the horrifying eddy, lunging from the bottom of my fears, and gasp in the life-affirming oxygen of my heart. It calls, *Remember me. I am your strength. I am your salvation. Do not submit to the mind's control. I am your ruler – and I will save you with my power.*

I turn to Christian. Although my tears are abating, my balance is not quite yet reestablished. "Thank you, my friend," I whisper, as I can barely will my lips to move. "Thank you." Christian starts to say something, but I hold my hand up in a move to silence him, and he does remain silent. I nod, and quickly leave his shop, wondering what the hell I'm going to do next.

What the hell am I going to do?

Upon arriving back home I throw my purse on the entry table and wander zombie-like into my studio. I stare, despondent, at my two commissioned paintings. The little dog, who has come along very nicely, breathes with a life that is palpable. I know this dog's arrival, this dog's homecoming with the woman who wants him with all her heart, is inevitable. It is assured. My gaze turns to the other work. The man. His sneer sends chills down my spine. I'm the one who painted that, I remind myself. I'm the one who put that smug sneer on his face. Why did I do that? Yes, he does wear that obscene smile at present, but he says he wants to change. He wants enlightenment. Or does he? I ask myself.

Or, does he?

I slowly walk all around the painting, as though I'll gain insight from a different angle. But I gain no new insight. Just the same uneasy feeling I've had all along.

I should never have accepted the commission. That's all there is to it. I should never have accepted.

Going back to the dog I pull on my smock, lift my brush, no paint on it, and gently stroke its fur. The image seems to shimmer and pulse. I take my finger and stroke its head, and its eyes seem to gain a shine, a sparkle that I hadn't seen before. "You are ready," I whisper to the beautiful little life on the canvas. As though it agrees, I sense a nod. Gently lifting the canvas from the easel I carry it to the north window. It truly is a beautiful work. One of my best. I know the woman will love it—both the painting *and* the actual dog, when it appears in her life. It will be one of the world's great love affairs. I am sure of that.

I choose a piece of silk, peace silk, because that has the most gentle vibe, and I wrap the canvas with a caress. "You are going home, now," I whisper. And I mean both the painting and the actual little dog the woman and I have called forth together. Setting the painting on the special table I reserve for finished canvases, the one I've had blessed by all higher entities that have wished to participate, I give the canvas one final, loving caress through the silk. It will be the last time I touch it. When it next feels a human hand it will be the hand of the woman who commissioned it. I'll call her later this morning.

My god, it is still morning! It seems I've lived a month in the last few hours. But it isn't even 9:30 yet.

Time to shake this funk and get to some serious work.

With dread I return to the portrait of the sneering man. I grab it and fling it across the room, instantly regretting the violent air that spins from the act.

"I'm sorry, I'm sorry!" I cry to the sacred space of my studio. "I'm so, so, very sorry," I cry softly. I sink to my knees, then puddle down on the floor in a spineless lump. Lying on my side I pull my knees into my chest and hug them there. I close my eyes and breathe slowly, fully in. I hold it, then release it, slowly, slowly. I do this again and again until the dizziness of full oxygenation has its hold on my brain. Then I place my awareness in my heart. "Dear heart," I murmur, "dear, dear, dearest heart. Help me now." The command triggers a physical sensation in my actual heart, not a pain, but almost. More than a twinge, but less than pain. And so, I know my heart hears. I place my hands gently on my chest, over that wise heart, and release two rogue tears. Then I am done.

I rise to my feet, stretch, and smile. Forced at first, but then the smile becomes real.

Thank you, my dear heart. I will be fine now.

Striding across the room to the broken canvas, I grab it off the floor, beam joy and light into all corners of the studio to erase any last vestiges of the violence unleashed, and take the canvas to the garage, to the trash can, where I stuff it unceremoniously into the garbage, just like the garbage that it is.

I will do better by you, I assure the man. To cement the promise I shout it aloud. "I – will – do – better!"

Refreshed, chastised, and determined, I return to my studio and grab a virgin canvas. I place it firmly upon the easel, and admire its purity, its total accepting blankness. Ready to give itself to anything I put there. Ready to change its very being, to breathe life into whatever passing fancy I demand of it. As is my habit, my ritual, I stroke it and give thanks for its being. For its willingness to accommodate my every whim. With regret for the lost life of the canvas I stuffed into the trash, I send it my sincere apology. I feel a sweet smile come in return. "It's okay," it says to me. "Don't fret. I understand. And I will rebirth myself into something else. All is well." I sigh in gratitude for its wise assessment, caress it in my mind for one last time, then release it.

Turning my full attention to the clean slate before me I squirt a slice of gold metallic paint onto my palette, pick a round brush with long silky hairs, and dip it into the gold. With loving care I inscribe my symbol of eternity onto the blank canvas. I do this in all my work. It gets painted over, so it's never seen. But it's there, underneath whatever conspires to manifest. A mirror of reality. Eternity beneath all things.

I'll let it dry, which won't take long in the dry desert air, cooled by the dry savior of refrigeration. Then I'll start anew on the portrait of the enlightened man. And I'll do it right.

I remove my smock and march into the kitchen. God I love this kitchen! Swinging open the refrigerator door I peer inside. Unlike many single women, my refrigerator is well stocked, and it's stocked with things that are actually nutritious! When Jazzie and I first met she raised an eyebrow of disdain at me. Jazzie, who not only communicates with animals but sees auras as well, informed me that mine sucked. When she inquired about my eating habits, she snorted in disbelief when I recounted my menus. "No wonder your aura is a mess! Garbage in, garbage out," she'd clipped. From that day forward I've taken much better care of myself.

Jazzie says my aura is very pretty now. At least most days.

I reach for salad makings and carry them to the counter where I throw the salad quickly together, remembering to give thanks to all the components, and then put the remains back in the frig. I realize it's nowhere near lunch time, but I don't care. It's been a long day already and I'm famished. I eat standing up at the sink, staring out the window at the expanse visible through my iron fence. Through the bars I spy a cottontail nibbling on some sage. Soon another hops into view, and I smile through my chews. They are just so cute. I finish the salad and dump the plate and fork on top of the dishes from breakfast.

And decide to call Jazzie.

I'm expecting to get her voice mail but she answers in person.

"Hi, Jazzie, it's me," I sing, glad to make a real connection.

"Hi, Alli," she replies. "How're you holding up, kiddo?"

"Fine," I say, fully prepared to slide over all that has happened this morning since we've spoken.

"Christian called me," she says. Shit. So much for that.

"Really?" I answer, with as much nonchalance as I can muster. After all, maybe he didn't discuss my visit this morning.

"Yes, really." From her tone I know I can kiss that thought goodbye. "Were you going to tell me?" she asks.

I thought about that for a few seconds. The truth is, I've never kept anything from Jazzie, at least not for long, so I reply in all truthfulness, "Of course I was going to tell you! You don't believe for an instant that I would keep that from you, do you?" As she snorts her disbelief, I laugh. "Okay, yeah, I would definitely *consider* not telling you. But in the end, you know I would."

"That's better," she says. "Full disclosure is good for the soul. So now that we've got that over with, tell me again—how're you doing?"

"All things considered, I really am doing fine," I reply. "I had some rough moments after my visit with Christian, but I'm over it now."

"Good!" she answers, and her willingness to so thoroughly let it go surprises me. But I'm grateful. "Guess what!" she continues.

"Okay, what?" I laugh.

"Remember how sad we were when Robert closed El Bistre Perdido? Well, be sad no longer, my friend, because he's opening a new restaurant!"

"Wow—really?"

"Yepper! It's going to be in Spanish Square, right where his old restaurant was, with the addition of the space next door. So it will be almost twice the size!"

"How cool is that?" I laugh, again.

"Very, very cool," she answers seriously. "And get this, he's going to feature a Spanish guitarist and flamenco dancers!"

"That really *is* cool!" I reply. And it is. I adore Spanish guitar and flamenco. Even though I'm auburn-haired and hazel-eyed I suspect there is some Spanish ancestry somewhere in my gene pool. When I am in the presence of fine Spanish rhythm I definitely want to shout *Olé!*

"So anyway," Jazzie continues, "the restaurant will be renamed just plain Roberto's, and should be open for business sometime later next week. Want to go and grace the opening?"

"Sure!"

"Then plan on wearing something that exudes passion and romance—with a bit of slut," she says over my puritanical objections, "because one never knows what can happen when two beautiful women such as ourselves beam aboard. Gotta go. I'll let you know what night they open when I find out."

And before I could get another word out, she was gone.

Beautiful women such as ourselves, I mumble to myself. Uh-huh. I shake my head with a chuckle. Now, Jazzie *is* beautiful. She's typical Scottsdale beautiful—blonde, silky, shoulder length hair, flawless skin with perpetual springtime tan, blue eyes, toned, shapely bod. That's why we call her Jazzie—because she is! Her actual name is Jasmine, but that sounds too staid for her. Jazzie suits her much better. Unlike me, Jazzie has a wardrobe that makes a definite statement. She has all her clothes made by a friend of hers (an acquaintance of mine) who specializes in whimsical. Silks, rayons, colors of the cosmos, everything that flows, floats, dazzles, sparkles. Metallic threads, sequins, beads, pearls, shells, even gemstones. Evie's creations are art in themselves, and Jazzie is her best model and spokesperson.

I, on the other hand, am not a shining example of otherworldly grace. I tend toward jeans (although I prefer white), and tee shirts (although I'm fussy about the colors and cuts), and I live in sandals year round. Sometimes they are slinky and sparkly, sometimes they are earth sandals—and, yes, I do wear socks with my earth sandals in the winter. So you see, I'm no fashionista. I wonder, do I even have anything that is passionate, romantic, and slightly slutty? If not, I guess I'll have to go shopping!

But not right now. Now it's time to return to "the portrait".

I saunter back into my studio, and without looking at the canvas I grab my smock and pull it on, unceremoniously, without grace or awareness, matter-of-factly, like a workman approaching road work or a farm hand cleaning a stable. Noticing this I chide myself. This is part of what is wrong with this commission. I am not offering myself to it as I should. So I strip the smock off, take some deep breaths with my eyes closed, filling my lungs to their fullest, then let the breath out in a swoosh. Again and again. When I feel dizzy, I know I'm oxygenated. I gaze out the window a moment, offering reverence for the landscape that meets my eyes—the clear, dry, turquoise sky, the saguaros and sage, the palo verde I've had pruned into a spectacular work of art, the windswept mesquites. I let the adoration surge through my heart, opening it wide. I feel the familiar sensation in that heart, like butterflies in your gut, only in the heart, and I know I'm ready to paint.

Turning to focus on the eternity symbol glowing gold, pulsing in its call to me, I walk to it as a bride down the aisle—slowly, joyfully, and scared. I arrive at the altar of my canvas and slowly slip my arms into the smock, never removing my gaze from the symbol. I shrug the smock on fully and tie the sash, still at one with eternity. I stand and sink into the spiral, following it from one end to the other. Breathing, breathing.

Now, I'm truly ready.

I slide my gaze from the painting to my stand which holds my paint, brushes, palette, and water. Deciding on a lavish, highly textured background for the portrait I mix a rich scarlet with heavy gel for a stiffer texture. I start at the upper left and work my way in a diagonal to approximately two thirds of the way down the canvas. Then I mix a deep, royal purple, and put a splash of violet on my palette. I blend the purple into the border of the scarlet, swirling, jabbing, and slipping, until I'm satisfied with its beauty, then continue on down the canvas to finish at the lower right. I wet the brush and remove only part of the water on the edge of my jar, leaving it wet so I can use the violet as a wash. I wash the violet here and there over the purple, which adds glow and spice. Then I dab violet here and there over the scarlet, just enough to bring balance between the colors. I aggressively swish my brush clean in the water, leaving a stain in it that looks much like blood half robbed of its oxygen. I spread a dab of dark metallic gold on my palette and a dab of copper. Wetting my brush, I highlight the hills and valleys of the textured scarlet and purple with metallic accents. When I find it mesmerizing, I put my brush into the water jar, and reverently remove my smock. I give thanks to my guides, my Higher Self, and to the Divine.

Then I turn and walk out, without a backward glance.

I feel better about this commencement. But I am still uneasy.

On my way to the kitchen I spy Rico and Bonnie in the living room window, sprawled on the long, narrow table I put there specifically for them to lie upon. They are both fast asleep, Bonnie's feet twitching. Chasing something elusive, no doubt. I smile at her earthiness. So unlike Rico who is one of the most evolved beings I know. Rico loves everything and everyone — except my ex.

Crap. There the bastard is again. In my mind, when I had managed to forget about him for an hour or so.

Moving to the kitchen I pour myself a glass of vegetable juice I made yesterday. Not as good as fresh, but I'm glad I don't have to run the Vita-Mix and disturb my kids. I pour a small bowl of pecans and sit at the little wrought iron table, gazing out at the desert. It is definitely midday—I can tell without looking at the clock. In the summer, at midday, things start to look a bit flat, a bit washed out. The sun is too bright, and it steals color and dimension from those enduring beneath it. I turn back to look at my food while I'm eating and drinking—mindful that I owe it my gratitude and awareness. Beth taught me that. She's a neighbor Jazzie introduced me to. She has greenhouses she grows food in all year round. In the summer she can do this because she cools them with swamp coolers a company in Tucson makes. They run off marine or golf cart batteries that can be charged with solar panels. They work very well, and if I ever find myself without the electricity to run my air conditioner, some oppressive summer day, I'm running over to Beth's greenhouses!

I smile at the thought of Beth and her harvests. She grows vegetables, herbs, and flowers. She sells to locals, and also makes her own herbal medicines, and body care products. She's one of the most energetic and accomplished people I know. I'm in constant awe of her. I can only do so much in a day, then I'm through. I'm basically very lazy. I am very much a Human Being instead of a Human Doing—that little distinction the New Thought Community is always bringing up. Beth is both a Human Being *and* a Human Doing. A very admirable accomplishment.

Finishing the last of my pecans, I pay extra attention to the firm but silky body as it submits to my teeth. I notice the mellow, earthy taste as I chew it into butter, then I swallow, giving thanks. I raise the glass for my last swallow of juice. The sweetness of the carrots, the tang of the watercress, the smooth taste of spinach—I bring them all into my awareness—then I drink it down, and give thanks. Sitting with my eyes closed for a moment, I envision all the good this meal is going to accomplish in the circle of life. It will provide me with health, energy, and beauty—which I'll pass on.

I rise and go to the sink. This time, however, I open the dishwasher and load the glass and bowl into it, then add the dishes I had left in the sink and close the door. Maybe tomorrow I can run it. Spritzing the sink with a bit of soap I give it a quick wash and rinse.

Ceremony over.

I need a nap.

Chapter 4

Instead of lying in bed I decide to use the loveseat. I pile a couple of pillows on one arm, to drape my legs over, and a narrow pillow at the other end where I lay my head. I close my eyes, and within two minutes I'm sound asleep.

I dream.

I'm somewhere festooned with lights. There is wonderful music floating in the air, and I am awash with joy. I don't know why—I just am. My gaze turns to the sight of a tall, lanky man with shiny, light brown hair that ends halfway between his chin and shoulders. His back is to me. I can't yet see his face, but my gut stirs and the thought, *He's the one*, sweeps through my mind. My heart swells in agreement. *Who is he?* I ask my mind and heart. They chuckle.

You shall see, they tease.

Just then the man turns. He's in his late thirties, maybe early forties. He's handsome in a comfortable way. Even, chiseled features, sensuous mouth, large, kind eyes beneath straight dark brows. Not GQ material, but, most definitely material for me. I lock eyes with him, unabashed in my stare. He moves to me with a languid stride. He arrives before me, never having unlocked eyes. He sits down, still locked into my eyes. He reaches and touches my face, gently, possessively.

"I want it," he says.

Startled, I reply, "You want what?"

"The Ultimate Cell," he says. "The cell that has lived forever, that has been through all the great lovers, all the great artists and musicians, all the greatest creators of all time. I want it." I just continue to stare at him, lost in the liquid that is his eyes.

After a minute he asks, "Do you know where it is?"

I start to say that I don't, but my heart and gut both jump. Butterflies swirl, making me almost nauseous in the intensity. But just as suddenly as it started, it settles, and a voice in my head gently demands my attention. With great love it says, "*You* have it. Give it to him."

Confused, I don't know what to do. However, I make note that I haven't moved a centimeter during the whole revelation. I've been locked into those chocolate eyes, and they have been locked into mine. Suddenly my lips start to tingle. I feel like little fairies are kissing me all over my mouth. Back and forth the tingles go. Then it comes to me. I am supposed to kiss him. I lean across the table and caress his face in return. Our mouths move closer and closer. Slowly, slowly, slowly. I shut my eyes, butterflies dancing throughout my body, from the tips of my toes to the ends of my hair. Our lips touch. His are so soft I melt. They touch, touch, touch. Tease, tease, tease. Then his lips are on mine firmly. They don't depart, as before. His lips move mine apart and his tongue does a slow, reverent slide into my mouth. My tongue obedient, submissive, aware of the importance, gently moves to touch his. Respectfully. Carefully. Lovingly. Our tongues caress.

And, with that kiss, I pass to him the Ultimate Cell.

I awaken with a start, flushed from the dream. In awe of its impact on my body. My lips still tingle, my gut still flutters, and I realize I want him. Whoever this man is—I want him. Very, very much.

I lie there another couple of minutes, regaining control of the present, then lift myself off the loveseat. In a daze that still has its grip I slide into the studio. Selecting a new canvas I place it on my second easel. I paint the spiral in my finest gold. Then, in an inspired joy, I paint all the symbols I've ever known of love and foreverness. The once virgin canvas is now filled with golden love. I smile, then leave the studio, closing the door for the day.

I move to the window where Rico and Bonita lie, and stroke them. Rico immediately goes into belly position, and I stroke his long, silky fur, sending little angel hairs floating off on the breeze of the air conditioning. Some catch the light as they go, flashing little sparkles like miniature fireworks. I gently pet Bonnie and she doesn't move a muscle, except to purr. Which she does with earnest appreciation. Soon a little droolie appears on her lips and drips to the paw on which she rests her head. She doesn't care. She just smiles, eyes closed, purrs filling the quiet room.

"I love you," I whisper to my two children, and leave them to their afternoon naps.

I pull a comb through my tousled hair—even more tousled because of letting it dry naturally this morning—some of that drying accomplished as it was tossed by the wind in my convertible. Assessing the wild look that that decision created, I'm not so sure it was such a great idea. Oh well. It is what it is. I grab my purse and head to the garage. Once again, I'm not sure where I'm going. But I'm going.

I back the car out of the garage and hit the button to shut it. Swinging the car around in the space created just for that, I head down the long, dirt driveway. In the morning the air is so filled with birdsong that it sounds as though I live in an aviary. At this early afternoon hour, it is dead silent. In two or so hours the doves and mocking birds will take up the chorus again, to be joined a little later by the woodpeckers, quails, and verdins. For now, everybody rests.

I pull onto the dirt road that intersects my driveway and move slowly past my neighbors' houses. The ground is its driest right now—the point where the winter rains have been a memory for many months, and the summer monsoons have yet to begin. I drive slowly

because I know what a bitch it is to have dust from the road constantly coating your windows, dimming your view. My license plate says
"Live the Golden Rule". So I try to not raise dust. Not that that is
possible. But at least I try.

Soon I'm at the main road, paved, thankfully. I turn onto it, traffic
is exceptionally light. The winter visitors have returned to their
homes in cooler climes, and the year round residents are avoiding the
heat. I turn on the radio to KYOT and Jesse Cook is gracing the
airwaves with his special brand of rumba guitar. I sigh deeply, in love
with the sound. The song finishes just as I pull up to my destination.
Seems I knew where I was going all along.

I depart with the usual routine of sunshade and beep, and enter
Evie's shop.

"Hi, Alli!" she calls, surprised, delighted.

"Hi, Evie," I return.

"What brings you here? I'm surprised to see you without Jazzie.
Did she send you to pick up her order?" Wow, that girl has more
clothes on order from Evie? Lucky little angel, I think to myself.

"No, actually, I'm here for me, today," I tell her.

"Really?" she asks. And the way she asks makes me a bit defen-
sive. I mean, I'm not that boring, am I? Okay. Maybe I am. But that's
why I'm here. To fix that.

"Yes, really," I answer with a chuckle. "I need a special dress.
However, I need it quickly, like in a week. Can you do that?"

"Of course, honey," she replies with the assurance of those who
have total control of their lives. I so envy them. "No problem. What is
it you need the dress for?"

"Well, Jazzie has convinced me to go to the opening of Roberto's,
and—"

Evie cuts me off. "Oh, isn't that great!" she enthuses. "I am so glad Robert is opening a new restaurant! Bill and I were just crushed when the Bistre closed."

"Yes, I know," I reply. "Everyone was heartbroken."

"So you and Jazzie are going to the opening. That's wonderful. Did you have something specific in mind, dear?"

"Well, Jazzie said I should wear something passionate and romantic, with a bit of slut." Evie bursts out laughing.

"That sounds like our Jazzie, all right."

"Does that description bring anything to mind for you?" I ask, hoping it does, because I'm clueless.

She starts an assessment of me, all professional dressmaker, now. She puts her finger to her lips and looks me slowly up and down, all objectivity. She circles me, her eyes calculating, her expression lost in her work.

"Pile your hair up on the top of your head," she commands. So I do, grabbing it with a twist and holding it atop my head. She scrutinizes for another ten seconds, then says, "Yes. I know exactly what to make." Wow, I think. Cool! Wish I was that sure of what I wanted!

"Let me get your measurements, sweetie, and I'll start today."

"Thanks so much, Evie," I offer. "I hate to just barge in on your time like this."

"Nonsense, girl," she bellows through the door to the back room. "Except for Jazzie's dress, I'm kind of slow right now. Just some alterations and such. I'm happy to do it."

She returns with some fabric swatches, resembling the colors I've just laid down for "the portrait", and I don't know whether to take that as a good sign or a bad sign. She holds them up to my face, nodding and grunting to herself, her eyes filing, sorting, assessing. Satisfied with whatever she has decided, she whips out her tape measure.

"No need to remove your clothes, sweetie," she says to the question I didn't express. "I know how much jeans and tees measure. You don't have fat underwear on, do you?" she teases.

"No," I laugh. "Just regular, regular."

"Great," she answers. She makes note of all her findings, then comes out of computer mode, personal and gracious once more. "Have everything I need, dear," she says, smiling broadly.

"How much will it cost," I ask, a bit afraid to know.

"We'll see," she offers, off hand.

Oh boy, I think. Okay. Whatever.

"Thanks so much, Evie," I say, as I stoop in for a kiss goodbye on her cheek.

"Don't worry, honey," she assures, a kind, knowing look lighting her capable eyes. "You'll love it."

And, suddenly, I am absolutely sure of that.

Chapter 5

Leaving Evie's shop I decide that I'll invite Christian and Ben over for dinner tonight. I'll do it last minute, however, and that will facilitate my cooking, no matter if they accept or not. Too often I eat out of a can, although it may be a healthy can, instead of bothering to cook if it will be only for myself. I turn on Tom Darlington, which becomes Scottsdale Road further south, and point Ms. Sebring to Whole Foods Market. On the radio Dave Koz's sweetly happy "Together Again" is filling my heart with little staccatos of joy. When it's finished I turn off the radio, opting for silence. The drive from Carefree to Scottsdale displays spectacular desert vistas, hiding large, stuccoed abodes, scattered about in lush landscapes. The McDowell Mountains tower in the east, a splash of homes dripping down the west slope. The trees and shrubs are green and healthy from the ample winter rain we had. A roadrunner shoots across the road in front of me, and I'm glad I wasn't speeding or I might have hit it.

Little by little the vegetation becomes more sparse, the lower elevation, though slight, exerting its affect. The traffic thickens, affluent people in flashy cars dominate the road.

I'm in Scottsdale—affectionately known as Snottsdale to those with a sense of humor.

I pull into Whole Foods. I put up the sunshade, grab a canvas bag from behind the front seat, beep Ms. Sebring secure—and stride into the upscale store. The Whole Foods down by Paradise Valley has a feel like Trader Joe's, but this one—the big kahuna—is like a mall without the walls. Each department is huge and gorgeous. Everything about this store shouts money—in a tasteful way, of course. But it is the best stocked store around.

Grabbing a basket I head to pick up the few dry goods I'll need. Then to the wine department, the produce department, and finally to the seafood department. No, I'm not a vegetarian. Yet. Though, I suspect, someday I will be. After making all my selections I head to the checkout where a surfer-looking blonde with Hawaiian shirt, blue bandana, and a thousand tattoos stands cheerfully behind the register. I didn't realize surfer types got tattoos. Live and learn. After receiving the nickel he insisted I take, when he forgot to credit my canvas bag on my receipt, I head out the door into the now blasting heat. Once in my car I turn the air conditioner on full bore and wait a minute until it turns ice cold.

Perfect.

I turn back onto Scottsdale Road and head north to home, the undulating road providing a calming rhythm. My thoughts float over the events of the day—an interesting 11 hours, indeed. Once again I wonder what my ex is up to. And once again I decide I don't want to know. So, instead, I dwell on my dream man.

Much better.

Home, I unpack and put away the groceries. I kiss Rico and Bonnie hello and put down their evening meal. I pull out the necessary pots, chopping board, spoons, and other weapons of creation and take down my favorite cookbook. Sitting at the breakfast bar I peruse recipes—then decide on what I had decided on all along. I love when that happens. Otherwise I might find myself at the local market procuring some last minute item. I assemble the ingredients I need to start and begin preparation. That is, until my phone rings.

I answer it quickly, without checking caller ID, because I have to wipe my hands before reaching for it, and it's on the last ring. I assume its good intent, like it's offering a connection to Jazzie, giving me the date for our grand opening event. But the phone deceives me. The intent is far from good. The little bastard has conjured a connection with Don.

"Hi, Alli," his slimy voice oozes snakelike through the receiver. "How're you doing?"

Bile leaps to my throat. I open my mouth to say something — something like what the hell do you want? Why are you inflicting your horrid self upon me? Why are you even still alive?

But instead, I bring my trembling lips back together, and silently hang up the phone.

Then I unplug it.

Wrapping my arms around myself I turn toward the window. I stare hard at the beautiful view, the view that never ceases to bring me joy and comfort. I stare and stare, willing myself to be in the present. The present is me, here in my perfect little home, gazing upon this God-given landscape, readying to cook a delicious meal to share with close friends. This is the present.

But I can't hold it. The present keeps slipping away.

Don used to kill things just because they were beautiful, just because they were free. He detested anything that was closer to God, closer to truth than he. That meant he detested most everyone and everything. I search my heart to ask myself for the millionth time — what did I ever see in him? But, I already know the answer, however little comfort it brings.

I believed him when he said he loved me — and I needed to be loved. I believed him when he said he wanted to marry me — and I needed to belong. I believed him right until the second month of marriage when he started hitting me. Where had the polite, romantic man that I had dated and then lived with for more than a year, gone? Who was this monster? I didn't know. But I did know one thing. I didn't have the strength to leave. I had married him for all the wrong reasons — need, insecurities, a search for love outside of myself and Source. And I was miserable.

It took me eleven years to gather enough strength to *start* to leave. I rented a storage room in Phoenix, and one day a month I would load my car with boxes I had packed, and drive the 125 miles to drop them off. I did this for two years. Then I gave nine weeks notice at the clinic where I worked and, on the first day of spring, I left.

Rebirth.

And now, with Don insinuating himself into my life again, I feel like death.

I cannot let him do this. I cannot! I remind myself that only one's *self* can do anything to one's self. It's only my interpretation of the event that is important, right? Right? I release my arms from the tight embrace I've been giving myself and hold them out. I close my eyes, breathe deeply, and declare that I am free, I am happy. I am living the life I love, and being the person I love to be. This is who I am, this is my life. All is well. All is truly well.

I almost feel it's true.

I go back to preparing dinner, but I eat it alone. Then I give in and go to bed. It's early, the sun is still settling into a sunset, but I'm exhausted. I need to check out for a while. I need the escape of darkness and dreams. So, I escape. And the dream comes.

I'm in a beautiful place. There are candles flickering by the hundreds. The air is balmy, it is velvet. I'm surrounded by blue — dark royal and electric blues, undulating, mixing, shimmering. The golden yellow of the candlelight halos them with tender touch. Then suddenly, there is music. It's guitar — slow, soulful, each note a caress. Each note a word of a conversation. A conversation that speaks of love. Then as my eyes soften in their focus I notice movement in the air. It starts very dimly, but grows brighter as I watch. Whatever it is it's swirling and dancing to the music. Wait! It *is* the music! I'm watching the notes. As they grow stronger in my sight I notice something else. They are leaving trails which are solidifying into a gossamer net. Soon the air is filled with this net. The music has wrapped the entire area in a gossamer net of love. It holds the moment together. It holds the blue together. It holds me together.

I am supported by the music. I am loved by the music. I am safe.

I awaken. My bedroom is still dark, but I see the beginning of the glow of the promised new day. I still feel the sweetness of the music. It was the last dream of the morning, and I'm glad. It will stay with me throughout the day.

I rise and draw the drapes open, then glide open the sliding glass door peering into the growing light. The air is cool and inviting. The first mockingbird starts his call. It is always the mockingbird who sings first. He calls. It is answered from the distance. He calls again, this time in a different voice. It is answered from a different spot, the reply a mirror of his own. On and on this ritual goes until everyone is awake — and the cacophony begins. The sun kisses the top of my saguaro, then the top of the mesquites and the palo verde. Soon it is kissing me. Hello, beautiful. Thank you for coming up today. I smile, then turn and start my day.

After feeding myself and the kids I remember that I unplugged the phone last night, so I plug it in and check my voice mail. There are messages.

Message one: "Hey, Alli! It's Christian. In case Jazzie didn't already tell you, Robert is opening a new restaurant next week. Ben says maybe we should all go together to the opening. What do you think? Talk with Jazzie and let me know. Bye!"

Message two: "Hi, Alli, it's Beth. Just wanted to let you know that I've made a new batch of the facial cleanser you like. The lavender is my most fragrant batch yet. You'll love it! Come on by anytime. See ya!"

Message three: "Hi, Alli. I've called and called, but it just goes to voice mail, so I'll leave a message. I need something from you, and I will get it. Don't think I won't. You're not that smart."

I spit on the phone, then wipe it off with my breakfast napkin. "Sorry, dear phone," I tell it. "It wasn't you, it was el creepo." The phone says it understands. It wishes it had the choice of discernment, but it has to do its job. I tell it I know.

I'm glad Don wrapped up his little threat with saying I wasn't smart. That makes me mad, and being mad makes me tough. The asshole will not be getting whatever it is he thinks he's getting. I'll be making sure he gets something entirely different.

I stroll to the studio, ready to create. I look first to the portrait. The background is lovely, and I flash on the fabric samples at Evie's. I'm excited about my new dress. No wonder Jazzie has Evie make her clothes. It adds a layer of enchantment that cannot be found in a department store. I look again at the background for the portrait.

"Sorry," I tell it. "I'm going to work on *my* painting."

After preparing myself and my tools, I stand before my canvas of gold symbols. They dance, awaiting their assignment. "What are we going to empower?" they ask me.

"Wait and see," I tell them.

Then I begin to cover them in breath-snatching blues, splashed with golden yellow highlights. When this is dry I'll paint the liquid chocolate eyes.

Chapter 6

At lunch I realize I forgot to call the woman yesterday about her little dog. So I do that, and then straighten the house up a bit, to prepare for her arrival. She arrives in half an hour, flushed, eyes shining.

"Hi, Alli!" she says, her excitement infectious, causing my heart to stir.

"Hi, Brenda," I reply warmly. "Thanks for coming over so soon. I appreciate it."

"Happy to do it! I'm so excited to see my little dog," she squeals. "Show me, show me!"

Laughing, I lead her to my studio. She takes in the two canvases I'm working on and mumbles her ritual admiration, but I know she wants her dog, so I don't waste any time with explanations. I direct her to the table where her painting sits wrapped in the peace silk.

"There it is," I tell her. "You should be the one to touch it next, so, please, help yourself."

She approaches the painting with careful excitement. Her hand trembles slightly as she reaches for, lifts, and removes the silk. She gasps. Tears form in her loving eyes.

"It's him," she says.

"Him?" I ask. "You've learned it's a him?"

"Yes," she says simply, and doesn't elaborate.

We stand in silence for a minute, Brenda unwilling to take her eyes off her precious dog, and me unwilling to spoil so touching a moment. Finally she's able to break her eyes away, and I take the opportunity to return her photo.

"I think he looks very at home on your couch," I say as I hand the photo of same couch to her.

"Yes he does," she affirms. "And he will be, when he comes to me." I smile, and as she hurries to the door with me in her trail, she adds, "I will most certainly call and let you know when he appears."

"Good," I tell her as I walk her to her car. She gently sets the painting on the front seat, as though it's fine china, and turns and gives me a big hug. "Thank you, Alli," she whispers.

"My pleasure," I whisper back.

And, it really, truly is.

I wouldn't trade this gift for any other in the world.

I wave as she drives off and return inside. Rico and Bonita have been strangely independent these past two days and, in the back of my mind, I notice this—and wonder why. In reality I'm grateful. I have so much on my mind, I enjoy the gift of having free choice of focus. And for now, my focus is on chocolate eyes.

Donning my smock I stand in front of my painting. I rough the eyes in, and stand back for perspective. They look good. Now it's time to breathe life into them. Choosing my brushes and paints carefully, I mix the colors with love and devotion. I stroke them onto the canvas as though stroking a lover's cheek, because that's exactly what I am doing. I recall every detail I can, and transfer the memory bit by bit to the canvas. Soon the eyes are alive, and staring back at me as I stare at them.

"Hello," I whisper.

They whisper back, "Hello."

"I love you," I tell the mesmerizing eyes, and a sparkle appears where I had painted none.

"We love you, too."

"Thank you," I say.

"Our pleasure," they reply. And I believe them.

I remove the painting from the easel, and though it is not quite dry I begin choosing a frame. I soon realize, however, that no frame is right. Probably never will be. So I hang it across from my bed just the way it is. My lover's eyes, watching over me. Orchestrating my dreams. Gifting me peace, and safety. And, most important of all, gifting me love.

Now that my painting is done I return to the studio and stand before "the portrait". I think hard on the man who has commissioned me this job. He never did tell me who told him about me, and it's not like I'm in the yellow pages under *Reality Creation*. People only know of me by word of mouth. I get the sick feeling that Don has told this man about me. But you know what? It doesn't matter. It really does not matter. I'm warming to this project and I'm warming to this man. We all deserve the best from everyone else, and we deserve the best from ourselves, as well. And that is what I'm going to do. I am going to give this man the best of myself. And I'm going to do it for both of us.

Taking his photo I study his skin tone. It's actually very nice. Very even and unblemished, sporting a nice golden tan. His cheeks have natural color and his eyes are blue. They're almost Caribbean blue. If I put my hand over his mouth, which I do right now, his face is wonderful. When I remove my hand I see that all that stands between who he is now, and who he says he'd like to be, is his mouth. So I get to work on his face minus his mouth. I'll paint the beauty that is already there, then I will meditate and ask for guidance to create a mouth that represents his enlightened self.

And, trust me, I know I'll need guidance for this one.

The portrait goes quickly and easily. His skin and eyes look radiant against the scarlet and purple background, and I'm glad I chose those colors. I add some of the same gold and copper highlights I used on the background to his light brown hair. He looks positively regal. Now I'll put away the paints and wash the brushes. The mouth will have to wait.

After I've finished cleaning up I check in on the kids. They are sound asleep in the front window so I just blow them a silent kiss and prepare to sneak out. I grab the phone from its cradle and go out on the patio. There are three seating areas in my backyard—one each on either side of the pool, and one under the fullest mesquite. I choose the pretty little table under the mesquite and call Jazzie.

"Hi, Alli!" she sings upon picking up. "How's things?"

"Actually, things are great," I say. "Brenda came by for her dog's portrait, and she loves it."

"That's wonderful," Jazzie says. "And I mean that in all sincerity. She loves that dog already, and she needs to have another companion. It's been a while since Brutus passed, and I can see in her aura that there's a hole that needs filling."

"I agree," I tell her. "You should have seen the joy in her eyes when she saw the painting. It was truly one of my best commissions. She's a darling lady."

"Yes, she is," Jazzie says. "So, not to change the subject or anything, but I found out the restaurant is opening next Friday evening. Is that good for you?"

"You bet!"

"Great. I'll make a reservation. Christian informs me he and Ben would like to be our escorts," she laughs. "That okay with you, or would you rather we wing it on our own?"

"I don't know," I answer. "Part of me would rather just go alone, us girls, but I suppose it would be impolite to turn down such a gallant offer." Jazzie laughs again and says she'll let Christian know they have a date. We say our goodbyes and break the connection.

Oh, I think. I forgot to tell her about my dress. Oh well. Next time.

I call Beth and ask if now is a good time to drop by and she says it is. Since it's only a five minute walk to her house, I walk—even though the sun is cruel. I wear a hat and bring a bottle of water, and arrive at her house none the worse for wear. Besides, when I get home, I'll go swimming.

Beth shows me her new herb garden in her smallest greenhouse. She grows most everything in self-watering containers. Saves a lot of water, and keeps things from suffering a constant, daily, hydrate/wilt cycle. In the desert, one simply can't water enough times a day to keep some things from wilting in the heat. Unless, of course, you use self-waterers. And swamp coolers in your greenhouse. I envy Beth her set up.

I make appropriate ooh and ahh noises, and she selects my cleanser for me. She wraps it in the bag I've brought, and adds a small vial.

"What's that?" I ask.

"A new fragrance I've created," she replies, mischief in her eyes.

I laugh at her lewd expression and thank her. Who knows? Maybe it will come in handy.

Arriving home I strip off my damp clothes, toss them in the laundry hamper, pull on my favorite swimsuit, and hit the pool. The coolness of the water provides an initial moment of discomfort, but then it becomes pure pleasure. I swim some laps, halfway between languid and serious, enjoying the exercise, but relishing the feeling that I have nothing in the world I must do. Nothing except live in joy to the best of my ability. Which isn't the best ability in the world, by a long shot. But as long as I'm trying, that's all that matters.

After my fingers start to prune I climb the steps out of the pool and select my favorite lounge chair. I spread my turquoise towel on the peach colored chair and lay myself in my pretty floral and gold swimsuit upon them. I revel in the colors, and let them revel in me—the one who brought them together. Enjoying the sun, which has now relinquished some of its fierceness, I close my eyes, stretching my arms out over my head. My hair dries in minutes, as does my suit, and I decide *that* is indication enough that it's time to retreat to the protection of the interior.

In my bedroom I glance at the eyes of my lover. They seem to be changing in depth. They are becoming even more than I painted them. More soulful, more wise. More beautiful. Smiling, I blow them a kiss.

I select a sundress the color of pink shells to put on after my shower, and I freshen up for the evening. I plan on having company tonight, and nothing will stop me this time. After my shower I loosely put my hair up, letting tendrils fall here and there. I slip into my dress and select gold sandals with shell and pearly accents. I slide a silver and brass Mexican bracelet on my wrist and adorn my ears with gold and shell chandeliers. Ending with a bit of lip gloss, I declare myself good to go.

I pay my lover's eyes one more glance of respect and adoration and go to find Rico and Bonita.

When I find them they are in the kitchen, side by side, waiting for me. They look at me as if to inquire about my present state of mind and I tell them I am fine—more than fine, really. I am very fine. I select two different flavors of cat food and place the cans, unopened, before Rico. He sniffs each one, lingering over the second.

"Rico's made his preference known," I tell Bonnie. "Now it's your turn!"

Placing the same cans before Bonnie, she sniffs the first, and then the second. As she finishes sniffing the second can she rubs her cheek on it, then looks up.

"Okay!" I say, happily. "You're in agreement! Hallelujah!"

I open the second can and divide it onto two blue plates, then place six crunchies on Bonnie's food. She was a Humane Society kitty and, having started out her life with dry food, she actually prefers it. But I won't let her have it except as a treat. Bonnie and I call them cherries, as in "cherries on top". She has to have her cherries on top or she won't eat her canned food. As I'm preparing dinner for my kids the phone rings. Looking at the anxious little faces on the floor I decide to let it go to voice mail, rather than interrupt dishing out their food. They look grateful when they see me continuing on. After setting the plates before them I check my message. It's from Brenda. She has found her dog.

"Hi, Alli!" the message starts. "I found my little dog! And you won't believe how it happened!" I hear little yipping noises in the background—little yelps of joy, and I'm glad to feel the dog is happy. "I was at the market," Brenda continues, "and when I was done shopping I decided to leave the parking lot by going around the back of the store—you know, so I could come out at the east drive where I figured it would be easier to get out in the afternoon traffic." She takes a big breath. "Anyway, I never go that way! I mean, I honestly don't think I've ever done it once! But, today, I said to myself that that was what I was going to do. So I did. And as I'm coming around the back of the store I see two young men throwing something into the dumpster there! When they see me, they take off running to their car, and hightail it to the street. So I got curious! And I stopped at the dumpster, and I heard this little whimper come from in there! So I banged on the back door of the store and a clerk opened it and helped me dig the poor little kid out of there. Can you imagine someone being so cruel? I mean, in this heat, no less! The poor little thing would have died of exposure before anyone would have even noticed he was in there!" She takes another deep breath. "Anyway, when the clerk handed him to me I about fell over. I really did. Because, there he was! My little dog! Just as I dreamed him and just as you painted him! And, oh look! He's lying on the couch, just as you portrayed him! Oh, Alli. I am so, so happy." I can hear tears in her voice. "I just can't thank you enough. I just really, really can't." Now there are audible sniffles. "I have to go now, dear." A small sob of joy. "After he's settled in a couple of days I'll have you over to meet him, okay? Okay. Bye now!" End of message. By now I'm in tears, too.

I love my work.

Glad I had foregone eye makeup, I pat them dry and decide exactly what I should do for dinner. I decide I could make a nice pasta dish with what was left over from my meal last night. Actually, most of it was still there, but I'd made enough of a dent to make me think it would be better to kind of fluff it up. Besides, Ben and Christian won't know any better. They are the easiest dinner guests ever.

I give them a call to see if they're game, and as usual, I receive an enthusiastic acceptance. Good, I smile to myself. I'm glad to have their company tonight.

I busy myself, as they will be by within the hour. They will bring the wine—which is great because, while they aren't that savvy about food, they are very savvy wine connoisseurs. I hum a little tune, slow, soulful, wondering what it is. Then I remember. It's the guitar lick from my dream. I like it. It's very pretty. I place everything in the oven to get it up to temperature, then I'll transfer it to the warming drawer. I put the water in the pot for the pasta, but I won't actually start it until we are well into the first bottle of wine. Everything good to go, I head to my bathroom for a last minute look, in case I need a touch up. Gliding happily into my bedroom I catch sight of my lover's eyes. I swear. They are even more intense and beautiful than before. "Those eyes will save me," I whisper. But I don't know why I say it. I shake my head, to clear the thought away, and continue into the bathroom. Gazing at myself in the mirror, I wonder—is it wrong to think that sometimes I'm beautiful? I hope not. I'm a child of God, so I should be beautiful, right? Nothing wrong with being a beautiful child of God. Happy that I look good tonight I pin up a strand that has snuck down on its own. There, I think. Much better. A few strands, yes. Too many strands, no. I reapply the apricot gloss and call it good. On my way back to the kitchen I make a detour to the studio. I look at the mouthless man in the portrait. I really wish he'd told me where he got my name. Maybe I should require that information as a part of my contract. I'll think about it. I reach out to touch his face, which, for some reason, is looking kinder than it had before. If I just keep this up, I think I will be able to paint him a nice mouth. We'll see.

The doorbell rings. Ben and Christian are here.

Stepping quickly to the front door, I swing it open wide with a smile. But it's not Ben and Christian. It's Don. I say nothing, just stare at him.

"Aren't you going to invite me in?" he sneers.

I still say nothing. And I *don't* move from the door.

"Well, this is going just great," he smirks, nodding condescendedly. "Come on, Alli. Let me in." He's getting perturbed. I stand still as stone, and just look at him. I look *at* him, *into* him, and *through* him. The once handsome face is lined with the million sneers he's forced onto it. His skin is sallow, his flesh sags. That's what I see as I look *at* him. Looking *into* him I see a big black hole where his heart should be. Looking *through* him I see Ben and Christian's car pulling into my drive. Don turns and watches the vehicle approach, not knowing who it is until they park and depart their car. Then he turns back to me.

"Ahhh," he says. "Saved by the queers." I swallow the impulse to spit at him, though I firmly believe he deserves it. I remind myself that what is best for everything, everywhere, is to resist such impulses of violence, whether they are only implied or actually executed. I, instead, need to swell my heart and beam love. So I do just that. To the best of my ability.

It isn't much, but it's better than nothing.

By now Ben and Christian have arrived at my door. Ben looks confused. Christian looks threatening. He stares at Don, as though waiting for permission to take him down. Any little provocation would be permission to Christian at this moment. Don seems to sense that, and knows when he is out-manned. So he puts on a fake cheery face. "Well, Alli," he exclaims. "Seems like my little surprise visit will just have to wait for another time! I can see you're going to be *busy* tonight." He speaks the word busy with all the lewdness he keeps in his soul. And that's a lot of lewdness. I see Christian start to raise a fist, so I quickly give him a slight shake of my head.

"Yes, keep the beast under control," Don sneers. "Ta ta—for now," he ends flatly. "For now" being the threat he hopes will tear a hole in my sanity. Well, dream on, asshole. I intend to keep all of me in perfect working order.

As Don pulls down the drive Ben, Christian, and I watch silently. When the jerk is finally out of sight Ben suggests we all go in and have a glass of wine. So that's exactly what we do. The three muske-teers.

Hip, hip, hurray.

After our first glass of wine the mood is much merrier, as tends to happen after one's first glass of wine. We start to discuss Don's visit with much lighter hearts, and soon we're laughing uncontrollably.

"Did you see the look on that asshole's face when Christian was giving him the evil eye?" Ben giggles, proud of the stud he lives with.

"Oh shush, Ben," Christian blushes. Then a beat later we're all doubled over in peals of laughter. God it feels good to laugh like this.

After we gain control I get going on the pasta, and serve dinner to my heroes.

Later, alone in the dark of my bedroom, I light a single candle and watch the light play along my walls and ceiling. I think of the day, all of the good, and all of the bad, and remind myself—it's all good. My lover's eyes are flickering in rhythm with the candlelight, and they seem to know. I'm not sure what they know. They just do. I blow out the candle, thank it for its moments of beauty, and fall fast asleep.

This time I remember nothing of my dreams.

The next dawn finds me eager to begin. I fling aside the drapes and admire the rosy break of sunrise. I choose a cool rayon top the colors of mountain meadows, white jeans, and broken-in flip flops. I add diamond earrings for their strong energies—energies that I've put in them myself. You have to be careful with diamonds. They retain energy so completely that, unless the energy in them is good, kind, and pure, they can really mess up your day. Their energy can be cleansed, however. It's just that most people don't know that. I'm glad I do, because I need all the positive energy I can get. Thus attired I stroll to the back patio and check the moisture in a few pots. The potted plants that need the normal amount of water, that potted plants generally require, are all on a drip system. This saves their lives if I forget to pay what amounts to constant attention in the summer heat. However, my cacti and succulents are on their own, dependent on my attention—if only infrequently. They all could use some water so I fill the watering can at the spigot and offer them all a drink as I tell them how pretty they all are, and how much I appreciate them. Then I offer a blessing to everything in my yard, living or "not", and return inside.

I put down breakfast for Rico and Bonita, make coffee and oatmeal for myself, nourish myself, then head to the studio. Gazing at the mouthless man, I wonder about him. What would compel a man to ask for a painting to help him gain enlightenment? It still seems weird to me, but I'm feeling easier and easier about the man, himself. I pick up his photo and study it, comparing it to the painting. There is already an improvement, which I hadn't noticed before. I thought I'd painted him just like his photo, except for the highlights in his hair. But his portrait is looking more angelic, now. I don't know. Maybe the painting is changing itself, in response to the reality that now exists — like the painting of my lover's eyes. I set the photo on the table that holds my paints, brushes, and water, and wonder if it's too early to call Jazzie.

What the heck, I think. It's not like she's never woke me up, before!

Returning to the kitchen (I don't keep a phone in the studio) I dial Jazzie's number. She answers on the second ring, sounding perky and fully awake. Good! This means I know she'll be fully understanding my concerns, when I talk with her.

"Mornin', Alli!" she sings in her melodic voice. I've always wished I had a voice like hers, but then, she is in a profession where voice is important. I'm not. I rarely speak with anyone, whereas Jazzie talks all day.

"Hi Jazzie," I reply. "It sounds like you're already up?" I inquire hopefully.

"Up, and at 'em," she returns.

"Good! Because you know how much I abhor waking you." I finish with a laugh.

"Yeah, I know. But only because I'm a bitch when my sleep is disturbed."

"Yes. There is that," I chuckle. "Say, listen, do you have any time this morning to help me with something?"

"As a matter of fact, I do," she replies. "Why? What's up?"

"Well, I have this painting I'm working on — a portrait of a man."

"Commission?"

"Yes."

"What does the commissioner want from the man? Love?"

"It's not exactly the normal thing I'm asked to do," I explain. "The commissioner is the man himself."

"Really!" she exclaims. "What does he want for, or of, himself?"

"Enlightenment," I say simply. There's a beat of silence while Jazzie processes this information.

"Enlightenment? Seriously?"

"Yes."

"Wow. That's a new one."

"I know. And I'd like your input for the painting."

"Okay," she replies. "But I'm not sure I can be of any help."

"That's okay," I tell her. "Just talking with you about it may be all the help I need."

"Okay then! Should I come over, or do you want to come over here?"

"I'll go over there," I tell her. "See you in about half an hour?"

"Sounds good, sweetie," she says. "See you then!"

We break our connection and I go to gather up the mouthless man.

When I arrive at Jazzie's I have this vague feeling that I've forgotten something, but I've no idea what it could be. The problem with having vivid dreams, whether I remember them or not, is that often times, what I think I'm forgetting, is something that I would be forgetting if I was in my dream. So I decide that that must be the case here, because I honestly don't think I've forgotten a thing.

I gather the portrait, (wrapped in plain muslin, which is my habit before I'm actually finished with it), grab my purse, and head to Jazzie's door. Jazzie lives in a more "civilized" part of the Valley than I do. She lives in North Scottsdale, in one of the finer gated communities. She says some of her neighbors are real snooty-tooty but, for the most part, they are nice folks. I ring the bell beside her massive front door and she answers immediately.

"Hola, amiga," she says. "Come on in!" I follow her through the foyer to the living room with the wall of sliding glass doors that show off the view of her immaculate backyard. Her pool is almost Olympic-sized and dominates the view. She has queen palms and California palms—the latter towering almost sixty feet in the air. She has a mesquite that blew over when it was young, so it has been trained and pruned to look like it lives in the Serengeti. A dozen humming-bird feeders hang from its branches and the hummingbirds are currently fighting off the sparrows and woodpeckers who seem to think that the feeders are there for them. And, because this must be so, why do they all have these annoying flower guards on them? Eventually the woodpeckers and sparrows give up, and push off the feeders, spilling a bit of sugar water to the ground when they do. This, of course, attracts ants, which is a real pisser. Oh well.

"Where would you like to talk?" she asks. "In here, or the kitch-en?" I think a moment.

"The kitchen," I reply. Not only is it not quite as grand, it offers a beautiful view of the mountains. We head to the kitchen and I set my purse on the granite countertop and pull the muslin from the portrait.

"Nice," she says. "I especially like the fact he has no mouth," she teases. "The perfect man." I roll my eyes at her and shake my head, giving her a lopsided grin. I just might agree with her if I didn't know that my lover was on his way. Maybe I should offer to paint a lover for Jazzie. Ever since her husband, Alan, died five years ago, she has been alone. She dates now and then—after all, she's beautiful, and men are forever falling over her. But she's had no one special in all those years. Make a note to yourself, I think. A lover for Jazzie. Check. Okay. Down to business.

I gaze at the painting myself, engrossed in the way his face is be-coming more handsome.

"What're you thinking about?" Jazzie asks. I tell her about the changing painting and she nods knowingly. "Changing reality," she says. "You know, most people don't even perceive the change. We're lucky that way. Makes life more interesting!"

I laugh, and say I agree. But as of yet, I don't mention my lover's eyes.

"So, what is it that you'd like my help with," she inquires.

"I would like you to give your opinions and/or insights on his mouth."

"Oh! He's going to have one?"

"Yes!!!" I tell her. "Of course he's going to have a mouth!"

"Well there goes his status as 'perfect man,'" she frowns. Jazzie, Jazzie, Jazzie.

Pulling his photo out of my purse I place it on the countertop beside his portrait. Jazzie takes it and holds it up, comparing the two. "Well, there is a definite difference between these two men," she says. "This one," she remarks, waving the photo, "this one is definitely a lower energy. He could use some enlightenment, if you ask me. He seems rather base."

"Yes," I agree. "He was rather base when we met. I didn't like his energy at all. Up until this morning I didn't like *him* at all. I also didn't like my first portrait of him."

"You've already done another portrait of him?" Jazzie asks, surprised.

"Yes, though I hadn't quite finished it." I explain further about the difficulties, including flinging it across the room and breaking it. But I leave out the part about puddling on the floor, letting him and Don make a mess of me.

She continues to study the man in the picture, then moves her attention to the painting. "You say the portrait is changing?" she asks again.

"Yes. I actually painted him as I see him in the photo—with the exception of the highlights in his hair and the omission of his mouth."

"Ah! Highlights in his hair!" Jazzie exclaims. "No wonder he's evolving! You know what highlights can do for a person!"

I laugh. Jazzie is such a goofball. That's one of the things I love about her.

"Okay," she says. "I'll be serious now." She takes the portrait to the light of the window and moves it slightly, side to side. "You know, Alli, this background you've painted is absolutely beautiful."

"Thanks," I say. "Oh! And that reminds me! I'm having Evie make my dress for the opening of Robert's restaurant."

"Really?" Jazzie squeals. "Oh cool, cool, cool!"

"I know," I laugh. "I can't believe I'm doing it! But it just seemed like the right thing to do, so I went for it. The reason I remembered right now is because the fabric swatches she brought out to place next to my complexion were the same colors as the background of this painting."

"Totally cool," Jazzie says. "Totally cool, yepper. You know what?" she asks.

"What?"

"In my opinion you don't need to worry about what his mouth will be like."

"No? Why not?"

"Because, if you just wait a few days, I think the painting itself will guide you. I think if you wait, it will all become perfectly clear." I consider that a moment, then agree.

"I think you're right," I tell her. "No, I know you're right." She brings the painting back over to me and I rewrap it in the muslin. "Well, it's been wonderful seeing you, but I better go," I say.

"I'm afraid I have a reading in about forty minutes anyway," she replies. "So, yes, you better go." She reaches for the painting, sets it down on the countertop and gives me a big hug. "Take care of your-self, Alli," she says, giving me a little shake.

"I will," I assure her. And I mean it. I'm also grateful that she doesn't speak the name of the one I have to take care of myself because of. She walks me to the door, and I move out into the ripening day. One stop at the store, as long as I'm down here, then home.

Chapter 7

When I arrive home I'm met with a sight that stops my heart. My front door is standing wide open. Pulling the car to the side of the drive, I stop a good fifty feet short of the garage. I consider turning around, and calling for help. I don't turn around — but I do call 911. I'm advised not to go inside my home and I say okay, and hang up. I think of the kids. No way I'm not going in. That's when I remember what was nagging me on the way to Jazzie's. I forgot to set my alarm. It's still relatively new to me, and being so preoccupied with the mouthless man I simply forgot all about it. I pull to the front and get out quietly. I realize that if anyone is still in there they most likely have been aware of my presence for many minutes. But it just seems more prudent to be quiet. Approaching the open door, I listen. Hard. Nothing. I tiptoe in and stop just inside, listening hard once more. Nothing. I continue tiptoeing through the living room into the kitchen. Nothing. Into the studio. Nothing. Into the bedroom. Nothing. Including no kids. I get down on my hands and knees and look under the bed. Two kids. My heart leaves my throat and returns to my chest. *Things* are not important. My kids are.

"Come on out, sweeties," I say as coaxingly as I can manage. However, my voice breaks a little. "Come on, sweeties."

Rico rises and crawls out from under the bed, with a purr, and a thrrpp. Bonnie stays put, not moving a hair. I'm still observing Bonnie as I reach to pet Rico and my hand jerks back in shock. I grab him and look at his back. He has a huge *D* shaved onto his back, right down to the skin.

"Oh my God!" I cry. I pull Rico to my chest and rock him back and forth, while he still purrs away. "Why did you let him do that to you?" I ask him, furious at what Dickhead has done. "Why?" But I know why. Rico is a pacifist. He doesn't believe in violence. He only believes in love. Bonnie, on the other hand, would have tried to rip Don's eyes out if he had tried this on her. Which is probably why he didn't. And after a moment of panic, envisioning the scene, I'm grateful to God that Rico didn't try to resist. Don would have probably killed him.

I hear a car pull up to the front of the house, and I go to meet the officer. I still have Rico in my arms. I show the policeman his shaved spot and he asks if I have any idea who would do that. Why, yes, officer. I do.

I explain the situation to him and he asks if he can go in to look around himself. I say of course, and we go in together, giving the place a better looking through than I had on my own.

That's when he finds the note. The one that says, *Where is it, Alli? I want it. Oh, and by the way, if I don't get it — Rico is a goner. Love, Don.* The officer asks if I recognize the writing and I say, yes. It's Don's writing. He asks if I know what the note means, what it is that Don wants. I say no, I haven't a clue what it is he wants.

I honestly don't have a clue.

The officer asks if he may keep the note as evidence, and I tell him I don't ever want to see it again. Take it and keep it. He puts it carefully into a baggie and then asks if there's any more that he can do. No, I tell him. He advises me that he'll make the report, and it will be determined what, if anything, can be done at this point in time. Then he advises me to be careful, to take care. And then he leaves.

I go to the kitchen, Rico still in my arms, pull out his favorite treats, put some in a fresh bowl, and set him down in front of it. Then

I go to my studio, close the door, and sink to the floor in a puddle of useless tears.

When I'm done dehydrating myself, I pull myself off the floor and dry my face. I take several deep breaths and open the studio door. Bonnie and Rico are both sitting just outside, side by side, love and concern on their beautiful little faces. "Hi, guys," I say, trying to put a smile on my face. They are not fooled. Rico gets up and saunters over to me, stretching midway, and then bumps my ankles, twining through my legs like a serpent. A good serpent. A sweet serpent. The stupid, ugly *D* shaved onto his back is a wound on my psyche. Which, of course, is just what Don wants. Every time I look at my precious Rico I will have to think of Don. God! He is such a cruel man. I try not to hate him, but at this moment, hate is all I feel. And it's hard to imagine ever being able to feel anything else.

I bend down and pet Rico, stroking over the shaved area, as though to make him believe it does not exist or, at the very least, does not concern me. He purrs loudly and struts away. I don't know. Maybe he likes it. Maybe he's in a punk stage of life and thinks it's radically cool. Maybe Bonnie has told him she thinks it makes him look tough, or some other term for macho. I sigh and reach to stroke Bonnie, and she raises her head to meet my touch. She locks her eyes with mine, and blinks *I love you.*

"Thank you, my Bonita," I tell her. "I love you, too." She seems satisfied with that and walks off to follow Rico.

I make my leaden feet follow the two of them.

They have gone to the slider leading to the patio. "Okay," I say. "Let's go see how the morning is shaping up."

We head outdoors and find that the usually oppressive heat is less today. There's a brisk breeze tossing the mesquites and palo verde. In the distant east thunderheads are forming. They tower high into the atmosphere, a single front lining to the north. The wind means they will most likely be here by afternoon, so I decide to take a swim, while I still can. I strip off my clothes where I stand and hit the water. It's still refreshing. Now that it's thunderstorm season, however, the humidity will make it seem less so in a few days. Yes, there really is a difference between humid heat and dry heat. We here, in the Sonoran Desert, are very blessed to have mostly dry heat.

I swim lap after lap while Rico bathes on top of one of the patio tables and Bonnie sits and watches intently for anything that moves. Most of the yard's fellow creatures are napping after their busy early morning, so Bonnie gets bored and joins Rico on the table. They nuzzle each other for a short bit, then wrestle a while. Rico always lets Bonnie "win". He always has, and I suspect he always will. Feeling I've finally worked out my frustrations, and cooled my core, I step out of the pool and realize I have no towel. Oh well. I stand and drip, and let the sun dry me. Rewarm me. Cleanse me. Bake me.

Ding! Done.

I push the button to send the pool cover gliding out over my lovely little play pool, putting it safely to bed before the fury of the thunderstorm fills it with dirt, dust, and leaves. The first fluffy sentries sent by the towering forces in the east are already here, causing the sun to play hide and seek. Every time the clouds obscure the sun, the temperature takes a noticeable drop. I actually feel a chill when the shade hits. My still-wet hair, I think. Time to go inside and put on fresh clothes — and do something with my mop.

I call the kids inside and they obediently follow. They're such good kids. They continue on through to the kitchen as I stop in my bedroom and search my closet for just the right inspiration. I find a scarlet tee shirt, trimmed in gold that matches the power of my heart. I pull on white jeans below it and add garnet and gold dangle earrings. I apply some red raisin lip gloss and put a splash of blush on my cheeks. I look a bit pale today, and I want to remedy that. I want to wipe out any reminders of the shock I've had this morning, but with Rico's *D*, I know that will be impossible. I decide to think of something else for the *D* to stand for. Something wonderful or inspiring. Something that makes me smile to see it. Nothing comes immediately to mind. Oh well. It will.

I wander into the kitchen and find Rico and Bonnie licking their empty plates clean. Finished completely with breakfast, now, they head in lazy zigzags to the living room window and jump up on their lookout table. They curl up, side by side, close their eyes, and are in dream land within thirty seconds. Oh how I envy them.

Feeling lost and unmotivated, I desire to do nothing but take a nap myself. But I don't. I head to my car, which is still parked out in the drive, and pull it into the garage. I reach into the backseat for the mouthless man—and he is gone. In his place is a note that says, *Thanks, Babe. I guess this means that Rico is spared. Love, Don.*

Oh. My. God.

Quickly closing up the garage, I enter the house and lock the door. I speed around the house and make sure all the doors are securely locked. The kids momentarily raise their heads to watch, then go back to their naps. I wrap my arms tightly around myself, feeling violated. Not only has Don stolen the painting, he probably watched me swim naked. The thought sends shivers of disgust all through my body. I feel nauseous. Grabbing a glass of water I drink it slowly down, washing my throat, diluting the bile. It doesn't help much so I reach for the teapot to make some chamomile tea. My hands are shaking so badly I can barely fill the damn thing. I set it gently upon the burner and turn it on high. No fooling around. I want this tea now.

When the tea has steeped I cradle the cup in my hands and sip the sweetness it contains. The chamomile calms me and settles my stomach. As I feel a better grip on life, I consider all that's happened. I hear a crack of thunder in the distance, and moving to the window I notice the clouds are barreling in much more quickly than usual. The storm will be here soon.

I rinse the cup and set it on the counter, as I'll probably want another soon. No need to dirty a second cup. I grab a few cherries and strawberries and sit as I slowly munch them, savoring, savoring. Another crack of thunder causes all of us to jump, but we settle back in seconds. Thunderstorms are a way of life in the desert, and we are no stranger to them. As the clouds race in, the sky is suddenly dark and foreboding. I rise and go to the sliding glass door and stare at the roiling dance in the sky. Lighting flashes pink between two competing giants bearing down on the thirsty land. The snap of thunder hits seconds later. A few seconds after that the crashing torrent of rain arrives.

The storm is here.

I watch, fascinated as always, and the kids are also watching out their window. I'm glad they aren't afraid of the thunder, like so many animals are. They seem to find the whole show an adventure of sight and sound, as do I. The rain is hitting the pool deck so hard the huge drops are bouncing back up almost a foot. It looks as though it's raining upwards, along with downwards. The wind whips the trees, tearing off the last of the seed pods. Any last bit of dust is being blasted and washed off the deck. After the storm passes the yard will be a mess, but my deck will be spotless — as will the tables, chairs, and lounges. Suddenly I have to be out there, out with the forces. So, I step out.

I'm drenched in seconds. I don't care. My hair is plastered to my face, neck, and shoulders which is good. Otherwise it would be whipping me to death. Eyes closed I hold out my arms and raise my face to the sky. The rain beats me. Stings me. Almost bruises me.

I love it.

The power that dwells in all of us begins to assert itself—a response to the power of the storm. Turning to the east I thank the forces of light, and draw them into me, making me wise. Turning to the south I thank the forces of love, and draw them into me, making my heart swell. Turning to the west I thank the forces of darkness and creativity, and draw them into me, igniting me. Turning to the north I thank the forces of my ancestors, and draw them into me, making me whole.

I'm now ready to fight the good fight. I'm now ready to get my painting back. I'm now ready to face Don. And, I am ready to win.

I laugh and whoop out there in the rain, wind, thunder, and lightning. I stay out as long as there is storm enough to empower me. Then I go in and dry off.

It's time to make a plan.

I spend the rest of the day considering options. When I've considered them to the best of my ability, and have examined my idea every which way, I find myself smiling broadly. Yep—it's going to work.

Putting on something slinky and sexy, for no good reason other than I feel powerful and energized, I decide to head to Jazzie's. I'm going to surprise her with an invitation to dine at Arrivederci tonight. Arrivederci is our favorite Italian restaurant in Scottsdale. It's small and intimate, comfortable and tasteful—the food is always wonderful, and the waiters always flirtatious. In other words, it's perfect.

I arrive at Jazzie's around sixish. There's still a lot of daylight to be had, now that the clouds have disappeared, but Jazzie and I don't mind an early dinner. I knock on her door and find her dressed in a beautiful, gauzy, mid-calf dress of exquisite color and design. She looks like an angel of the sunset. My heart sinks a bit. I think I'm going to be eating alone, but she grabs her purse and says, "I'm ready when you are!"

Confused, I ask, "Where are we going?"

To which she replies, "Well, I thought you wanted to take me to Arrivederci."

"I do!" I exclaim. "But how did you know?"

She rolls her eyes and pushes me out of the way of the door in order to lock it. "I asked the kids," she says, like I should have already known that. "Come on!" she orders as she sashays down her front walk. "Move it! I'm starving!"

Sometimes I hate that my kids tell her things without consulting me first. But other times, I admit—you gotta love it.

We chat on the way down Scottsdale Road, me telling her about Brenda's little dog, and how she found him—she telling me how grateful she was that she'd been led to tell Brenda about me. Then she asks how the kids have been behaving lately, and I tell her that they seem a bit more independent than usual. She smiles and says that's good. I ask her what she means by that, and she tells me she had a discussion with them.

"I told them their Mom needed to focus her energy on the problems at hand," she says, "and they said okey-dokey, Smokey." She says this with utter seriousness, and I glance at her to see if there's a smirk on her face. There isn't. But then she snickers and says, "Well, okay. They didn't exactly say that. But they promised they wouldn't cause you any trouble. Well, at least not more than is absolutely necessary. After all, they *are* cats."

I adore those two.

We arrive at the Restaurante and park in front. Giovanni calls out "Buona sera!" as we enter through the door and gives us each a hug and a peck on both cheeks. Which we return, of course. He leads us to our favorite table and inquires about our wine preference for the evening. As he heads off, to procure such preference, we look around the room. Even though it's barely six-thirty the restaurant is filling up quickly. We wave hello to Marilyn and Eduardo (the other two servers extraordinaire) and to the two young busgirls. The hostess, who Giovanni always intercepts when we arrive, so as to place us at the table he knows we prefer, comes to say hi, and we exchange a few pleasantries.

So far it's a typical, lovely night at Arrivederci.

But in our glancing around, I've seen something—someone?—that has raised a red flag. I look around the restaurant again, but don't see anything or anyone who should disturb me. Giovanni returns with our wine and the glasses, which he sets before us as he opens the bottle. He pours a small amount in Jazzie's glass, which she samples, and gives him a thumbs up. As he pours for us, he takes our appetizer order and tells us the special for the evening. He tells us about his latest trip to Canada to visit his family, then leaves to give the appetizer order to the kitchen. As I'm sipping my wine I look up just in time to lock eyes, for a brief second, with the man in the corner table. I gasp and choke on the wine. It's the mouthless man. As Jazzie expresses her concern over my sputtering, the man rises from his chair and drops cash on the table, all in one motion, then walks directly to the door, eyes straight ahead, not a glance our way. Before I can catch my breath, he is gone.

"Did you see him?" I manage to eke out.

"See who?" Jazzie answers, looking all around.

"He's gone, now," I tell her with regret. "He left as soon as he saw me see him."

"Who?!"

"The mouthless man of my portrait."

She looks relieved. "I thought you were going to say it was Don! But I'm surprised he didn't stop to say hi and ask about your progress," she adds.

"It's just as well he didn't."

"Why?"

"Because." I hesitate. I wasn't sure I was going to tell Jazzie tonight. I'd thought maybe I'd sleep on it, to make sure my plan looked as good tomorrow. But it looks as though the time is now, so I forge on, knowing this is not going to be a calm revelation.

"Because," I begin again, "I don't have the painting anymore."

"Why?! You had it just this morning, and it was going so well!"

I take a breath, and another sip of wine, firmly swallowing before I attempt to speak.

"Don stole it. He broke into my house while I was at yours this morning, and looked for it. Then he left a note that said he wanted 'it', and if he didn't get 'it' he would kill Rico."

"That son-of-a-bitch!" Jazzie says, too loudly, and a few patrons turn to give us warning looks. "Sorry," Jazzie says meekly, and they turn back to their own business. Jazzie leans in close to me and whispers intensely, "That son-of-a-bitch!" And I laugh. Then I remember Rico and his shaved fur and the laugh shrivels in my throat. I tell Jazzie about the *D* and she turns scarlet with rage.

"He's okay with it," I soothe. "Even Bonnie doesn't seem to mind it."

"Those brats didn't say a *thing* to me about it when I checked in with them earlier. You know, when they told me you were intending to take me out to dinner tonight."

"Well, maybe they feel it's no longer a big deal since Don apparently got what he wanted. Which was the portrait. He returned when I was out back for a swim, and stole it out of my car before I remembered to bring it in."

"But why in the world would he want it?"

"I have no idea," I tell her, shaking my head. "However," I say firmly, "I fully intend to get it back. And I'll need your help. And probably Christian's and Ben's."

"You got it," she replies. "And I speak for all of us!" I laugh at her conviction. Good friends are such a blessing.

In bed, later that night, I stare at my lover's eyes in the moonlit room. The doors are safely fastened, as are the windows, and the alarm is set, but I know there's really no need. Don is home in Sedona. He has what he wanted, and I'm out of present danger. I gaze at the full moon through the high window above the sliding door. It lights the sky like a spotlight, obliterating the normally showy stars. I think of the town of Sedona, a place I once called home. A magical place of very rare beauty. Filled with magical people of very rare talents. But no matter how special a place is, there are always some bad seeds. Well, perhaps one day soon, that will no longer be true. However for now, the bad seeds still exist. And Don is definitely bad seed. And Sedona is definitely, for all its sophistication and depth, a *very* small town. When you can't stand the sight of someone, it's a very, very small town. I return my gaze to my lover's eyes and blow them a kiss. "Goodnight, my love," I say.

The eyes sparkle back. I feel their *goodnight*, and I am content to drift off to dreamland.

In my dream the mouthless man is trying to tell me something. Something important. But he can't. Because he has no mouth.

I shouldn't have left him without a mouth.

I float from my bed, through the door, out over the desert behind my yard. I land gently on a small outcropping of granite, and lift my eyes to the moon. The desert is wrapped in silence. *In dead silence*, I think, but I know that isn't true. It is very much alive—but the desert can dwell in silence like no other place on earth.

It can be so silent, you can hear your tears fall.

Chapter 8

The next several days find the skies dark with thunderstorms. I allow the power of them to propel me through two fine paintings, which I finished late yesterday. I'll take them to the gallery on Friday. Tomorrow. I wash the brushes I've left soaking in water and make sure the caps on all the paint tubes are tight. I throw away the wax-coated paper I affix to my palette, having used every square inch. Sometimes twice. Staring at my empty easels I think of the mouthless man.

I've wrestled with the idea of painting just his mouth, then intending it to be together with the rest of his face—but being unconvinced of the rightness of it, I've done nothing. Which is a decision in itself. One I also wrestle with.

I stand at the window of my studio and look out at the rain drenched landscape. The mesquites and palo verde are showing signs of the extra water that they so love. They are greener. They are tough trees that can survive the harsh desert conditions—but everyone loves a bit of ease, don't they? A bit of caressing. An extra dose of God's love. Affirmation that one is cared for, and cared about.

In the desert, rain will do just that.

Evie called this morning and told me to come pick up my dress. It's ready. She told me she set aside a "sample" of the dress so I could match it to some new shoes and purse, if I wished. She doesn't want me to actually look at the dress until I'm ready to pull it on Friday evening.

But what if it doesn't fit? I had asked her. She just said it would. Count on it.

Okay. Whatever.

I figure now is as good a time as any to go pick it up, so I ready myself and head out the door after calling my goodbyes to the kids, and assuring them I'll be back soon. Pulling out of the garage and heading down my driveway, I'm thankful I don't have to deal with dust today. Just mud. But mud is good when you don't have much of it.

I arrive at Evie's shop several minutes later and park in front. The bougainvilleas look tousled, but happy. Everything is fresh and clean. One doesn't realize how much dust coats everything most of the time, until one sees things without the familiar shroud. It's very pretty. The colors sing. They're beautiful.

"Hi, Evie," I call as I push the door and enter.

"Oh, hi, Alli!" she calls brightly from the back room. "Be right with you!"

I browse the selections of fabrics she has displayed in neat racks, and the drawings she's done for ideas on wardrobe creations. I notice she's a very fine pencil artist. She could probably make a living at it. But I suppose she considers her clothing her art. And she would be right.

Carrying a long, black garment bag that is zipped tightly shut, she finally comes through the door of her back room.

"Now, remember what I told you," she scolds, like a grade school teacher.

"Yes," I reply obediently. "Don't open the bag or look at the dress until it's time to put it on."

"That's right," she says. Satisfied that I'm a good girl.

"And here is the sample," she says, handing over a patchwork of those gorgeous colors of scarlet, purple, gold, and copper. They are hand sewn together in a loose ruffle.

"Pick out some special shoes and a kick-butt purse to go with your dress," she commands. "Check Monica's for your purse," she adds.

"Okay," I say, simply.

"And make sure the shoes are comfortable enough to dance in."

"Why? Am I going dancing?" I ask, because I hadn't heard that there was going to be dancing at the restaurant, besides the flamenco dancers.

"I'm just saying," she replies with a dismissive wave of her hand. "Now go!"

"But what do I owe you?" I ask, pulling out my wallet.

"Oh, jeez, Alli!" she exclaims. "You don't honestly think I'd waste a creation like this on mere money, do you?" She's knitted her eyebrows together in a severe expression of exasperation. Mine is an expression of pure confusion. We stand a short moment, exchanging these energies, before she illuminates me. "Alli," she says, "when I need payment from you I fully intend to get it. But it will be worth more than money. It will be a painting."

"Oh," I say. Feeling humbled. "I would be honored to paint whatever it is you wish."

"I know, dear," she replies. "That's the point. So, go now! And enjoy your special dress!" She waves her hand at me again. Dismissing me. And heads back to her cave. When she disappears through her door I carefully gather my piece of art, my sample, my purse, and head to my chariot.

I drive home, hang the dress carefully in my closet, check to make sure the kids don't need anything, fill my stainless, lidded travel mug with RO water, and head out to shop for shoes and purse.

Shoes I can dance in, I remind myself. And a kick-butt purse.

I find the shoes at DSW, and the purse, just as Evie had suggested, I find at Monica's. I'm all set.

Spending the rest of the day catching up on the trappings of personal life, I do the laundry, tend to the yard, and swim and float in the pool. My laundry I allow to hang dry in the studio, since it is all very pretty stuff and I feel it won't interfere with the vibes of the studio. I try not to let anything ugly in there—with the exception of an occasional mood, as has been the case in this past week and a half. In my yard I remove dead flowers and leaves. I rake the sand, gravel and mulch, and move a couple of pots to better position them for the remainder of summer. The trees I have to leave for a professional. Keeping up with the voracious growth of mesquites and palo verdes is too much for an amateur—which I definitely am. In between these activities I swim for exercise, and float for enjoyment. The day is mostly dark with rain-laden clouds, but they hurry through and leave nothing in the desert. Instead they save it for the north, the high deserts and the forests. For Sedona, Prescott, Flagstaff, and the Hopi and Navajo Indian Reservations.

I am happy to share.

The sky is breathtaking where the clouds break for moments, ripping my heart out with the deepest turquoise imaginable— magnificent against the dark, brooding gray of the thunderclouds. The air is coolish, though muggy. The water in my pool is still coolish, amazingly, so it is very refreshing. I spend the entire afternoon in these activities, my mind slipping now and then to tomorrow night. Robert's last Bistre was wonderful. We were all shocked, and disappointed to death when it closed. I'm so relieved he will have another. It sounds fabulous, this new restaurant of his. I drift into dreamland for an undetermined amount of time, there in the womblike environment of water and floating. The breeze, blowing the clouds on their way up north, has created an almost imperceptible rocking of the water as it skitters across, and I guess I find the combination of it all an irresistible invitation to nap.

In my dream I dance.

As a few large raindrops sting my face, I awaken with a start. The clouds have returned after all, and are ominous in their darkness. I see torrential rain reaching for the ground in the distance, so I roll off the floatie and swim a quick lap. Grabbing my raft so it won't blow away, never to be seen again, I climb out of the pool, pull on my terry robe, and close the pool cover. I move to the overhang of the patio, and watch as the wall of water approaches closer and closer. Then I go inside, making sure all is tightly shut.

I shower a minute, just to remove any chlorine from my skin and hair, and dress in some rayon pants and a black tank top. The pants are rust, brown, black, and cream—the design vaguely Native American. The comfort, in heat and humidity, is unparalleled. To honor the memory of the afternoon sky peeping through the clouds, I add a turquoise necklace and earrings, then head to the kitchen. Rico and Bonnie are waiting. I pick each up in turn and hug them tightly, kissing each numerous times on their silky heads. They purr their approval and leave me gobs of fur on the front of my tank top as my reward. I'll feed them first, then I'll use my taped roller to "defur". I admit, this past week I haven't brushed them every day. I thought they'd finished shedding, but I was wrong!

The kids are now happily eating, my tank top is fur-free, and I'm standing with the frig door open, contemplating what to feed myself. I decide to shut the frig and grab a can of Amy's soup. I'll eat light until tomorrow night—that way I can pig out at Roberto's.

Good plan! I think. I congratulate myself.

After dinner I curl up in bed with a book, but the steady sound of rain and thunder lulls me to swift and deep sleep. I sleep so deeply I don't remember my dreams. I sleep so deeply I don't awaken all night. When I do awaken, it's morning, and the sun is already beating in a cloudless sky.

The storms have gone. Friday is here. I experience an intense flutter in my gut and heart, like a child anticipating the first day of summer vacation, or the day of their grandest birthday party yet. I'm excited beyond belief, and I don't even know why.

I do my morning routine, clean up the house (which generally means removing dust from any and all surfaces), then gather my paintings to take to the gallery. After dropping them off I'm at a loss as to what to do now. I'm antsy to the point of being nervous. Not having anything, really, to do, I decide to drive by the restaurant, perhaps to pop in and say hello to Robert. I head on over, only to find an organized, high-energy chaos—one I know I have no place in. I hate to be in the way, so I leave, and go home, where I know I'll be welcome no matter what my mood.

There, I get out the Furminator and go to town on Rico and Bonnie. They release enough fur to make another cat and I apologize for having been remiss in my mom-duty. There was an article once on a woman who had enough fur saved from her long-haired cat to have it made into yarn. She then had someone knit her a sweater from it. I have to say—it was gorgeous. She was posed with her cat, and they looked spectacular together. But I don't know. I'm not ready to go there just yet. However I'm not willing to just throw it away, either. So I put it in the bag I use to save it until I can bury it in my yard. Hair and fur are actually nutritious for soil. And I like to think of us all as part of the pretty landscape. Togetherness and oneness.

Bonnie, as is her ritual, goes in to finish eating her breakfast after the brushing. Rico, as is his ritual, steps outside to show off. He is a good-looking boy, and he likes to share his beauty with all who might admire it—especially after his brushing. I tell him the birds and lizards are probably not impressed—but what do I know?

With that uneasy excitement still nagging me, I go around the house and gather my crystals. Each has a particular area of expertise, so they are displayed where they can do the most good. I gather the compassionate healer from the bedroom, and the manifester from the studio. The one I call Nike, because he's the one that's always shouting *just do it!*, I gather from the kitchen. I take them all to the living room and grab the little rug from in front of the couch, which I place in the middle of the floor. I rescue my meditation pillow from the corner, set it upon the rug, myself upon the pillow, and place my crystals around me. I close my eyes and relax, my hands loose in my lap, palms up. I breathe in and out slowly, concentrating on the sound and feel of my breath. I listen to the silence. I ask the crystals to send me their energies. I ask my angels and guides to send me their energies. I ask the Divine Universe to send me its love and energy. I do this for 15 minutes until I feel calm and centered. Then I open my eyes, thank them all, arise out of the circle of crystals, leaving them there for now to chat among themselves, and select oracle cards from the bookshelf in the corner of the living room. Sitting on the floor in front of the coffee table I place the piece of red velvet fabric, I've acquired just for this purpose, on the table before me.

I'm ready to see what my higher mind has to tell me.

At least I think I am.

I open the box and spill the deck, upside down, into my hand. I place the bottom card, now face up, on the red velvet. I always consider that the bottom card is my first card for a reading. It's just something I do. Upon finishing a reading I always shuffle the cards thoroughly before returning them to their box. I figure higher mind energies know when I'm going to be next asking them for help, and that they know exactly what help I'll be asking them for. So the card they place at the bottom of the deck, when I'm shuffling to put the deck away, is the first card I'm going to see, and the first card of my next reading. At least that's the way I look at it. And since there's no right or wrong, I go with it.

That card is *Rest*. I shuffle the deck until another card falls out. *Passion*. I shuffle again and a card flips over. *Beginnings*. I shuffle for ten more times, and nothing else falls out or flips over. So I consider myself done. I take the booklet provided, and read the interpretations — though little interpretation is needed. I stare at the cards. I had hoped a reading would provide a sense of calm, but instead it has created even more of a stirring in me. Such is life.

Finally, not knowing what else to do, and afraid that no matter what it is I choose I'm just going to be more and more on edge — I decide to take a nap. Perhaps that is my "Rest".

When I awaken three hours later I can't believe I slept that long or hard! It must be the strain of the last week and a half. I'm normally a person who craves a lot of sleep — but not this much! I lie in bed for a minute longer, letting my head clear as I crawl out of the well. A slant of sunlight slashes the eyes on my wall. The look is disconcerting, so I don't speak to them, just stare. For now they have nothing to say, and neither do I.

I get up, snatch the clothes I stripped off earlier, and hang them back up in the closet. Taking a long hot shower I wash my hair well, paying particular attention to conditioning it all the way down to the ends. Then I add a bit more conditioner to the ends. It just feels right. I shave with care, and exfoliate with tender awareness, my body brimming with sensual tensions I haven't felt in years. I rinse thoroughly, every bit of the shower ritual seeming to take on special meaning. Seeming to speak of extreme importance. I exit, towel off lightly, leaving my skin damp, and select my favorite lotion. It's one of Beth's, and it both smells and feels like heaven itself. Slathering it all over, I leave it to finish melting into my thirsty skin as I turn to my hair. I only partially dry it, mostly at the roots, leaving it damp enough to turn into waves and curls as it dries. Evie had said to wear it up, and waves and curls add interest when I do that. I check the time, loving the feel of walking through the house naked. I still have two and a half hours before I need to meet everyone at the restaurant so I go to the kitchen, still naked, and make myself some tea. While it's steeping I select a nail polish and set up my manicure kit on the little table in the breakfast area. The tea is ready and the lotion has all soaked in, so I grab my silk robe and slide it over skin that now matches its beauty.

Gliding back to the kitchen, feeling cloud-like and heady, I pour the tea into a porcelain cup I bought at a consignment shop—one of those works of art painted in colors that suck the breath right out of you. All the gold is still completely intact around the rim, so I wash it very carefully when I use it—which, truthfully, isn't often. I select a scarlet party napkin to set it upon, as it came with no saucer, and arrange the manicure supplies and tea on the table just so. Pulling the second chair over to have handy for doing my toes, I get to work.

In a little less than an hour my hands and feet are works of art. I even did a little gold detailing over the scarlet polish, which is totally not my style. Jazzie's, maybe! But not mine. Tonight, however, is going to be special. I just know it.

Still having an hour and a half before our reservation I revel in the luxury of time as I step carefully back through the house to my bathroom, keeping my toes spread as I walk. The nail polish should be dry, but why take chances? When I'm in front of my sink I carefully touch each fingernail, testing them. They pass that test so I give them a firmer rub. If one is going to screw up, better to know now than later. They're all good to go so I arrange my hair styling supplies on the vanity and assess my reflection in the large three sided mirror. I remember my frustration sometimes, at messing with my hair for an hour, thinking it will never look right, then saying screw it and doing my makeup. Afterwards, lo and behold, my hair looks wonderful—because I did my makeup! So instead of risking a similar situation tonight I push the hair stuff aside and put out the baskets of makeup. Not that I have a lot of makeup—they are small baskets. I just like to keep things I use regularly in one, and the not so regular stuff in another. Tonight, I'm sure, will require bits of both.

I start with a dusting of mineral foundation. Jazzie turned me on to mineral based makeup, and I really like it. I lightly brush here and there, anywhere my skin is less than perfect. Then, choosing my largest, softest blush brush, I add the barest of sunset to my cheeks. I dash a dusting of gold and bronze where I think it will be sexiest, then spritz my face to set the powders. While it dries I pick my dark brown eye powder and seriously line my eyes. I don't usually even wear eye makeup, but, you know, if there are to be flamenco dancers tonight, I'll have a lot of smoldering eyes to compete with. Don't want to be a washed-up wall flower! Tonight is all about standing out. So, I put it on in lavish abundance, them smudge it into appropriate smolder. I enhance the crease of my eyelid with a brown that is slightly lighter, place light touches of orchid on my lids, and stroke a bit of gold over the brown liner. I spritz and let dry. Then, very carefully, I apply mascara, making sure every lash has its fill. Standing back a little I assess my appearance. Wow. Maybe I should wear makeup more often! Of course, then, how would I look special when I wanted? Better this way, I guess. I leave my lipstick off for now, and turn to my hair again. I comb it gently with a wide toothed pick, then grab the majority of it, twirling it into place on the top of my head. I apply the appropriate number of hair pins to hold it, then stick some decorative picks in. I brush the tendrils that hang until they are silky, then lightly mist them so they will curl in a nice spiral when dry. My hair looks awesome. I line my lips with light rusty-scarlet liner, then fill them in lightly with the same. Over that I put my favorite apricot lip gloss, and then turn my head this way and that. Very nice. Floating into the bedroom I check the time. Forty minutes until the reservation. Perfect.

I slip off my robe and hang it on the gilded hook behind my bathroom door. Being that it's summer, any kind of nylon stocking is out—and, besides, I don't even know what my dress looks like yet. So I choose a bronzing lotion with a touch of gold sparkle and smooth a very tiny amount over my bare legs and feet. When I wiggle my toes the sparkles dance in time with the gold decorative touches on my toenails. I love it. I choose my sexiest thong with the matching strapless bra, then decide against the bra. I know it's not the norm, but I like to go braless when I can. So I will. I admire my half naked self in my full length mirror and take a deep breath.

Time to don my dress.

Moving to my closet I gently remove the garment bag from the rod. I lay it on the bed and unzip it slowly, carefully, anxious to see what is inside, but wishing to prolong the experience. I chuckle to myself as I realize this is what a man does with the object of his desire, especially the first time he unzips her dress. I guess I know how they feel, now.

As I part the folds of the garment bag I suck in a gasp. The fabric shimmers and shines at me in tantalizing little golden stars set in the now familiar scarlet and purple sky. Even though I was familiar with the fabric it seems even more magical in the caress of the garment bag. I pull the bag off and lift the dress out fully, like when a man finally unhooks his lover's bra and allows her breasts to seek their freedom.

The dress seems to sigh with relief, and I'm glad to be its rescuer. I hold it up in front of me in the mirror. My god, it is stunning. I carefully pull it on and zip it up the back. It fits like a glove, but a comfortable one because the fabric has some stretch, which I hadn't noticed before. The neckline is sweetheart, the straps are designed to wear either firmly placed on your shoulders, completely off your shoulders, or somewhere in between. I choose to place one strap off, and the other in between. The skirt falls with a slight godet flair, just below where it clings to, and accentuates, my butt. Its length is asymmetrical, with a slight, loose ruffle at the hem. I don't normally do ruffles, but I have to admit, this one is pure romance. I step into my golden, high-heeled sandals, with the tiny crystal accents, and turn to the mirror again.

I can hardly believe my eyes. Tonight I am a goddess.

Finally tearing my gaze away I take my new purse out of its bag, carefully releasing it from its tissue wrapping. It's beaded in the same colors as the dress, with an edging of miniscule stones of robin's egg blue along the top, below the clasp. You don't even really see them unless you look close. They just provide what seems to be an uniden-tifiable contrast that lights up the other colors. They make the other colors sing. I load the purse with my favorite golden hair pick, my little gold compact with the green-stoned gecko on it, my lace edged handkerchief, my lipstick and gloss, my tiniest wallet, and one small amethyst stone. Amethyst has many duties. It can prevent drunken-ness, encourage magic, and ward off evil. A useful stone for a night like this, I think. I glance at the clock, which confirms what I already know. It's time to go.

Checking the kids' dishes I find there's still a bit of dinner left for a snack later, so I just refill the water bowl and blow them a kiss, telling them I'll be home in a few hours. I arm the alarm, lock up, and set to the task of meeting my best friends for an evening that is sure to be special.

Chapter 9

When I arrive the place is already hopping, and I spy Ben and Christian's car next to Jazzie's in the parking lot. I have to park further away, but that's just fine. These shoes really are comfortable. Walking is a breeze—dancing should be no problem. When I glide up the steps to the arched entrance I hear a wolf whistle and a "Helloooo beautiful!" from the patio. It's Christian, which makes me smile.

Sailing to the hostess podium I let her know I'm with my three friends on the patio. She grabs a menu and leads me through the ornate dining room, and through heavy, wooden French doors that have been flung open to the evening breeze. I follow her to the large, round table where my friends sit with glasses of wine already before them. The last of the bottle they ordered is waiting for me to finish it. The hostess places my menu before me and asks if I'd like her to pour me a glass of wine and I tell her yes. As she does, Ben asks her to please tell our server to bring another and she says it would be her pleasure.

"My god, girl!" Ben exclaims. "You are positively ravishing to-night!" I blush at the compliment and thank him.

"He's right," Jazzie chimes in. "Is that the dress Evie made for you?" she asks, knowing darn well it has to be. Romance like this can't be bought just anywhere. I tell her it is, and sip my wine, to forestall any more compliments or questions. I'm not used to this sort of thing. It really is almost like magic. Tonight I'm even prettier than Jazzie, and I don't recall that ever happening before. Not ever.

Our server shows up with another bottle of wine that is, I must say, absolutely divine. He shows it to Ben, who nods, then he opens it and pours a taste into a fresh glass he has brought. Ben swirls it, inhales it, tastes it, then nods again. The server, an extremely handsome young man I must admit, pours Ben a half glass, and puts the bottle on the table. He places our fresh glasses near us, as no one but Ben is finished with their current glass yet, and removes the empty bottle. He politely inquires if we've decided on an appetizer, and Jazzie, who's the most experienced with food, orders for us. The server tells us that's a good choice, which I'm sure is true, because at Robert's restaurants there are no bad choices. When he leaves us to put in the order Christian turns to me.

"You really do look radiant, tonight, Alli," he says sincerely.

"Thank you, Christian," I reply. "I guess I was hoping for that effect, because all day I just had this feeling that tonight was going to be special," I tell them all.

Ben raises his glass and toasts, "To tonight being special!" And we clink, and drink.

The server returns with our appetizers and plates, a busgirl right behind him. She clears off the first round of wine glasses, which we now have emptied, and takes them away while the server arranges plates. We tell him no, thank you, when he asks if we need anything else at the moment, and he goes off to please other patrons. As the aromas wash over the table in a spicy wave, we dig into the succulent food, and catch up on our day. Ben is close to finishing his latest sculpture, and Christian almost has his new employee whipped into shape. Jazzie is working her way through her present appointments, but scheduling any new ones for no earlier than week after next. All these things are good news to me because, what my friends are doing, is clearing their calendars for me and my planned escapade—the one where I get my painting back from Don.

"Have you been able to tune into Sadie?" I ask Jazzie, while sipping some water to keep from drinking too much wine too fast. Sadie is Don's large black lab.

"No, not yet," she says with a frown. "It can be difficult, if an animal doesn't know to expect me," she explains. "They may just kind of sit there, and look at me like 'who the hell are you?' if no one has warned them I'll be tuning in. And, of course, it's not like we're going to tell Don to tell his dog we'll be tuning in," she finishes with a swig of her wine. I can tell she's frustrated. Jazzie doesn't even usually drink wine. She tries to keep her diet as pure as possible. It helps her work, keeps her more sensitive.

"That's okay, Jazzie," I reassure her. "It will happen. When we need it, it will happen."

"I know you're right," she says. "But after all, this is my most important contribution. Everything could hinge on it! And the stupid mutt just sits there like a bump on a log!"

"Well, my dear," Ben interjects, "maybe you shouldn't talk about her that way if you want her help."

"Good point," adds Christian.

Jazzie laughs, losing her edge. "Yes, my darlings," she admits, holding her glass up for another toast. We all clink again as Jazzie says, "To Sadie! The smartest, most beautiful, most cooperative dog in the whole, wide world!"

"Hear, hear!" the rest of us add, and we all take a big sip.

"So, Miss Alli, how're things going on your end?" Ben asks.

"Fine," I tell him. "I have no commissions, and won't take any until this is all over with. I'm just doing regular paint work, finished two earlier this week. I've taken them to the gallery already, this morning."

"Any good?" he teases.

I just punch him in the arm and don't reply.

We've finished the appetizers by now and the busgirl appears, to efficiently clear our table. Our server arrives and takes our dinner orders, pours wine into our stemware, and calls the water girl over to top off our water glasses. We pause a few minutes in our conversation to just sit and take in the new restaurant. Like Robert's first, it's a work of art. The Spanish décor is elegant enough to make a patron feel like they're in a classy place, but the rustic heaviness of it invites exuberant conversation. I like that. I totally detest those restaurants where everything is so hoity-toity and delicate that all you can hear is whispering and the clinking of crystal. I enjoy a little more meat on my experience.

The patio where we're sitting looks out over the courtyard. A huge, gnarled tree dominates the center of the yard, surrounded with cobbled stones that are edged with weathered brick. Benches are scattered here and there to accommodate diners and shoppers who just want to sit and enjoy the shade. There are dozens of Mexican pots strewn about, filled with every kind of flower that can tolerate the summer in a place like this. Festive lights are strung haphazardly from the tree branches, reaching to the patio roof, and winding down the wooden columns. Large candles in heavy, colored glass, flicker from several points in the courtyard, everything combining to create a magnificent romance. The other patrons, who are lucky enough to be here tonight in an obvious sellout crowd, are as happy as we. The air is alive with energy. The smell of food is intoxicating. The music coming from the sound system, just barely audible over the din of the diners, strums and picks its way through one's consciousness, taking your senses to Spain and to Mexico—to all the Latin places of passion and intrigue. I notice two lovers lost in each other's eyes three tables over, and my heart swells. *Bless you*, I whisper in my mind. *Bless you and your future children*, I add, very much feeling like there will be. I bring my awareness back to our table, and to my three friends—just, it would seem, as they do, also. We look to one another, dreamy-eyed and immersed.

"Glorious place," Christian says simply, his voice barely more than a whisper.

"Amazing," Jazzie replies, her voice also a whisper.

"Magic," I add.

"To Roberto's," Ben finishes, holding up his glass. We all touch our glasses gently, reverently, and hold them together for a few seconds. Then we lower them to lips that are aching with longing, overcome with so much romance. I see the eyes on the wall of my bedroom and send them a silent kiss. They smile at me, then turn serious in their desire for me. I shudder with the strength of their longing. And blush. Fortunately it has grown too dark for my friends to witness the extra color on my cheeks. I smile to myself and take another small sip of wine.

Our entrees arrive.

Delicious beyond belief, dinner is magnificent. We share bits of our meals with each other, so that we can widen our enjoyment and our sensations. Our server insists we all have flan for dessert, on him, so we agree. Ben orders aperitifs for us all, telling us it will be the perfect enhancement of our dessert. Everything arrives just as the music on the sound system melts away. As the music, the dining room, and the patio grow quiet, a guitarist appears at the far end of the main room. He is in shadow, and no one can really see him, especially we who are out on the patio. But through the open French doors I can see his silhouette. A short, staccato rift bursts from his instrument, followed by utter silence. Another rift erupts, this one a bit longer, a bit more soulful. Then silence. Finally a soulful, tantalizing string of notes ebbs quietly, steadily from the guitar, not ceasing, but calling, calling. Drawn by the demand of the notes, the dancers appear. There are two of them, a man and a woman. The man is medium tall, lean and muscular. He's wearing a white shirt of fabric that moves with him, draping, fluttering, sighing as his arms first caress the woman, then fly away to do their own thing, high above his handsome head. His black pants drape over a small, tight butt and, like the shirt, the pants are fluid—just like is he.

The woman, stepping into a spotlight, is drop-dead beautiful. She wears a dress of flaming red, with black satin insets in the full-length skirt. Her sleeves are pulled off her flawless shoulders, her neck is long and expressive. Her dark hair is pulled back into a severe chignon, decorated with a single red rose. She wears no other adornment. Her beauty is adornment enough.

They move out into the dining room, heeding the command of the guitar, ebbing and flowing together, then apart. The tempo quickens, and they obey. The passion mounts, and they obey.

A silence erupts—and they obey.

Then a slow, soulful conversation of notes begins to flow from the guitar, and they come together, circling each other with wonderment, questioning the attraction. The male dancer bursts forth with a demand, his feet pounding their dominance, then admitting their vulnerability. Her feet answer quietly, understanding the power her beauty holds over him, agreeing to be gentle with his heart. They stare, breathless, at each other, their chests heaving with both desire and exertion as the music suddenly stops.

And, like that, it is over. A beautiful first dance. The diners erupt into a deafening ovation, and *olé* and *bravo* is shouted time after time. The dancers bow and curtsey as gracefully as they danced, and hold their arms out to the appreciative spectators. Then quietly, unobtrusively, the guitarist leaves the shadows. The light hits his hair, his body, his guitar, but he holds his face down, still in shadow. Slowly he raises it. His eyes are looking across the dining room, through the doors, straight at our table. Straight at me. My heart jumps as I gasp out loud.

It's him. My lover.

And he knows it.

With his eyes locked into mine he begins to play. The dancers work their magic, I'm sure, but I can't take my eyes off the guitarist. As the trio crosses the dining room, step by step, twirl by twirl, engaging all who are in attendance with an up close experience, his eyes never leave me. Some patrons are starting to stare our way, curious as to what or whom the guitarist is looking at. I feel my cheeks burning, and my stomach begins to lurch. I start to feel the need to gulp air, to will control of my senses, my body. I'm definitely losing it, but don't know what else to do but remain under his spell. So, that's what I do. Remain lock, stock, and barrel in his control. Under his magic. Helpless.

My body starts to tingle, and I realize he is probably scanning it. I feel caressing thoughts sweeping over my skin, and my nipples grow hard. I'm glad this dress is heavily patterned because, without the bra I so hastily flung on the bed, they would be on display for all to see. And frankly, I'm embarrassed enough. Embarrassed at the attention I am *so* not used to having, embarrassed at the adoration deep in his eyes, embarrassed at the way I'm swooning like an inexperienced virgin. When the music finally stops, the dancers bow again, and the guitarist nods almost imperceptibly at me, with a small smile on his full lips. As the crowd erupts into more shows of appreciation I feel a hand on mine, and I jerk my attention to it. It's Christian's hand. I look up at his face, and melt into the look of amusement mixed with genuine concern. I glance back quickly to the guitarist, whose gaze is now a stony question. He abruptly turns away, and heads back into the shadow. The dancers follow gracefully behind. The set is over, and so am I.

I stare dumbly at the empty space my lover occupied moments ago, my mouth open slightly in a daze. Christian's hand still rests on mine, and he gives it a gentle squeeze. Turning back to him, I close my mouth.

"Are you okay?" he asks.

"Yes, of course," I answer, perhaps too abruptly. "I'm fine. Why?"

Christian raises one eyebrow in question, and statement. He says nothing, and I gently remove my hand from under his. "I'm fine, really," I assure him and everyone at the table who, I now realize, are all looking at me with concern. "Really. I'm fine," I repeat, as though that is all it takes to make it true. "But, you know what?" I say, faking a lightness I absolutely do not feel, "I'm ready to go home." I start to rise from my chair and stagger a bit. Ben and Christian, assuming it's the wine—and who knows? it could be—immediately offer their services as escort home.

"We'll pick you up in the morning and bring you to get your car," Ben commands. I say that will be fine and gather my purse. Since Jazzie is in worse shape than I, and in her case it is without a doubt the fault of the alcohol, Ben and Christian take her under their wing, also, and the four of us pay the bill and head to their car.

"Please take me home first," I request, without explanation. Christian says no problem, and in minutes I am home. Home alone, except for Rico and Bonita. Alone with the shock of seeing my lover tonight. Alone with his stony misunderstanding.

Alone with his eyes.

It is, thankfully, a night without dreams.

Chapter 10

The next morning I awaken to the sound of the telephone ringing painfully beside my bed. Grasping my head I manage a meek hello when I finally get the receiver to my ear. So much for the amethyst helping to deter a hangover. But then, I *have* read it works best if you actually put it into your glass. You know, instead of just leaving it in your purse!

"Hello, Sunshine," a cheery Ben sings. "How's it goin'?"

"How do you think?" I retort, more testily than I should. Ben only laughs it off.

"When should we be by to help you reclaim your chariot?" he asks.

"Give me half an hour," I tell him, then hang up.

Moaning aloud, I drag myself out of bed. I splash water on my face, brush my teeth, comb my hair, stuff myself unceremoniously into jeans and a tee shirt and look at myself in the mirror.

"You're no goddess, today," I accuse the image in the mirror. "You are nothing but an *idiot*, today." The image nods in agreement.

I hurry to the kitchen to make a small pot of coffee. Pouring the first cup long before the pot has finished dripping, I know the rest of the coffee will be weak, but I don't care. I only have a few minutes before Ben and Christian will be here and I need my coffee! I stir Stevia and half and half into it, and gulp the brew. Mmmmmm. Good, strong, Italian roast. An eye opener extraordinaire. I slam the rest of it down just as the front bell rings. Hollering that I'll be right there, I grab my everyday purse, flinging the keys and wallet into it from the purse I carried last night. I call to the kids that I'll be back shortly to fix their breakfast, and feel a bit ashamed of myself that I took the time to make coffee instead of their breakfast—but then, I'm no saint, I remind myself. "You got that right," I chide, aloud.

I hurry out the front door, lock it, and trot to the car. I crawl into the backseat, giving my heartfelt thanks for the fine way they take care of their friends, and Christian waves it off. Ben is driving, so the ride will be less dramatic than if Christian were driving. Everything that Ben does is less dramatic than Christian, except his art. His art is plenty dramatic. Maybe that's why he can afford to be so safe the rest of the time. And, maybe, that's what Christian sees in him.

They drop me at my car, mine and Jazzie's being two of only three cars in the parking lot at this early hour. The quietness seems imposs-ible, in light of the roar that was last night, but I'm sure it will all be a roar again tonight. Robert has a hit on his hands, that is for certain. I get out and thank the guys. I tell them to say "hi" to Jazzie when they gather her and bring her to reclaim her Solara, and they say they will be happy to. Waving them off I dig the keys out of my purse. As I beep the door unlocked, and reach for the handle, I notice a piece of paper placed under my windshield wiper. I grab it, thinking it's a flyer for something or other I could care less about, and almost toss it inside without reading it. I'm glad I don't. It's not a flyer. It's a handwritten note. A note that claims in no uncertain terms that the writer needs to speak with me urgently.

I look around, as though the note's author might still be close by, then think what an idiot I am. But as I think this, there's movement in the third car in the lot, and a man starts to step out of the now open driver's door. It's my commissioner. He's looking straight at me, concern lining his face. But as he departs the car a shot rings out, and he quickly ducks back in. The engine roars to life and he spins his tires in the dirt, desperate for traction. Another shot rings out, but the mouthless man is now at the road and quickly disappearing from sight. I stand transfixed beside my car. I'm waiting, helpless, to see if I'm the next target. But nothing happens. After several tense seconds I hear a car on the next street pull slowly away, but I can't see who it is. I can surely suspect, however. Yes, I surely can.

When I no longer hear the car, I go to where the vehicle of the mouthless man was parked. I look to the ground. There's blood. Not much, but enough.

I pray for the mouthless man.

Then I get in my car and drive home in shocked silence. When I get there I call the police. Yes, I *know* I should have called from the scene, I assure them, but I didn't have my cell phone. And at that hour on Saturday morning the shops aren't open yet. There was no place to call from, I explain. Okay, they say. Can I meet them back there and answer the necessary questions, and give the necessary facts? Yes, I can. But I need to feed my cats first. Okay, the voice says. *Whatever* is implied. I put the food down for my kids, put out a fresh bowl of water, slam another quick cup of coffee, grab my cell phone this time, and drive back to the parking lot to meet with the officer. When I get there Jazzie is just stepping out of Ben and Christian's car, and the looks on their faces say it all when the police car drives up. I give them a small shake of my head when they raise their eyebrows in question, and they simply disappear, as though we did not know each other from Adam. I feel in my heart, however, that I will hear from them all before the morning is over.

The officer is the same one who came to my house when Don broke in.

"Miss James," he says in hello.

"Officer Trundell," I reply.

"You've had another incident, I hear," he says, opening his note-book.

"Well," I start, "it's not really *my* incident. More an incident with," I almost say 'the mouthless man', but catch myself in time. As a matter of fact I'm not sure I should say anything about our connection, so I just finish with, "more an incident with a man whose car was here in the parking lot when I came to pick up mine."

"And why was your car here in the parking lot?"

"Because I was borderline tipsy last night," I explained. "So my friends drove me home."

"I see," Officer Trundell says, scribbling in his book. "So, these same friends brought you by this morning to pick up your car?"

"Yes."

"And after they left, the man in the other car stepped out to say something to you?" he asks, repeating what I'd already told the dispatcher.

"Yes."

"Then what happened?"

"Well, as soon as he stepped out there was a shot. So he scrambled back in, started the engine, then tore out of here."

"And there was another shot?"

"Yes."

"Do you believe either shot found its target?"

"Yes."

His head jerks up. "Yes?" he asks, surprised.

I nod, and point to the ground several yards away. He walks over, still scribbling, then spots the blood when he finishes his note. He squats for closer observation, then rises and calls his station.

"Which shot was that, do you think?" he asks, upon his return.

"The first."

"Why is that?"

"Because his car was already moving when the second shot was fired."

"Any breaking glass, sound of metal, anything of that sort?"

"No. Not that I heard. However, his engine was pretty loud because he was spinning his tires in the dirt trying to get traction. So I couldn't say for sure," I finish.

Officer Trundell keeps scribbling. When he's done, he tucks his notebook under one arm, and puts his pencil to his lips, considering me. After several long seconds he asks, "Do you know the man?" Shit. I was really hoping he wasn't going to ask.

I lower my head, and look at the ground. Then I nod.

"Really?" he asks, surprised again.

"I know who he is, sort of. But I don't really *know* him, know him."

"Who is he 'sort of'?" the officer asks, intrigued.

"He's the man in the painting my ex-husband stole."

"Your ex stole a painting from you?"

"Yes."

"I thought he hadn't taken anything the day I came to your home," Trundell says, confused.

"He hadn't. He came back later. He found it in my car, because I hadn't pulled it into the garage yet. I had it with me that morning because I was asking a friend for her advice on it. Apparently Don was still hanging around after you came to investigate. Later, when I remembered my car was still in the drive, I went to put it away. When I reached for the painting in the back seat, it was gone. A note was in its place."

"What did the note say?"

"Something like 'Thanks. Guess Rico's off the hook,'" I answered, shuddering at the memory.

"Why would he want a painting of this man?"

"I have no idea," I answer. "I honest to God have no idea."

"Has this man tried to contact you any other time lately?"

I think of the encounter in Arrivederci and tell the officer that no, actually, he ignored me last time I saw him.

Then I think of the dream, and how he was trying to tell me something that night. But I decide to keep that bit of information to myself.

"What's the man's name?" he asks.

"John Smith," I reply. The officer looks at me with 'you've got to be kidding' written all over his face. "That's what he told me," I tell him, embarrassed at the truth. "And no, I actually didn't think a thing of it at the time," I admit. "I just spoke with him about his desire for the portrait, and gave him a price—"

"Which he paid in cash," Trundell offers.

"Yes. Which he paid in cash."

The officer makes some more notes in his trusty notebook, and just then another police vehicle pulls into the lot. A van this time. Officer Trundell gives them a short wave and turns back to me.

"That's all, Miss James," he says. His tone is a mixture of concern and suspicion.

"Thank you," I reply, and go to my car without a backward glance at him or the other officers. I start Ms. Sebring up, put her into gear, and drive slowly out of the parking lot, tears welling in my eyes.

"I'm so sorry," I whisper to the mouthless man. But I'm not even sure why.

At home I kick off my sandals, strip off my clothes, and shower away the sickness I feel in my heart. When I feel a little better I dress in fresh clothes, throw the ones I was wearing in the hamper even though they aren't dirty, and go to the kitchen, hoping I can eat something. But I can't. Not yet.

I wander aimlessly around the house, finally ending up in my studio. Pulling out a canvas I set it upon one of my easels. I'm still torn about whether or not to paint his mouth, by itself. Jazzie doesn't like the idea, but I'm getting freaked about being powerless to help him. I pray our trip to Sedona comes together soon. I close my eyes and talk to Sadie, myself. I'm thinking maybe she will listen to me, because she knows me, unlike Jazzie. I beam her love, good intentions, and comfort. I tell her Jazzie needs to communicate with her. That Jazzie needs to ask her some important questions, and that these questions, while they might seem intrusive, are very important to some very good people—me included. I ask her to please consider telling Jazzie what she wants to know. Then I mentally blow her a kiss, and break off.

Thinking about what I said to Sadie, that this issue was important to very good people, I wonder—am I good? I like to think so, but then I'm prejudiced. Is the mouthless man good? I don't really know. At first I didn't like him. But as time goes on, and especially after I started the second painting, he seems to be changing. And, yes. I now feel much more inclined to think of him as a good person. I sincerely hope I'm not misleading Sadie. She'll be pissed if I am. After all, we're going to be asking her to betray her master, and that's not something any self-respecting dog would want to be a part of. But I don't know. Maybe she's as sick of Don by now as the rest of us.

At this thought I smile. There is hope. Yes there is.

The rest of the morning finds me pretty worthless, so I give in and put on my suit for a swim. I'm shocked that none of my friends have called, but glad of it. I suspect they've agreed to leave it be for now, for whatever reason—that reason probably being to give me a little peace and quiet. And for that, I'm grateful. I swim laps today. Hard, strong, fast laps. I give my legs and arms a workout they haven't seen for quite a while. I keep it up until I'm sore and breathless. I depart the pool and pull a lounge chair under one of my umbrellas. Stretching out on the chair I revel in the silky warmth of the air. There are clouds in the sky, clipping along swiftly to the west. They are fluffy, both white and gray, but there is plenty of blue sky playing between them. Their shadows are sharp as they fly across my patio and yard, and in a few minutes I've been lulled to a trance. The events of the last two weeks fly before my eyes, crossing the expanse of my consciousness. The clouds are Don, his agenda, and the mouthless man. The blue sky is Brenda's little dog, friends who love me, and my lover. Or, I ask myself, is he a cloud, too? The way things were left is certainly a cloud. The way I felt when he looked at me was pure, blue sky. I fall asleep pondering the possibilities, and dream.

What I dream is that, one after another, my friends line up. Then my lover joins them. Then the mouthless man joins them. And as they all stand there looking solemnly at me, they suddenly merge into one, with a flash of light. They glow as one nova, blinding me, so that I have to shield my eyes. Then I feel a huge wave of love hit me. It nearly bowls me over with its might. But it doesn't. And soon I'm enveloped in a cocoon of love. It's warm and comforting. Then it's hot. Burning. I awaken to find the day has progressed, the sun has moved, I am no longer in the shade, and I'm getting sunburned. I take one more dip in the pool, then go inside.

After my shower I apply one of Beth's oil remedies to my red-tinged skin. It will heal it, and keep it from peeling. She's very good with this stuff, and I'm very thankful for that. No matter how conscientious I try to be, I'm frequently caught with my guard down.

It is now late afternoon and I'm feeling restless. I think of last night and blush from hair to toe. Or maybe it's just the sunburn. I decide to call the restaurant and see if there are any reservations still left.

No, they are terribly sorry, but they are booked up. However, I can always just come and take my chances, they offer. Diners sometimes don't show up, for whatever reason. Thank you, I say, and hang up.

Besides, was I going to make a reservation for one?

I call Jazzie. She has a reading tonight, for someone who really needs her. Sorry. I call Ben and Christian. They have previous plans. Sorry.

I hang up feeling a bit sorry for myself, then realize that, along with being busy, no one asked me about this morning. Very, very strange. Well, I guess it's just going to be dinner at home. Just me and the kids. I go to find them to tell them the good news, but they blink at me as though to say *whoop-de-do.*

Now I'm really hurt.

I fill the kids' dishes with dinner and dig through the pantry for a can of chili. Opening it, I dump it in a bowl, and nuke it. I try to avoid nuking whenever possible but, right now, getting a pot out, turning on the stove and all that—much-too-much effort. The chili's hot in a couple of minutes and I eat it standing up at the sink. No ceremony tonight. No place mat, pretty napkin, candle—that's for when one is celebrating life. And yes, I know. That should be every day, every moment. But tonight, I JUST DON'T FEEL LIKE IT. "So there," I tell that higher part of me that I imagine is wagging its finger, giving me stern, disapproving looks. Judging my weakness. Oh wait, that wouldn't be my higher self. That would be *me* right here. Alli. I stop eating the chili, pull out some plastic wrap and cover the bowl. Then I stuff it in the frig and put my spoon in the dishwasher. Time to get ready to go out.

I don't have anything as magical to wear as I did last night, but I choose something that is as nice as it comes for the remainder of my wardrobe. It's silk, slinky, draping, and my favored colors of sunset. I shower, style my hair hanging sleek and long, put on mascara, blush and lipstick, and stick some large gold hoops in my ears. I choose my barely there underclothes, slip on my dress, my gold sandals, and grab a casual little gold clutch, which I stuff with the necessities. I kiss the kids goodbye, turn on my alarm, lock the door, and drive off to whatever adventure awaits me.

When I'm restless I always assume there's a reasonably happy adventure awaiting me. Why else would I be antsy? Why would my guides and angels be pushing me into action? Does the Divine have a twisted sense of humor? Of course not. God loves me. And so, this must be a good thing, this ache to go to Roberto's. This ache to put myself on display. This ache to see my lover.

When I pull into the parking lot it's full, and I have to park way at the end. I beep Girlie-Girl locked, and tread carefully through the dirt lot, taking care not to raise dust and dim my sandals. I arrive at the front door relatively dustless and the hostess points out a spot at the bar. Okay. Better than nothing. Claiming my seat I order a white Zin. It arrives in seconds and the bartender asks if I want to start a tab. Sure, I tell him. I take a sip of my wine and turn my stool around to look out at the dining room. Just like last night it is full of happy, boisterous patrons. The aromas drifting from the kitchen are divine, and the golden glow of the lighting makes everyone look twice as spectacular as they probably do in ordinary life. But that's what restaurants like this are for. To elevate one above ordinary life. To give small reminders of what heaven is like.

I take another sip of wine, then turn my stool back around to face the bar. There is a mirror behind it, like many bars, but it mostly reflects the large liquor supply in front of it. The bartenders are whipping through their work with the efficiency of the young and strong, sometimes almost running into each other, but always just avoiding disaster. Practice makes perfect, I guess. I'm watching them without real focus, just letting their rhythm mesmerize me, when I feel a hand on my shoulder. For an instant I jump out of my skin. But then, through my obvious fog I hear, "Miss? Miss? There's a small table available if you'd like to have it." And I swallow my heart back down into my chest and turn to say yes, I would love that. The hostess moves aside and I'm looking directly into the eyes of the mouthless man. She adds, "Only thing is, you'd have to share it with him."

Not knowing what to say, I merely nod. She slips away and he holds out his hand to help me off the stool, waving at the bartender as he lays a bill on the bar. The young man takes it and says he'll be back with the change, but the mouthless man waves *no*, along with a shake of his head, and takes my arm to lead me through the crowded room. The table is in the corner near a potted palm. He sits me in the chair with the view out the window and I'm grateful. The sunset is just going into high gear, and it's a beautiful one tonight. The sky is aflame with hot embers of clouds. The blue between them is Maxfield Parrish blue. It's stunning. I gaze at it for a minute, then turn to "John Smith". He's looking at me queerly. I ask him how he is, and he just nods his okay. I ask him where he was shot and he gingerly touches the side of his calf. I ask him if he had it tended to. He hesitates, then nods yes.

I ask him if he can speak.

He looks at me long and hard. Tears begin to sneak into the corners of his eyes. Then slowly, painfully, his eyes never leaving mine, he shakes his head no.

It suddenly dawns on me. This is not the same man who commissioned the portrait.

"You aren't the man who hired me, are you," I state. He shakes his head.

"That man—he's your brother?"

Yes.

"Your twin brother."

Yes.

"He's an evil person, isn't he."

Yes.

"And," I say, feeling it strongly now, "he's a friend of my ex-husband, Don."

Yes.

"And they're up to something no good," I finish.

A long pause. Then, the nod *yes*.

"Are you mute because of your brother?"

Another pause, then a look up and to the left, pain in his eyes.

"Okay. We are responsible for ourselves," I agree. "But, are you struggling with this because of something your brother did?"

A shrug, a sigh.

"What can I do to help you?" I ask.

He considers this thoughtfully. His eyes look deep into my eyes, and they soften. He mouths the words *be careful*, waits a moment as if considering something else, then merely nods. *Be careful*, he mouths again. He stands, bends to touch my hand, and leaves.

I watch in dazed silence as he disappears out the door. And as I sit there, I hire myself to finish a painting. A very special painting. I'm giving this man his voice if it's the last thing I ever, ever do.

And I'm going to fulfill my contract with his brother, also. Tomorrow I'm going to start another portrait. I'm going to elevate that asshole someway, somehow. Also, if it's the last thing I ever, ever do.

And then, I consider the ramifications of Don stealing the portrait. He didn't know I had started a second one. How could he? But obviously he knew about "John Smith" hiring me in the first place. So, I reason, he thinks it's a portrait of the man who's in cahoots with him. So why steal it? Was there some sort of falling out? As I consider this the server comes to ask if I'd like to order. I say yes, and order what Jazzie had for dinner last night. Also, another wine—the house cab this time, please. He nods and sweeps away.

Then it comes to me. Don found out what excuse the man had given for his portrait. "Paint me enlightened" he'd asked of me. He'd thought it a big joke. But Don knows better. He knows I could do it. And that would reduce the man's worth as an accomplice. If he were any less of a jackass, he wouldn't be of service to Don.

Now the only real question is, why did John Smith involve me in the first place? He must've gotten my information from Don, but am I a real piece of the puzzle? Or was my being commissioned just some sort of joke John Smith decided to play on Don? Something to egg him on? As I finish my Zin I feel it's the latter. But I'm not positive. Either way, I'm part of the picture now.

Oh, yes. I most definitely am, now.

My server brings my dinner and wine and I eat slowly, indulging my ritual of savoring every bite. The din in the dining room fades away from my awareness and I eat while deep inside myself. I pray, and give out waves of love and healing energy to my kids, my friends, my town, my state, my country, my world. Myself. The exquisite aromas of the special food before me envelop me in wings of delight. The texture, the taste, send shudders of ecstasy up and down my spine. My fellow diners return to my awareness and I see them in their own special, glowing beauty. Everyone is beautiful, everyone is connected. I see the movements of the servers as a dance. The ebb and flow of the diners, as they lean forward and back, are like the gentle tides on a beach. Even the bartenders, in their more hurried state, are a dance. A fast one, I chuckle. The room is alive with rhythm. The voices and clinking of glasses and silverware on plates is music. The aromas are nirvana. I sink into bliss at being part of it, although I'm the most motionless entity in the room. Having finished my dinner I slowly sip on my wine. I push my chair back slightly from the table and feel a gentle touch on my shoulder. It's the frond of the potted palm. I smile at the palm and return a slight touch to its frond. Just a quick one. I realize that sometimes my actions cause amused interest from others, and tonight I wish to be as unseen as possible. But I feel a wave of love from the potted palm at my touch. So I'm glad I risked the encounter.

Suddenly the lights start to dim and the piped music fades away. It's show time. My lover appears in the shadow and starts the magic. The dancers appear, and continue the magic. At first it is slow and gentle. Then the woman starts to be demanding, and the guitar and the male dancer must keep up. She dances a dance of frustration, anger. She demands more and more of her partner until he has had enough, and stamps his end to the argument, even turning away from her. She continues on a few moments, but soon realizes that her partner is no longer playing along. So, she stops. Then gives a little patter of apology. Then a patter of inquiring. He answers with a firm, short step. He folds his arms across his chest and turns to glare at her. She begins a dance of seduction. Slowly she encircles her partner. Twirling gently, touching him with careful caresses. He lets his arms fall, then watches her as she picks up the pace of her seduction. She smolders, her eyes aflame with desire. He can no longer resist so he joins her. They seduce each other with fire and passion, all of it contained, calculated. Making it more seductive, flaming the longing. The guitarist is hardly playing at all, at this point. They need no music. They are the music. Love is the music. It is a stunning display and the audience sits mesmerized, enthralled. Finally the guitar begins to join, tentative at first, then more and more. The dance becomes familiar. The steps merge into one with each other. Then, in a burst of surrender, the woman ends in her partners arms. As the guitar fades the male dancer lifts her chin and gives her the barest kiss on her full, red lips. She lays her head on his heaving chest, and the music stops.

As the room erupts into applause I see women fanning themselves in mock displays of heat. Or, perhaps, it isn't play. I know I feel pretty enflamed! Taking a sip of cold water, I turn my attention back to the trio, only to find my lover's eyes heavy upon me. They smolder with the same intensity of the dancers', and I look away in embarrassment. When I raise my eyes again, the trio is gone. It's break time.

I decide I need to pay a visit to the ladies room. I place my napkin in my chair as I pick up my purse and head to where I believe the restrooms are. I turn down the hall with the familiar signs of men, women, and phone, and am opening my purse to check for a hand-kerchief when I raise my eyes and, suddenly, the world stomps on my heart. I stop in my tracks, and think of turning and making a quick exit, but it's really unnecessary. The two at the end of the hall are oblivious to me, or anything else, for that matter. At the end of the hall is my lover, with his arms around the female dancer. They are talking excitedly, and then she gives him a quick kiss on the lips and lays her head on his chest. He lays his head on top of hers and they just stand there like that. Like they deserve to be happy together. Like they aren't breaking my heart into a thousand pieces. Like I'm not the biggest idiot in the whole world.

I decide I can wait to use a restroom until I get home. After all, it's only a few minutes, and I'm leaving now.

Turning, I head back to my table, flag down my server and hand him two bills that will cover the cost of dinner and leave a very generous tip. Then I hurry out the door, before the tears begin. I run to my car, not caring about dust on my pretty sandals, beep her open before I'm even fifteen feet away, throw myself inside as the first sob hits, and drive myself home as carefully as a broken heart can.

Once in bed I stare at the eyes on my wall, once again bathed in light, this time from the stars, and I can't tell — is it my imagination, or are they laughing at me?

I am such an idiot.

That night I dream of dancing. I'm dancing with my lover, and he is demanding my attention, my love. He is demanding my submission to his desires. But I simply walk away, laughing. Laughing. Laughing until I'm out of earshot of the man who stands stunned with the rejection.

And then, I start to cry.

Chapter 11

I awaken to the ringing phone. It's Jazzie, and the tone of her voice brings me immediately out of my well.

"Alli! Alli!" she practically screams through the line. "I got through to Sadie! She answered me!"

"Excellent!" I reply, "What did she say?"

"She says Don has the painting in the hall closet under an old blanket. She showed me exactly where."

"She showed you?"

"Yeah. With the pictures in her mind."

"Oh," I answer, a bit embarrassed. Duh.

"Anyway, she says she thinks the picture needs to be finished. She says it looks dumb the way it is."

"She's got that right," I laugh. I love animals. They are a lot like children. Always honest. "Why do you think she finally allowed connection?" I ask, curious if Sadie told Jazzie.

"She says you contacted her, and explained the situation," Jazzie tells me. "Did you really?"

"Yes. I hope you don't mind."

"Why would I mind? I think it's great!"

"Well, I doubt I'd be able to communicate fully, like you do. But I thought it wouldn't hurt if I tried to at least put her at ease, being as how she knows me."

"Well, girl, it worked. She was completely at ease. She also added that she picked up a thought that you hadn't intended her to hear, after you thought you had signed off, so to speak."

"She did?"

"Yes. She said you thought that maybe she'd be as sick of Don as the rest of us—and, actually, that was the clincher for her. Because she is. Sick of Don, that is."

"Really? Why?"

"Well, the jerk has been leaving her without enough food and water when he goes."

"The asshole!" I yell, enraged.

"Not only that, but he's started calling her 'Stupid'—sound familiar?" Jazzie asks, knowing darn well it does.

"He's getting bored with her," I reply, suddenly afraid for Sadie. Don turns mean when he's bored with someone.

"So, she says, after careful consideration, she's willing to help us."

"Thank you, Sadie," I whisper to the image of her in my head. To Jazzie I say, "When do you think you can be ready to make the trip to Sedona?"

"I'm good as of this coming Wednesday. How about Ben and Christian?"

"I'm not sure—but I know they will have a good idea by now. So as soon as I get myself together, I'll give them a call, and see if we can get the show organized."

"Sounds good to me!" Jazzie says. "Let me know!"

"I will. And thanks, Jazzie," I tell her sincerely. "I am *so* grateful for your help. This will save a lot of time when we're there."

"Well, thank Sadie. She's the one who told us where it is." I laugh, we say our goodbyes, and disconnect.

I spring out of bed, refreshed, refueled, and happy—until I see the eyes on my wall. I experience a momentary pang of sorrow, then rally to the decision to be happy. Happiness *is* a *decision*, you know. If one thinks that happiness is based on something outside oneself, one will never be happy for more than brief periods of time. Because, as expanding beings, we always want more, once we've obtained what we desire. Therefore, if our happiness is based on *getting* something, we are constantly yo-yoing between happiness and unhappiness.

It's just easier to remember that happiness is an inside job.

Standing right where I am I close my eyes. I conjure up the feeling of joy in my heart. I give thanks for all the wonderful things in my life, and allow the joy and gratitude to sweep through me, over me, and out into the world. There. That's better.

With a huge smile on my face I take a quick shower, throw on some joyful clothes, and start the day.

After feeding the kids, and brushing them, they retire to the front window where they contentedly watch the show. That's what we call it. The birds, cottontails, and lizards are the actors, the yard is the stage, and everything the actors do is "the show". I'm glad my kids are so easily entertained. I honestly don't know what I would do with two-legged kids. Commit suicide, probably. Okay, scratch that. But I doubt I would be up to the task. At least not with any aplomb.

After a decadent chocolate muffin, strawberries, and kefir, I clean up the breakfast dishes and call the guys.

Christian answers with a "Hi, beautiful! What's up?"

"Hi, beautiful, yourself," I laugh.

"Why, thank you," Christian replies with bravado, but I can hear the blush in his voice.

"What's up is that Jazzie made contact with Sadie!"

"All right!" Christian whoops. "And, I take it from the upbeat tone in your voice that the contact was illuminating?"

"Oh, yeah," I giggle. "She's already shown Jazzie where the painting is, and says she's happy to help because Don is a jerk."

"All right!" Christian whoops again. "So, what's the plan?"

"Well, Jazzie is free as of this coming Wednesday. How about you guys?"

"Ben is free anytime, now, and Wednesday sounds good to me," he replies. "My new employee is doing great. She has learned the systems, the bookkeeping, and has a natural ability to suck up to snooty rich people."

"Terrific! How about the non-snooty rich people? Does she suck up to them as well?" I tease.

"They don't need sucking up to," he explains. "You can just be reasonable with them." I laugh, and we agree to keep in touch until Wednesday.

Bravo! This show is going to happen—and it will be one glorious performance. I can't wait.

Feeling smug I head to the studio. Then I realize I'm feeling smug. Not good. Wipe that smug feeling out of your heart immediately, my inner voice screams. Smugness is the prelude to downfall. So I stop where I am, spread my arms wide, ask forgiveness for my momentary lapse of good judgment, and concentrate on turning the smugness to pure joy—no meanness involved. It works. I'm happy.

I look at the easel I'd already filled with a blank canvas yesterday, and prepare to paint. I'm going to paint "John Smith". The original one. The "evil" brother. And he isn't going to stand a chance against my paints. He's going to get what he asked for. Yes he *is*.

My brushes practically fly over the canvas. The background materializes in minutes. His face springs into being within half an hour. His hair, his eyes, his nose, everything but his mouth. I set down the brush, close my eyes and say a prayer. I raise the easel higher so I'm face to face with where his mouth will be. I breathe deeply, flooding myself with oxygen. Then I pick up the brush once more, select the first color and paint the outline of his mouth. It has a sweetness that wasn't there before. A gentle knowing. Good start, I assure myself. Then as I fill in the lips, forming them, shading them, creating lips that speak only truth, I get a funny feeling. I'm not sure what it is. It's

just a fluttery feeling in my gut. I stand back and look at the portrait.
It is definitely not the voiceless twin. Now that I've met him I can see
the difference in them. The voiceless twin has the facial lines of
someone who hasn't spent years with meanness written on his face. I
believe *this* twin has practiced his meanness for most of his life. I pick
up his photo and study it. I doubt I can change the lines etched into
his face, but I can offer eyes that show remorse, a clear understanding
of where he has gone wrong. So I work on the eyes. When I'm finished I stand back. Yes. There is now understanding where once
there was none.

I look at the mouth again. It needs something more, but I don't
know exactly what. So I'll let it be for now. I'll paint it when I know
what's missing.

Removing my smock I study the portrait. It's good, actually. It's
very good. I move back and forth in front of it, eyeing it from different
angles. Except for what is missing in the mouth it's finished. I wash
up the brushes, tighten the caps on the paints, and call it quits for the
day.

I make myself a smoothie with whey and leafy green vegetables I
have bought from Beth, put on my suit, and go to the pool. I sit under
an umbrella and drink my lunch. Another storm is moving in from
the south, though it's still a ways off. The thunderheads tower what
seems like miles into the sky. Huge, scary monoliths. Staring at them I
see what appears to be lightning illuminate one of the giants. My skin
prickles, and I get the very strong feeling that if I'm to get a swim in
today I had better get a move on. I go inside and put my glass in the
dishwasher and grab a towel. When I return outside, in just those few
minutes, the thunderheads have grown noticeably closer. It's going to
be one hell of a storm.

I toss my towel on the chair and dive into the water. It's much
warmer than last week. One of those experiences where you almost

don't feel it because it's the same temperature as your skin. Soon it won't be refreshing at all to swim during the day. Like the convertible, enjoying the pool will become a nighttime activity. Which is just fine with me. One of the things I most enjoy about my work is that I make my own hours, design my own time just to my liking. Soon I will sleep more during the day and work and play more at night. In the city, in the main metropolis of Phoenix, the spread of concrete has created a heat island. It doesn't cool off much at night, anymore, in Phoenix. But here, north of town, where there is still lots of native desert and room for the breezes to play, it *does* cool off. For that, I am grateful.

I swim several laps, but then the wind suddenly picks up. I stop in the shallow end and look south. The sky is turning yellow ahead of the thunderheads. We're in for a major dust storm. Those suckers can come rolling in at race car speed, so I get out and towel off. Closing the cover on the pool, I say a pray of thanks that I could afford to have it installed. Cleaning a pool after a major dust storm is no fun at all. I make sure that everything that can blow around is secured, wish everyone in my yard good luck, though they are all seasoned survivors, and go inside. Just as I do the wind picks up to tree whipping strength, and the sky takes on a pall. I quickly hang up the towel in the bathroom and grab a robe to pull on over my suit. I don't want to miss a minute of the show.

For thirty minutes the dust storm is ferocious. The wind pounds the windows and dust cakes the outdoor furniture. Visibility reduces to almost zero, but I can't take my eyes off it anyway. Through the yellow pallor flashes become visible. Then the growl of thunder breaks through the roar of the wind. When the lightning and thunder become one, scaring the hell out of me for a second because the crack sounds like my house splitting in two, the rain starts. Torrential rain. In an instant the dust is reduced to mud. It's raining mud. Then, thirty seconds later, the rain is clear. The dust is gone. The sky is no longer yellow but a deep, brooding charcoal gray. The rain beats away the dust that had covered everything outdoors and, eventually, clears the dust from even my windows. The lightning and thunder drone on and on. For twenty minutes there is not even a second between lightning bolts. It's a strobe show. It's fierce, loud, and relentless. But eventually, there's a break in the rhythm. Bits of blue dance in miniscule portals amidst the angry clouds, quickly shut away again as the clouds race by. I can see the clouds more clearly now, as the rain is beginning to let up. One layer of clouds is moving east, another is moving west, and yet another is moving north. It's a fascinating dance. However, in the end, it will mean pure blue skies. Skies so blue and clear one will wonder if the storm had only been a dream. In the desert, that can happen within an hour.

God. I love this place.

Eventually the storm is gone. Not in an hour, but in an hour and forty minutes. I can still see some clouds out west and up north, but they are many, many miles away. Between here and there, there is nothing but the clearest, bluest sky imaginable. The humidity lingers from the water in the land, but the upper air is dry once more. The temperature has dropped considerably, and though it isn't exactly temperate out, I open the sliders and close the screens to enjoy the wonderful smell of wet earth. The creosote bushes are giving off their signature odor— the odor that says wet desert. I decide to go cut a sprig and bring it inside to romance the indoor air. Grabbing a large crystal vase, I fill it with water, and go cut some creosote. I place it on the kitchen table and enjoy the outdoors brought in. Dusk is beginning to creep in, and it brings even cooler temperatures. I think, for a crazy moment, that maybe I should sleep with the doors open tonight. Then I remember Don. And the imposition he has made on my life brings a flash of anger. Taking some deep breaths I dismiss the feeling. After all, allowing the anger to linger will only give him more power over me, defile more of my life and happiness. So I rekindle the joy in my heart. However, as evening falls, I close the doors and windows. And I lock them.

I fix myself a simple dinner and eat with the kids. Literally. I decide that tonight we should have a lot of together-time, so I sit cross-legged on the floor with them as they eat—I with my bowl, they with their plates. They actually think this is pretty funny and give me plenty of chuckling purrs between bites. But eventually we are all finished, and head off in our separate directions. I close all the drapes and make sure the alarm is set. Then I grab a book and head to bed. Yes. It's early. But I'm exhausted.

Crawling into bed, Rico joins me. Bonnie is already curled up in her favorite spot near one corner of the bedroom, between the dresser and a woven basket filled with dry desert twigs. Rico does his happy dance then curls up next to my leg and closes his eyes. Within seconds he is sound asleep. I decide not to read after all, and turn off the lamp.

Another day over. Another portrait largely created. Another reality almost in play. Another day closer to retrieving the painting of the mouthless man. Another day....

Chapter 12

Monday morning breaks bright and humid. During the night the land has released some of its gift of water, and it now hangs in the air. I pick out a rayon pants and top set. Because I feel like it, I pull the sides of my hair up and back, and clip them. Then, as the coolness rushes over the exposed skin, I decide to pull all my hair up. Yes. That's good for today. I stick a turquoise bracelet on my wrist and add matching earrings. Stepping into the kitchen I notice the creosote is still emitting the smell of wet desert, and I'm pleased. I add water to the vase, then spritz a bit of water on the cuttings. They turn the aroma up a notch and I smile. I set the vase back on the table and fix breakfast for all of us.

After we eat the kids seem restless, so we all go outside for a bit. The birds are busy comparing notes about the storm, and telling personal horror stories about how their nests were almost blown out of the trees. The lizards are scurrying through bushes, catching bugs that are just sitting out because they're too lazy or stupid to search for a dry spot, now that their old home is too wet to occupy. Lucky lizards.

In the distance I see a couple of cottontails drinking from a small puddle that will be gone by noon. But it's there now—and it's good to live in the present. Eventually the heat and humidity bear down too heavily, and we all decide we've had enough. The kids and I return inside, and they go off to have a nap. I feel like doing the same, but I decide I had better be more responsible.

Stepping into my studio I put on a subliminal CD. The music is rhythmic and seductive, and I find myself swaying to it as I study the portrait of John Smith. I still don't know how to finish his mouth because I still don't understand what's missing. As I stare, the desire to dance overtakes me, and I twirl with my arms upraised. I feel the earrings hit my face as I begin to shake my head back and forth to the music. The rhythm starts to accelerate and so does my pulse, and my desire. I let the music sway me and turn me and rock me. I close my eyes and give in to the music. It seduces me completely, and I'm glad to be a woman, glad to feel so free to give in to the music. I dance with the eroticism of all goddesses across the ages. My hips are undulating and graceful. I shimmy to feel my breasts move. All of me feels free and sublime beneath the gauze of the rayon. I dance like this for fifteen minutes, until I'm breathless and flushed. I stride gently around the studio, toe, heel. Toe, heel. Letting my pulse slow, and my breath steady. When I am calmed I give a final twirl to end up in front of the portrait again. A vision of wonderment slightly parts the center of John Smith's lips. Then the vision disappears as quickly as it appeared.

Now I know what's missing. A sense of wonderment! When we think we know it all, life becomes a drag, a box. When we're in wonderment life turns to magic. And we evolve. That's what Mr. Smith needs. A sense of magic. A sense that life is not only what he has been led to believe that it is. Life is much, much more. I know that, and I'm going to help *him* realize it by giving him the gift of wonderment.

I quickly don my smock, anxious to perform this life-changing deed. Preparing the palette with just dots of paint, the change is so small, I select my finest brush. In a matter of seconds his mouth is complete. His eyes speak of knowingness and understanding, but his mouth shows slight disagreement. His mouth says that it can still be surprised, still be open to magic. It's a good combination, and I'm pleased to have given John Smith a new life. I wonder how long it will be before it takes effect. Not long, I know, because it never takes too long. I kiss the tip of my finger and lay it gently upon John's cheek. It seems to blush under my touch. "I love you, Mr. John Smith," I tell the portrait. And I do. We are all God's children, and we are all here to help each other in the best ways we know how. I've helped him, and for that opportunity I'm grateful. It has added to my credit ledger. Now, it will be his turn to either pay it forward, or help me in return. It'll be interesting to see what happens.

I'm about to remove my smock when I think of my lover's eyes. And I chide myself for continuing to call them that, since it appears that he is someone else's lover, not mine. But I go and retrieve the painting off the bedroom wall and bring it into the studio. I reverently set it upon the open easel and give it quiet regard. The music is still playing in the background, luring me into another dance. So I remove my smock and fling it to a chair as though I'm in a timeless, erotic striptease. I return to the dance, and as I dance before the eyes, my body fills with desire for the man who owns those eyes. Not knowing how the music will lead me I carefully turn the portrait of John Smith around, so he is facing the wall. I apologize, but it can't be helped. I start the swaying again, and, as I stare into the beautiful eyes, I unbutton my blouse. I let it fall open and dance some more, revealing my breasts to him. As I twirl the blouse slips off my shoulders and I leave it there, like a shawl. Then with a hard twirl I send it flying across the studio, and my breasts are totally free at last. For a split instant I am washed with modesty, but the feeling passes immediately, and instead I walk with goddess surety to the painting and stand with my breasts right before the eyes. I reach up and, with the barest of touch, I slowly draw my hand across one nipple, causing it to stiffen. Then I do the same with my other breast, and move a few inches closer. The eyes are glowing with desire, just as I am. Feeling as though I've heard a command, I step back a few steps and unhook the pants, letting them fall to the floor. I slip my panties down and step out of the rest of my clothes.

I stand completely naked before my lover. I let his eyes take me in, totally. And, at this moment, I know. I know. He *is* mine.

With the exhilaration this knowing brings me I dance with sheer abandonment. I am every beautiful woman who has ever lived. I'm every goddess that man has ever worshipped. I am perfect in my feminine beauty and power. I dance myself to exhaustion then return to stand in front of the eyes. They are reverent. And with that single look, I know I've found the love of my life.

I blow him a kiss and sweep my clothes off the floor where I had flung them. Sashaying to the shower, I toss my clothes in the hamper. I shower, lotion, adorn myself in a long rayon dress, and pin up the hair that fell out of the confines of the pins while I was dancing. I put in gold hoops, my largest, and drape several gold chains around my neck. The realization of the goddess within me has driven me to an executive decision. I'm going to see Evie, and I'm going to add more of her creations to my wardrobe. I want it, and I deserve it. Even if I have to eat beans for a year to pay for it.

When I pull up in front of Evie's, Jazzie's car is there. I step inside the shop and call out my hello. They turn in unison and beam the same expression—one that says they are happy to see me. Which makes *me* happy. It is truly a blessing to have real friends.

"Alli!" Evie booms. "I'm so glad you're here!"

"Cool!" I laugh. "But, pray tell, why?"

"Because I have another dress for you!"

"Another dress?" I ask. "I don't recall ordering another dress," I tell her, confused.

"That's because you *didn't*," Evie replies, straight-faced, and faking a very good mope.

"But, that's what I'm here to *do*..." I offer, returning fake remorse.

"Good! Then we can cut to the chase." She brings out a garment bag, already zipped up tight, as Jazzie grins her co-conspirator smile. I give Jazzie a "you shouldn't have" look, and she just shrugs slightly with a tilt of her head. As I take the garment bag from Evie I ask if I can open it. Evie snaps, of course not. Sigh. I guess I should have known.

"Any suggestions on shoes and purse," I tease, but only half joking. After all, Evie did tell me where to get my last purse, and it is stunning.

"You can use the same purse and shoes you bought for the other dress," she says. "I know you aren't rich, like some people we know," she adds, leaning her head toward Jazzie.

"Oh, stop it, Evie" Jazzie laughs. "I'm *not* rich. Just extremely comfortable. Not at all the same thing."

"No, you're right," Evie agrees. "Comfortable is way better. Rich is overrated."

"So, you want to go for a second look at that guitarist tonight?" Jazzie asks. And then I realize I hadn't told her anything about Saturday night. She doesn't know about the mouthless man or seeing my lover kissing the dancer. However, now isn't the time to set her straight, so I just say, yes. Tonight would be good. Jazzie pulls out her cell phone and does a quick search. As she hits a button she asks if seven is good. I say sure.

"Hi!" she says brightly when the call is answered. "Would you have a table for two available around seven?" she asks, sounding hopeful. "Seven fifteen! Sounds good. The name is Jazzie," she says. Then, a second later she says, "Yes, you heard me right. Jazzie." Another couple of seconds. "Thanks! See you then!"

"You already have their number programmed into your cell phone?" I ask, incredulous.

"Of course," she replies, then looks at me with consternation. "What? You don't?"

"No!" I laugh. Tsk, tsk, is all she says.

"And are we sure that the flamenco show is on tonight?" I'm suddenly scared of being greatly disappointed.

"Already checked on the nights they perform," Jazzie replies. "Every night but Tuesdays and Wednesdays," she finishes.

"You are so organized," I tell her, a bit jealous.

"I know. You could learn a thing or two," she chides. And I laugh, because she is absolutely right.

We pay our farewells to Evie and head out into the hot, humid noon hour. I lay the dress carefully in the trunk, where I hope it will be fine until I finish my grocery shopping. Jazzie and I kiss cheeks, then go our separate ways. I make my weekly run to Whole Foods to stock up on the essentials, and while I'm there I decide to have lunch. It's as good as any café. When I'm done I fill my cart with a week's worth of goodies, including a few frozen meals from Organic Bistro. I add a couple bottles of wine that a vendor is pushing, but only because they really do sound good, and because one of the other shoppers tells me he has already tried them, and they are delicious. I check out with a cashier who is probably a really beautiful girl under all her studs and tats, and head back up the road to Carefree land. I pull into my driveway, thankful to see everything looking just as I left it. The last thing I need right now is an unpleasant surprise.

I gather up my groceries and put everything away. The kids come out to see if I've brought any special treats for them, and I have. I bring out the small bag of chicken livers I procured, and cut up two small plates worth. I set them down in front of Bonnie and Rico and they dig in. When they're finished, and primly cleaning their faces, I pick up the plates and put them in the dishwasher. I do a load of laundry and freshen up the house with a few licks of mopping here, and a little dusting there. Then I remember that John Smith is turned around, facing the wall in the studio, and I go in to give him his view back. As I turn the easel around and glance distractedly at the portrait, I gasp.

Tears have appeared on his cheeks.

Oh my God, I wonder. What now?

My heart begins pounding in my chest. Then suddenly, I have a moment of total lucidity. I'm in charge here! As long as this painting is in my control, I can change anything. So I quickly grab my smock and pull it on haphazardly. I grab paints, palette, and brush, and carefully, lovingly, paint away the tears.

"Don't cry," I whisper to him. "Don't cry. Everything will be all right."

I clean up the studio, glance again at John, then leave, closing the door.

It's not quite time to start the ritual of getting ready to go out, so I take a swim. My arms and legs are already sore from my dance "workout" this morning, so I just float, glide, and sidestroke—all the easy stuff. The air has dried, and only a few white puffs of cloud dot the sky. I'm glad for that. Maybe Jazzie and I can get a table on the patio, if there's one available. When the humidity is low, the misters that most restaurant patios have are very efficient. I make a note to be sure to wear my hair in a style that can hold up to mist, just in case.

When I've done all the swimming I care to do I get out and freshen up my sun glow for a few minutes. It's late enough I don't worry about sunburn, but the sun can still put a touch of blush on your cheeks, even this late in the day. When I'm mostly dry, from the sun and the warm air, I go inside to do my routine.

I can't wait to see what my new dress looks like.

Chapter 13

The dress is stunning. Not, perhaps, as elegant as the first, but stunning. It's rayon, and for that I say a thank you to Evie and Jazzie. The predominant color is turquoise, with accents of rust, scarlet, and purple. It is a simple sheath, but very form-fitting with a huge slit up the right side. A slit so high it almost precludes wearing underwear. Fortunately I do have a thong that works, and I notice that, when I examine my rear end in the mirror, my butt looks pretty good under the drapey fabric. I decide to wear a bra tonight, because if we sit outside under the misters there's a chance I might sweat under my breasts, and that wouldn't be good in this dress. I choose a very soft bra—more drip catcher than anything.

I add the same shoes I wore on Friday and they do look fabulous. I grab the purse and hold it up to the dress. Yes. It, too, looks fabulous. I have put my hair up very loosely and, now that I've seen the dress, I choose a turquoise clip to decorate it. I select some earrings made of jasper and amethyst set in gold, and call it good.

After loading the purse with my favorite essentials I see if the kids need anything. They say they don't, so I kiss them goodbye, make sure everything is locked up tight, the curtains and blinds are drawn, and the alarm is set. I glide out to my chariot, off to meet Jazzie. And, who knows? I remember the dance I did this morning, causing a blush. I was so sure that this man is to be my lover, I was shameless. But what if I was wrong? And then I remember the dream I had Saturday night—the one where I laughed at him and left him standing in humiliation and frustration. The one where I refused to dance.

Quite a difference between the two realities. Neither of which is reality, yet, I remind myself. Well, we'll see.

I'm at the restaurant, now, and the spot next to Jazzie's car is open. I pull in, check my makeup and hair in the visor mirror, and depart. As I walk through the lot toward the door I notice a car out of the corner of my eye. It seems to be crawling along, like it's following my progress down the line of cars. I turn my head just slightly, hoping it isn't obvious I'm trying to check it out, but the windows are tinted dark, and I can't see who's driving. That pisses me off, because it's illegal to tint front seat windows that dark in Arizona, but the cops don't ever seem to care. If they do, I haven't noticed. So, I just keep my normal pace, and stride confidently to the steps of Roberto's, like I haven't a care in the world.

Once inside I find that Jazzie has read my mind and requested a table on the patio. While we wait for one to become available (which should be soon, the hostess has assured her) we sit at the bar. I order a wine cooler, determined to keep my drinking to a minimum tonight. I like to drink, but I don't always like who I become when I do. I'm sure it must have something to do with hormones, but I've never figured out the rhythm enough to be safe from unwanted incidents. Jazzie is having a wine cooler, also. Even though she doesn't usually drink she informs me that, because she has no consultations for the next few days, she is going to imbibe tonight. It makes her more forgiving, she explains. Less judgmental. No one likes a self-righteous jerk, she says, and I ask her if, perhaps, she is protesting too much, explaining too much.

"What's wrong, Jazzie?" I finally ask, when she drops her head to her arm and rests on the bar for a moment.

"I'm jealous," she says.

"Of whom?!" I ask in surprise

"Of you!" she answers.

"Of me?" I can't believe my ears. "Why?"

"Because you have possibilities before you."

"Possibilities?"

"Yes," she states firmly. "Possibilities of love."

"Oh," I mumble. I take a sip of cooler and turn to face her. "There's something you should know," I start, but we are cut off by the hostess telling us that our table is ready. She instructs the busgirl, who accompanied her, to bring our drinks while we all follow obediently behind her to a table for four out on the patio. Jazzie makes sure we aren't being inconsiderate by occupying a table bigger than we need, but the hostess assures us it's just fine. I see a smaller table in a corner and point it out, but she says this is the table we are to have, so we sit as the busgirl places our coolers before us. The misters are on and feel glorious.

We silently work on our drinks for a minute, then Jazzie says, "Okay. What is it I should know?" That's when I explain to her about coming here Saturday night and seeing the guitarist with the dancer.

"They looked so comfortable together," I tell her, fighting a sudden onslaught of tears as I recall them in the hall. "They are obviously very close."

Jazzie starts to say something—something meant to be reassuring, I presume. But instead, she clamps her mouth shut for a moment. Then with sadness in her eyes, she simply says she's sorry.

We continue sipping our wine coolers until our server arrives to take our order. Jazzie orders some appetizers for us and we sit and peruse the menu while waiting. Just as we make up our minds our server returns with our tapas. We tell him what we'd like for our entrees, and hand over our menus. He asks if we would like more coolers, or would we prefer something else. Jazzie looks at me and raises her eyebrow. "What do you think?" she asks. "Should we live it up?"

"Sure. Why not?" I answer.

She orders an expensive bottle of Spanish wine, informing me that it's on her, and the waiter hurries away to fulfill our whim. When he returns he performs the wine ritual with Jazzie, who gives her approval, and he pours for us. He whips away our other glasses and we sit in barely disguised moroseness, drinking the heavenly wine.

"I'm sorry for setting such a stupid mood," Jazzie offers.

I laugh and wipe away a tear that sprung up at her apology. "I'm sorry I don't have anything wonderful to say, to sweep it away!" I return.

"Well, I guess I could say something good has come of it," Jazzie says.

"What's that?"

"I'm no longer jealous."

That gets us both laughing as we pick at the tapas, which are delicious, but don't raise our mood by much. By the time dinner arrives, however, the wine has worked its magic and we are laughing, in good spirits again. The waiter sets the plates down and asks if there's anything else at the moment, and we tell him no, thank you. He looks at us shyly.

"I know it's not my place, but I hope you won't mind if I tell you something," he says, looking at the ground.

"What is it?" Jazzie asks.

"You both look very beautiful tonight," he murmurs, then slips away before we can say a word. We look at each other and smile broadly. Okay, nothing like a sweet, young, handsome man to raise your spirits. We toast to that, and dig into food fit for the gods.

As we're finishing up, the music starts to fade and the lights begin to dim. Our shy waiter inquires if we'd like dessert and we say yes, but we'd need to see a dessert menu. As he goes to find one, the busgirl arrives to clear our plates, and gives me a shy smile. I smile back and she lowers her eyes, then swiftly retreats. The waiter returns with the menus, and as he refills our wine glasses, we make a quick decision and he hurries off to place our order. We toast again, without words, and sip our wine.

Jazzie sets her glass down and says, "I wonder what that was all about?"

"What was what all about?"

"The look the busgirl gave you."

"Oh," I say. I sit there a moment. Then, leaning conspiratorially toward her I confide, "I haven't the foggiest idea!" Which, while it isn't funny at all, seems terribly funny to us. Uh-oh. Too late. We've already had too much wine. And with no one to drive us home we determine we'll need a taxi. With that decision we say, what the hell? Might as well go for it.

So we do. When our waiter returns with dessert, Jazzie orders another bottle, explaining that we will call a cab when the time comes. He says he will be happy to assist with that.

Our waiter returns with the second bottle and pours our glasses. As he sets the bottle down and leaves our table, after we assure him we need nothing more at the moment, I raise the glass to my lips to sip. My eyes focus across the room and there stands my lover, arms crossed, leaning against the wall, staring at me. I give a slight little raise of my glass to him, as a salute, then quickly lower it, ashamed. He belongs to someone else, I scold. Then why is he staring at me? I wonder. If he's that kind of man, one who constantly plays the field even if he's involved, I don't want him anyway! I look up again and he's still there, still staring. I take a slow sip of wine, hiding behind the glass, then set it on the table in front of me, eyes again lowered. I slowly twirl the glass in front of me, watching the wine leave little legs, fidgeting with confusion—but when I look up again, he's gone. Then the music begins, the dancers appear, and the set starts. I watch in a kind of dazed entrapment. The dancers are so beautiful together, literally and figuratively — why can't *they* be lovers, instead of she and the guitarist? The way they dance, they *should* be together, I tell myself. But then, I'm definitely prejudiced. The set ends, the trio disappears, and Jazzie asks me a question, which, momentarily, I do not process.

"Excuse me," I apologize to Jazzie. "I guess I was a little preoccupied. What did you ask?"

"If you've heard from the guy who commissioned that portrait we're going to rescue. You know — the mouthless man."

And with that question I remember I haven't even told her about the twin. Or about the second portrait. Or any of it.

"Actually, I have heard from him — kind of."

"Kind of?" Jazzie raises an eyebrow.

"Yes. He's mute. He can't speak — at least not yet. So, I didn't actually 'hear' from him, per se."

"What do you mean he can't speak? You talked with him when he hired you!"

"Well, here's the thing, Jazzie. There are two men, the one who hired me, and the mouthless man — who happens to be his twin brother."

"Oh my god! Are you serious?"

"Yes, completely. Remember the cops on Saturday morning?"

"Yes," she admits sheepishly. "Just to let you know, Christian, Ben, and I decided not to ask you about the situation, because we thought you might like a break from all our hounding."

"Well, I appreciate that, actually," I tell her. "But I'll let you in on it now. When the guys dropped me off I found a note on my car. Whoever wrote it said they needed to talk with me. I kind of looked around and noticed that there was a man in the only other car in the lot besides yours and mine. He started to get out when I noticed him—but someone shot him."

"Shot him? Oh my god!"

"Fortunately it just grazed his leg, though I know that can be painful," I say. "Well, thankfully I don't know from personal experience," I add, "but I imagine it's painful." Jazzie just nods. "Anyway, I *thought* it was the man who hired me, as I didn't get an up close look at him. He took off when he was shot," I explain.

"I imagine so!"

"But then he showed up when I was here on Saturday night. He asked the hostess to arrange for us to have a table together, and that's when I found out he was the twin brother."

"How did he speak with the hostess?" Jazzie muses.

"Well, since he left *me* a note, I assume he did the same with the hostess."

"Oh," Jazzie says. "Good point."

"So, anyway, it was then that I realized there were two men, which is why the second portrait was looking different from the one I smashed and threw away. It's not the same man."

"Wow. How do you think you got mixed up in this?" she asks, her voice a slight tease.

"I haven't a clue. But I'm glad I did, because when we rescue the portrait, I'm going to give him a mouth—which will, I pray, give him a voice."

"He seemed like a good guy?"

"Yes. Very," I state firmly, thinking of the gentle vibes I felt when we shared those few minutes.

"I hope it works, then. You giving him a voice."

"Me too." As I sip my wine, Jazzie's eyes suddenly grow wide, and she looks at something, or someone, behind me. As I begin to turn my head to see what she's looking at, the object of her surprise appears at my side, and sits in one of the empty chairs at our table.

It's the guitarist.

I open my mouth to say something, but it just hangs there in shock. Up close his eyes are so goddam beautiful I can hardly breathe. And he is using those eyes to bore into me.

Jazzie clears her throat. "Ahem. You got a name, handsome?"

"Nate," he answers, never taking his eyes off me.

"Nate. Nice to meet you, Nate," Jazzie says. "I'm Jasmine, better known as Jazzie," she continues, "and the woman you're ogling is Allison, better known as Alli," she finishes.

Nate continues the lock on my eyes for another moment, then turns to Jazzie. "Nice to meet you, Jazzie," he says with true grace and sincerity, taking her hand for a kiss. Jazzie fans herself with her free hand and giggles.

Then Nate turns back to me. He takes my hand in his, gently stroking it for a few seconds, running his long fingers over mine. I can feel the calluses on his fingertips. He raises my hand to his lips, and once again locks his eyes with mine. He gives one light kiss, then another longer one, his lips barely on my hand, his warm, moist breath brushing my flesh. "Nice to meet you, Alli," he says.

Jazzie fans herself again. I just sit in a stupor, and stare at the vision before me. Suddenly Nate rises out of the chair and says simply, "I have to go." He strides off to the back of the restaurant, where his guitar and the dancers await him. As they begin the second set, the busgirl comes and clears our dessert plates, giving me a broad smile and a wink before she scurries off.

"Oh," Jazzie says. "Now we know what that look was about!" She laughs as I blush my brains out. However, I recover soon enough as I remember the kiss he gave the dancer on Saturday night.

"The man is scum," I tell Jazzie.

She almost spits out the wine she has just taken a sip of and says, "What?! Why in the world would you say that?!"

"Becaaaause," I begin, self-righteous and snotty, "remember that when I was here Saturday night, I saw him hugging and kissing the female dancer."

Jazzie stares at me in wonder. "Oh my god. How could I have already forgotten that?" she asks, incredulous.

"Yes," I scold. "How in the *world* could you have forgotten that?" I pause, covering a smile with a sip of wine. "Could it have been those eyes? Or those lips? Or maybe it was the electric touch of his hand?"

Jazzie stares at me. "You know—if it weren't for the fact that he's yours, I'd go jump his bones right now!"

"He's *not* mine!" I say with exasperation. "Haven't you been listening?"

"Oh, I've been listening, all right," she says offhand. "I just haven't been hearing." She sips her wine and sets the glass down with a firm clunk. She looks at me with her head cocked, and squints her eyes at me with appraisal. "Have you painted him?" she asks. I blush and quickly look away. "That's what I thought," she laughs. She reaches across the table and gives my arm a quick squeeze. "Don't worry, girlfriend," she whispers. "He's yours. You'll see."

I take another sip of wine, as tears begin to creep in. "I certainly hope so," is all I can say.

By now we are too tipsy to enjoy much else, so we call over the waiter and ask for the bill and his help with procuring a taxi. He brings the bill and informs us that the restaurant's personal limo will be our ride home.

We are very cool with that.

After we ante up he escorts us to the front steps where the limo awaits, and the driver opens the back doors for us with a flourish. We giggle our thanks, climb in, and in minutes I am safely at my doorstep. I offer him payment, and he says no. I offer a tip, and again he refuses. He tips his hat, and he's off to deliver Jazzie.

I unlock the front door, disarm the alarm, then set it again for bed. I throw my purse on the entry table and stagger to the kitchen, where I pull out the bottle of ibuprofen. Actually, I hate feeling like this. I sometimes don't know why I drink at all. Maybe it's time for a change.

Maybe it's time for a lot of changes.

I find the kids already in their preferred bedtime places, Bonnie tucked between basket and dresser, and Rico in bed. They blink and squint when I turn on the light, so I quickly dim it way down, leaving just enough light to see what I'm doing. I undress and carefully hang up my lovely sheath. I take my hair down, remove my makeup, brush my teeth, strip off my underwear, and fall into bed. Because I'm drunk I do not remember any of my dreams.

One more reason to quit.

The next morning I'm okay because I took the ibuprofen the night before, but I lack energy. I wander aimlessly around the kitchen, staring out the window, staring into the refrigerator, sitting at the table with nothing more than a cup of coffee I warmed up from yesterday's leftovers. I'm wishing I could feel something. The greatest problem with alcohol, for me, is that it deadens my feelings. I suppose if one wants to deaden their feelings, this would be okay. But I don't. I want to feel joy. I want to create the feeling of ecstasy in my heart. And when I'm hungover those things elude me.

I finally have had enough coffee, so I put the cup in the dishwasher and go to pull on some clothes. I choose jeans and a tee shirt, as usual, and do no more than comb my hair, and dab some gloss on my lips. I remember that I need to get my car, so I head to the phone to call Christian, to see if he can help out. But before I get to the phone the front door bell rings. I'm startled, as no one ever shows up unex-pectedly, unless it's bad news, like Don, so I warily go to the door and look out the peephole. The limo is out front, and the driver is at the door, politely turned away, wearing the same hat as last night. I open the door and he turns around. It's Nate.

"Morning, Miss," he says, sweeping the hat off with a flourish. As he returns it to his head he says, "I assume you would like a ride to pick up your car? After we go collect your friend, Miss Jasmine, of course."

I just stare at him, suddenly aware that I look like a slob. Shit! Why didn't I do more with myself this morning? Oh, yeah. Probably because I'm hungover.

"Uh," I say smartly. "Uh," I say again. Jeez! Think of something to say, you idiot! "Sure. That sounds good!" I say a little too brightly. Crap. What a way to make an impression. "I'll get my purse," I mumble, and leave him at the door as I grab my everyday bag and stuff the necessities in it from the purse I carried last night. I entertain the thought of running in and changing clothes, or putting on more makeup, but then I realize the damage is already done. He's already seen me in all my dumpy glory. Guess mom was right. If I'd just assumed I was going to end up in the hospital today, I would have dressed nicer. I yell goodbye to the kids and say I'll be back in a while, then set the alarm and lock the door. As we head to the limo Nate asks if I have children. I tell him yes, I have two. When he looks surprised I tell him they have eight legs between them. Oh, he says. And grins. Then he opens the front passenger door, and bows for me to enter. I hesitate, which brings a raised eyebrow in reply.

"You would rather sit in back?" he asks, hurt and surprise creep-ing into his voice.

I picture him and the dancer and tell him, "Yes. I would rather sit in back." So, he quietly shuts the front door and opens the back one.

He looks at me hard, and gives a silent sigh, almost like it hurts to breathe. As I approach the door hesitantly, about to change my mind, he does another flourish of a bow, sweeping his hand toward the backseat, and I lose the moment to reconsider.

I step into the limo and plop down on the seat with all the grace of a walrus. Shit. What an idiot.

Nate doesn't seem to notice, but closes the door and takes his place in the driver's seat. He backs the car expertly down the drive and turns onto the road.

"You'll have to give me directions to Miss Jasmine's home," he says.

"How come?" I ask, with a snottier tone than I would have liked. What's wrong with me? "I mean," I try to explain, in a more friendly manner, "you knew where *I* lived. Why not Jazzie?"

"Because," he answers, "I only asked Carl where *you* lived. I did not inquire after Miss Jasmine."

"Oh stop with all the 'Miss' stuff," I scold. "It sounds stupid."

I see him glance at me in the rearview mirror, and his eyes crinkle in a smile. "Okay," is all he says. I tell him to head south on Scottsdale Road, and that I'll give further directions as needed. "Okay," he says, again.

To make conversation I continue, "So, the driver's name is Carl?"

"Yes."

"And you know him well enough to take his limo, his hat, and pump him for information as to where the patrons he drives live?" Uh-oh. There's that snotty tone again.

His eyes crinkle again. "Yes," is all he says.

"Must be a good friend, then."

"Yes, he is, actually. Has been a good friend for years—even before he became my brother-in-law."

"Oh!" I'm surprised. "He's your brother-in-law?"

"I believe that's what I said."

I stick my tongue out at him, thinking he won't see it but, before I can get it back into my mouth, he has glanced in the mirror and caught me at it.

Crap, crap, crap.

Nate continues, as though he didn't notice me being a stupid moron. "Carl's been married to my sister, Maribela, for almost five years."

"And what does Maribela do?" I ask, making conversation.

Nate gives me another glance in the mirror, then looks away, not saying anything for several seconds. Then he smiles.

"She dances," is all he says.

"That's interesting," I begin. "Where does she dance?"

Nate doesn't say anything. But I see the wheels turning in his head, and comprehension spreads in his eyes. He looks at me again, and with that look I suddenly see the light. "The dancer at Roberto's," I say slowly. "She's your sister?"

"Yes. Why—did you think we had something going on?"

Suddenly I don't know which emotion is more appropriate, or more overwhelming. The feeling of relief, the feeling of joy, or the feeling that I have to be the biggest idiot on earth.

"Stop the car," I command. Nate looks startled, but he pulls over to the shoulder, and stops the car.

"Is something wrong?" he asks, concerned.

"Oh, yes," I say. "Something is very wrong."

"Tell me," he starts, but I'm already opening the back door and I close it with a slam as I get out. I see the consternation in Nate's face as I stand a moment and glare at him through the window.

"Well," I say, putting my fists on my hips. "Aren't you going to open that door for me?" I scold, as I nod toward the front passenger side.

The look of pure happiness on his face will always be etched in my mind. He is such a joy, that man is. So handsome. So talented. So open.

So easy to love.

He springs out of the limo, rushes to the passenger side, and opens the door with his biggest flourish yet, but before I can step in, he grabs me, hard. He pulls me to him in a clutch so tight it knocks the wind out of me, and I grunt with the force of it.

"Oh. Sorry," he says, releasing his grip just a bit. Then he places one hand under my chin and raises it up. With gentleness I've never before experienced, except in the dream when I met him, he kisses me. Wondrously.

With joy written all over his face, he releases me and guides me into the front seat.

The only person happier than him, in the whole, wide world, is me.

As he puts the limo in gear I scoot over next to him, glad this big old car has the good sense to sport old-fashioned seats, without a console between them, and we head off to Jazzie's.

When we arrive she's all ready to go. She opens the door, purse under her arm, sunglasses perched on her perfect nose, and steps out, key in hand, which she uses in one quick motion. Nate and I stand there, totally confused.

"Hi, you two!" she says brightly.

"Uh, hi," I return. "Jazzie?" I ask, as she's already sashaying down the walk to the limo.

"How did I know you were coming?" she interrupts.

"Yeah," I say as we catch up with her.

"Asked the kids," she says.

Nate gives me a very confused look, as I just say, "Oh."

Hurrying to beat Jazzie to the car, Nate opens the back door for her. She glides in with grace, then reaches over to shut the door before I can consider whether I should sit in back with her.

"Don't bother playing games," she says. "I can see your auras," she adds.

"Oh."

So I slide in up front when Nate opens the door for me, and he hurries around to the driver's side, and we take off, back up to Carefree and Robert's restaurant.

After we drive a couple of miles in silence Nate says, "Okay. There's something I have to know."

"What's that?" I ask.

"I thought you said your two kids had eight legs between them, right?"

"Yes," I say with laugh, because I know where this is going. In the back seat Jazzie snickers.

"So, okay. Go ahead and laugh. But, Jazzie, please explain how they told you we were coming."

"I'm an animal communicator, handsome."

"A what?"

"You heard me. But I do it telepathically. I invite animals to communicate with me, mind to mind, heart to heart, and they almost always oblige. I've communicated with hundreds of pets, both here and on the other side, which I usually do for clients. For myself, I've talked with dolphins and whales. And, once, with a hawk," she finishes, obviously pleased with herself. As well she should be. It's an awesome gift she has. And she's not boastful or arrogant about it— she'd be just as pleased if it were someone else's gift. She's pleased with the gift—and the fact that she is the one who happens to have it, just makes it better.

"So," Nate starts, "how long have you been doing this?"

"Since my husband died, five years ago," she answers.

"Oh," Nate replies. "I'm sorry."

"Well, thanks. But it's been a long time, and I'm pretty much over it. It was just that, without Alan, I needed something to do. And, Mutton, that's the Bichon we had at the time, was so sad when Alan died that I wanted to be able to comfort him. In a very real way. I wanted to know exactly how he felt. So I studied with a well known communicator in Prescott, and found I have a gift for it."

"What did Mutton have to say?" Nate asks, intrigued.

"He said he was sad because he never got to say goodbye to Alan before he left. Alan had a heart attack, and died at his office. Mutton knew Alan was on the other side, and had said hi to him and all, but it wasn't the same as saying goodbye on this plane. He felt cheated."

"What did you do?"

"I set aside a night, lit some candles, brought out all the happy reminders of Alan I could find, and Mutton and I spent the whole night just remembering how much we loved him. We went over every important time, every funny time, every sad time — every time we could remember. We laughed and cried. And sighed. We smiled, mostly, until we could remember nothing else.

"Then, as I blew out the candles, one by one, we sent him all the love in our hearts. And when it was finally dark, we said goodbye."

I've heard the story before, but her telling of it this time brings tears to my eyes, as if this were the first. When I look at Nate, his eyes are also filled with tears.

We ride the rest of the way in silence.

I return home a short time later. When Nate dropped us off in the parking lot he'd wanted to make arrangements for lunch or dinner, but I told him that today, unfortunately, was not a good day. He had then suggested the same for tomorrow but of course, that, too, is out. I told him Jazzie and I have business in Sedona tomorrow, and he had wanted to come with us, being that Wednesday is a day off. I had to turn him down as gently as possible, without revealing what our "business" was, and Nate was a gentleman about it. I agreed to come to Roberto's on Thursday, and be his guest. We exchanged telephone numbers, and that is where we left it.

After saying hi to the kids, and giving them both a good brushing, I go to the studio and lovingly retrieve Nate's eyes from the easel where I had left them. It is so good to be able to give a name to them. I study the painting, and admire how good a job I'd done capturing those wonderful eyes. I absolutely adore the fact that my dreams are so vivid and foretelling.

Then I remember Don dead on my kitchen floor, blood ruining my grout, and I shudder.

Okay. Maybe it's not *that* great a gift.

I carry the eyes back to my bedroom and place them once more upon my wall. I blow them a huge, smacking kiss, and leave the room smiling. And flushed. I recall the kiss Nate gave me beside the road, and the flush travels all through my body. My stomach turns to butterflies and my heart swells. The phone rings and when I answer it, Ben is on the other end.

"Alli," he starts, "I am sooooooo sorry!"

"What about?" I ask, alarmed.

"About tomorrow," he says, a sniffle in his voice.

"What about tomorrow?" I prompt.

"Christian and I can't go!"

Uh-oh. "Why not?!"

"Because Christian's mother arrived today, unexpectedly, and plans on staying for a week!"

"Oh, crap," I blurt, before I can stop the words coming from my mouth.

"I'm so sorry! I'm so sorry!" Ben cries.

"It's okay, Ben," I try to assure him, though I'm not sure it is. "Really! I understand that it can't be helped. I do!" I say with all the sincerity I can muster.

"You know we'd be there if we could be, don't you?"

"Of course I do, Ben," I say. And I mean it. I do know they would be there if they could be.

"Well, if you can put it off a week then Christian and I can—" but I cut him off.

"No, I think this needs to be taken care of ASAP," I tell him. "But don't worry, Ben," I say. "Everything will be just fine."

"Okay, dear," he says. "Talk with you later."

"Okay, sweetie. Bye."

I call Jazzie to give her the bad news, and to ask her opinion. She listens intently, then says she wants to check something before she decides. She says she will call me back just as soon as she can. I say okay, and we disconnect.

I grab a jar of organic peanut butter and stir it up as best I can. The effort leaves my fingers with an ache, but the stuff is really good. Worth the trouble—I think. Selecting a small spoon from the drawer I eat the peanut butter right from the jar. I flash on a conversation I had once, with someone who got on my nerves, a lot. He was complaining about his dead wife, telling me how much of a nutcase she had been, and he used the example of her eating peanut butter straight from the jar as proof of his pronouncement. When I told him that I, also, ate it straight from the jar, I never had to put up with him again. He just looked at me like I was from Mars, stomped away, and spoke to me nevermore.

Honestly, from that day forward, peanut butter has tasted even better.

I eat so much my mouth is stuck together and I go to get a glass of water from the RO. When I've washed it all down I screw the lid back on the jar and put it away. Nice thing about living alone—I can eat out of jars and drink out of cartons, and never worry about spreading my germs. At that thought I decide I should reconsider my bad habits. Because, you never know.

Just then the phone rings. I see Jazzie's number on the ID and answer it cheerily, but I'm met with an entirely different mood.

"We have to go tonight," Jazzie tells me with a catch in her voice.

"Why?!" I ask, wishing I had more time to pull myself together, to work up to this escapade.

A sob breaks from Jazzie's throat.

"Oh my god, Jazzie. What's the matter?" I'm afraid now.

"He's hurt her," Jazzie whispers, trying to keep her voice steady.

"Sadie?"

"Yes."

"How?" I ask, fear ripping my guts.

"He's broken her leg."

"Oh no," I whisper back. "Oh no."

"He kicked her when she was trying to get his attention for breakfast this morning, and laughed when she fell. Then he just left, telling her if she had a brain in her head she could go get her own breakfast. She's not sure it's broken, but she can't get up. She's in pain, and she's scared."

Fighting nausea and hatred I swallow hard, several times. Then I say to my quietly crying friend, "You are absolutely right. We have to go tonight."

"Thank you, Alli," Jazzie says.

"No," I reply. "Thank you. Thank you for being such a wonderful person and honing such a wonderful gift."

"We'll need someone to help us with Sadie, you know. She's too big for us to carry alone. And there's no way we can leave her there."

I think for just a split second then tell her, "I'll get someone. Don't cry, Jazzie. We are going to do a double rescue, tonight. Everything will turn out wonderfully." With that we disconnect, I pray for guidance, and, with the answer clear in my head, I call Nate.

To keep the day from being one of agony, I paint. I paint Sadie standing up, smiling from ear to ear, wagging her tail and being in love with life. I hope it helps. Then, when it's late enough to get going, I gather up the supplies we're going to need. Just as I'm finishing this task, Jazzie arrives. A minute later Nate arrives and we all pile into his truck. We've decided to take Nate's vehicle because Don isn't familiar with it, in case that should become an important point. We head out Carefree Hwy. and take the exit north on I-17. In an hour and a half we'll be in Sedona.

I'm riding up front with Nate and Jazzie is in the backseat of the king cab. Nobody speaks for the first leg of our journey. Everyone just stays locked in their own thoughts. Eventually I turn in the seat and look at Jazzie in the back. She appears to be sound asleep, stretched out on the seat. Her arms are folded across her chest and her face is impassive. I turn back to Nate and, upon impulse, I give him a kiss on the cheek. He smiles broadly but keeps his eyes on the road. The sun is now low enough that it is hidden behind mountains that have sprung up in the west. The shade is soothing. We climb higher and higher, eventually arriving to the flat lands of Sunset Point. We don't pull off at the rest area, however. These days it's always a zoo, and the romance that once pervaded, when it was a quiet and lonely outpost, is long gone. In a while we pass Arcosanti and Cordes Junction in the now high desert. The turnoffs for several quaint towns, snuggled on plains and in valleys between here and Sedona, come and go. We cross the Verde River and I know the turnoff for Sedona is not far, now. Dusk is on its way, and we've made good time. We should be at Don's just as it gets dark enough to shelter our activities from the neighbors' sight. We already know that Don will, most likely, not be home until later, as that's his pattern. We aren't positive, but it's probable.

Suddenly Jazzie sits up and asks from the backseat, "How long till we're there?"

"I guesstimate about 35 minutes," I answer.

She is silent for several seconds then says, "I hope that's soon enough."

Fear grabs me. "Why?"

"I've been trying to get through to Sadie since we've been on the road, and I can connect, but she's very, very fuzzy. I don't know why—so I'm worried."

I look at Jazzie, and her face is a mask of concern.

"Well, please *don't* worry, Jazzie," I soothe. "I painted Sadie today, happy and healthy. She should be all right."

Jazzie meets my eyes, and they soften. "Thanks," is all she says. She lies back down, crosses her arms across her chest, and closes her eyes. Nate steals a glance at me, his eyes full of sympathy, and assessment. I realize he is probably still processing my revelations of this afternoon—when I gave him the details of our mission tonight...the stolen portrait *and* why its retrieval is mandatory. I admit—any normal person would question what I revealed about my work. Nate flicks on the headlights, and we continue to Sedona in silence.

Chapter 14

As the first red rocks loom ahead, my stomach knots. Both the past and the future contribute to this, so I gaze at Nate—my present—and the knot fades. I hold onto this feeling of Nate, this wonderful gift of the present, and am able to watch the landscape change into that unique beauty, which is Sedona, without further incident. Finally we arrive at Don's.

The driveway is empty. As is the case with many Sedona homes, there is no garage or carport. Because of this we assume that we've been correct in our assessment, and that Don isn't home. It has just become dark enough to make colors lie, and shapes deceive, so we disembark from Nate's truck, grab our supplies, and sneak around back.

Don's yard is large, wooded, and fenced. Helpful things for our purpose. I take out the lock picks I bought at a consignment store, and try one on Don's back door. It immediately opens to my touch. I'm both shocked and grateful.

"Wow," Jazzie says. "Either you and those picks are very good, or Don is a stupid cheapskate who should have spent more money on his locks."

We chuckle softly, turn the knob, and carefully open the door. It is quiet as death in there. We tiptoe in and turn on a flashlight. So far so good. I whisper, "I'll go get the painting from the closet while you two look for Sadie," and I hand Jazzie a flashlight. She and Nate head to the kitchen, where Sadie should be, and I head to the hall closet. I open the closet and push aside the coats, parkas, and sweaters that hang there. Behind them, there is nothing. My heart skips a beat, then starts beating faster to make up for it. Panic flushes my face and gut. Crap! Where is the painting? I can hear voices calling quietly in the other part of the house, and I head toward them in haste. We're going to have to ask Sadie where the painting has been moved to—if she can tell us. We don't want to be spending too much time here. If Don comes home while we're here it will be a very ugly scene. Don has guns. We do not. And while *we* don't have guns because we would never want to shoot someone, Don would not hesitate a second.

I follow the voices and find them in Don's study.

"Have you found Sadie?" I ask.

"No!" Jazzie answers, frustration lining her face.

"Well, we need to find her!" I say. "The painting isn't where it should be, and we need to talk to her!"

Jazzie snaps, "Screw your painting! Sadie is more important. And I don't need to find her to talk to her. But I do need to find her to save her life."

Shame washes over me. "Forgive me," I whisper. She steps in and gives me a quick hug.

"What we need to do, at this point, is to let me try once more to contact Sadie." Nate and I agree, so we go to the kitchen and sit at the table. Nate and I keep our mouths shut as Jazzie closes her eyes, relaxes, breathes slowly in and slowly out. She then begins to speak out loud to Sadie.

"Sadie, honey," she says. "It's Jazzie. Can you hear me?"

"You can?! Good!" Jazzie continues, "Where are you, sweetie?" Silence. "You don't know?" Silence. "You are definitely not at home, but the place seems familiar. Okay. You feel funny? How so?" Silence. "Dizzy, thirsty, heavy." Silence. Then Jazzie raises an eyebrow. "Sadie, darling, are you lying on a cement floor, and is there a wire cage around you?" Silence. "Yes?! Okay! Sadie, do you think you might be at the vet? Yes? Okay! Good girl. Okay, princess, one more question. Do you know where Don moved the painting to?" Silence. "Are you sure?" Silence. "Okay, Sadie. Thank you. And don't worry, beautiful. We will be rescuing you shortly." Silence and a smile. "We love you, too, Sadie. We most certainly do."

Jazzie opens her eyes and looks at me.

"Well?!' I demand.

Jazzie shakes her head. "Sorry, Alli. Sadie doesn't know where Don put it. She's sure of that."

"Shit!"

Nate pipes up, "We'll just have to search for it, and the sooner the better I'd say."

"Let's get a move on," I reply. We split up and start a methodical search of Don's house. We search as neatly as possible, hoping beyond common sense that we can find the painting without Don realizing anyone has been here and taken it. Because, who else would, but me? Nate has gone to park his truck around the corner, since we don't have to be carrying Sadie to it, and that makes us feel a bit better. But as the hour drags on, and we come up empty, we have another pow-wow.

"Now what?" Jazzie asks.

I start to say that I haven't a clue, when a clue pops into my head.

"Jazzie," I start, "did you get any impressions on who dropped Sadie off at the vet? Do you think it was Don? Because, I have my doubts about that."

Jazzie's eyes brighten in agreement. "Good point!" she chirps. She immediately closes her eyes, breathes deeply, relaxes, and contacts Sadie.

"Sadie, darling—we have a question for you. Who brought you to the vet today?" Silence. "Karla? Who's Karla?" Silence. "Pretty lady who comes every week. She makes the house nice." Silence. "Thank you, Sadie. I know you're tired. It's getting late, and I don't know if we can come by tonight, but trust me, beautiful, we *will* come for you, okay?" Silence. "We love you, too. With all our hearts," Jazzie adds with a choke. She opens her eyes, and looks at me. "Any ideas?"

"His housekeeper. I'll see if I can find a number. Don's memory isn't great, so it's probably written down."

I find the address book by the phone, and flip through. There it is, nice big letters. I pull out my cell phone and dial. A woman answers on the third ring.

"Hello?"

"Hi, is this Karla?"

"Yes. Who's this?"

"You don't know me, but you clean house for my ex-husband, Don Winters..."

"Yes?" she asks, bitterness clouding her voice. *Hmmm.*

"Did you take Sadie to the vet today, possibly with a broken leg?" There's silence on the other end for several beats.

"Yes, I did. How did you know?"

"A friend found out for me," I say, with a shrug to Nate and Jazzie. But Karla takes this as sufficient explanation, and goes on.

"That creep of an ex-husband of yours told me to get my boyfriend, Jake, and take Sadie to the woods and dump her. He said she'd make some coyote or mountain lion a great meal!" Her voice drips with venom. "He is the biggest scumbag I have ever met in my life! That poor, sweet dog!" She's on a roll now. "I can't believe he actually thought I'd do it! But I just said 'sure, whatever', and he just nodded like he truly believed I was as big a scumbag as he is. Then he said, while I was at it, I could dump a painting for him, too."

"A painting?" I asked, my voice catching in my throat.

"Yeah. Some painting of a man with no mouth." Yes!

"And, did you dump the painting?" I ask, holding my breath for the answer.

"Well, since there was no trip to the woods for Sadie, obviously, I didn't make a special trip for the painting. I have it here. My sister paints, and I thought maybe she could add a mouth. It's good enough that we thought maybe we could sell it to one of the galleries and make a buck. Perhaps enough to pay for Sadie's surgery, because, frankly, we don't have that kind of money. The doc said we could pay over time, though. Which was nice of him."

"Does he know whose dog it is?" I ask.

"I don't think so. It was a new guy. A new partner, or whatever."

"Okay, Karla, here's the thing. I would like the painting, and I could give you a little something for it. But I would also like Sadie. So you don't have to worry about the bill. I'll take care of it. All you have to do is call them and tell them that I'm paying, and that I have permission to take her, okay?"

"Sure, no problem. When do want the painting?" she asks.

"Can I get it tonight?"

"Tomorrow would be better," she answers. "Jake and I have plans for tonight."

I'm disappointed but, since she's been so nice, I agree to call her tomorrow and arrange a place to meet. We disconnect, and I tell Nate and Jazzie all the news.

We take a quick run through the house, and try to put right anything that may have been put amiss. Satisfied, we make sure we have all our stuff, head out the door through which we entered, and I make sure it's locked tight. We creep through the backyard to the gate, just in time to see Don's car pull into the drive. Shit! We all freeze as Don gets out and beeps his car locked. He takes two steps toward the house when another car comes skidding in behind him, raising dust, which blows our way. Jazzie stifles a sneeze as we all hold our breaths. Double shit.

A man leaps out of the second car, and Don takes an easy stance as he watches him approach. "Hey, Michael," Don sneers. "What's up?"

The other man grabs Don by the collar and hollers, "Why did you do it, asshole?! Why?!"

"Whatever do you mean, Michael?" Don returns, nonchalantly.

"You hurt her!" the other man screams. The thought flashes through me — is he talking about Sadie? But the man continues, "You hurt that innocent little girl, you fucking creep!"

"Jeez, Michael. She wouldn't tell me what I wanted to know! And it was only a slap, for chrissake. She wasn't really hurt," Don finishes, trying to appease the other man with his scummy logic.

"You knocked her to the ground, you goddam asshole. You knocked a little girl to the ground!"

"I'm getting tired of this conversation," Don says, as he starts for his house.

"This partnership is at an end, bud," the other man yells. And that's when I realize two things — the other man is "John Smith", and I now know what his tears were about.

"Fine with me," Don says dismissively, with a wave of his hand. But then he stops in his tracks and turns. He folds his arms over his chest, and raises his chin to look down his nose. A man faking his importance. Faking his power.

"Just remember one thing," Don sneers, "you have nothing without me. Nothing."

"We'll see about that," John Smith growls. But Don is already at his door, so the man stomps back to his car, throws himself into it, roars it to life, crams it into reverse, and leaves in a cloud of dust. Which forces all of us to stifle a sneeze. Lights are already coming on in Don's house, so we beat it as fast as we can while still being sneaky.

We arrive at Nate's truck, climb quickly in, and slam the doors to snuff the lights. Nate cranks the engine, and we're out of there.

Once we're on the main road we all breathe a sigh of relief, and the shaky nerves, that had hold of me previously, finally slow to a mere flutter. "Are you okay, Jazzie?" I call to the backseat, but there's no answer. I turn around quick to see what's wrong. She has her hand over her mouth, and looks pale, even in the starlight.

Finally she pulls her hand away. "I think I need to be sick," she says simply, and Nate is already pulling off to the side of the road. Jazzie springs out and wretches, as Nate and I look at each other. Then, as Jazzie wretches again, Nate grabs me and pulls me to him, in a tight embrace. We sit there, just like that for a minute, neither of us moving except for our breaths. Then Nate releases his hold and pushes me slightly away, so he can look me in the eyes.

"I could say, next time you and Jazzie want to go somewhere, and I ask if I can come, that I sincerely hope you refuse. And that I would *stay* refused!" I lower my head, ashamed of getting him involved. But he lifts my chin, catches my eyes again, and continues, "However, the fact is, beautiful, that I am so very, very glad I was here for you tonight."

I throw myself into his arms. "Oh god, Nate. Me, too! Me, too!" I rub my head into his chest, wishing I could crawl inside, be completely safe inside his warmth and strength. He kisses the top of my head, and I start considering a good make out session, but Jazzie opens the back door just then, and crawls inside. She reaches for her purse and pulls out a tissue.

"Do we have any water left?" she asks. I grab a bottle and hand it over. She wets the tissue and rubs it over her face and mouth. She wads it up and looks for a place to put it, then just drops it to the floor. "I'll deal with it later," she says. Her breathing has evened out, and the color appears to be returning. Suddenly, she snickers. Nate and I glance at each other, wondering if she's okay. However, Jazzie then puts her head back and just howls with laughter. Genuine laughter. In a moment we are all laughing ourselves breathless, and, actually, it feels pretty good. After we're done relieving our tension I give Nate directions to the local "dive" motel, Sugarloaf Lodge. It really isn't a dive, except by Sedona standards. But I figure we don't need a resort to stay in tonight. Besides, at a resort they want to pay all this attention to you, and we need to keep a low profile while here. We pay cash for two rooms and take our keys. We decide we'd better get something to eat, so we pick a restaurant and send Nate in to order us all something to go. Jazzie and I stay with truck, and stand in awe of the stars.

"You know," I tell her, "the only thing I really, truly miss about Sedona is the stars."

"Don't blame you there," she answers.

After that, we just stand and gawk in silence.

Nate returns in just a few minutes. "That was quick" Jazzie tells him.

"They weren't busy," Nate explains. "I guess it is getting kind of late."

That would help explain why I'm dead on my feet, I think to myself. Nothing to do with this adventure, tonight. Nope. Just plain old late.

Nate asks where we should go to eat—back to the rooms, or...?

I say let's go drive north of town just a bit, and find a place to pull off the road. I'm really into these stars tonight, and I'd like to see more. The other two agree that it's a good idea, and we find a good spot in a few minutes. We unpack our food and set upon it like a ravenous pack of dogs. I think of Sadie left out for coyotes and shudder. But I push the thought immediately aside because, the fact is, she's safe. And so are we. And so is the painting. And while there stands a night between us and the end of this adventure, I am happy. Truly happy.

All aglow—like the stars.

We finish and go back to our rooms. I'm suddenly aware that no actual arrangements have been agreed to—do I sleep with Nate, or do I sleep with Jazzie?

I'm not sure if Jazzie read my face or what, but she grabs my arm and smiles sweetly at Nate. "I know you probably *want* her for the night," she says, "but I *need* her. I need some company tonight."

Nate, with eyes that don't reveal anything one way or another just smiles and nods. We unlock our rooms, say goodnight, and before I can say boo Jazzie is fast asleep. I slip into the bathroom and call Christian, asking him to use his key and feed my kids in the morning. He says no problem, asks how it went, and I say I'll tell him tomorrow. Falling into bed is the last thing I remember, as I'm fast asleep and in dream land as quickly as Jazzie.

In my dream everyone is dancing. Jazzie, Nate, the mouthless man, John Smith, Don, Sadie, Rico, Bonnie, and I. It's kind of a circle dance, and we don't look particularly happy, but we don't look unhappy either. I guess you could say we look determined. And resigned. And, perhaps, even relaxed—as though this was all expected even though there is obvious effort involved.

It's the only dream I remember.

As light is breaking in around the curtain over the window there's a knock on the door. Jazzie sleeps through it but I get up and go to answer it. I smile as I realize that Jazzie probably sleeps more soundly than I because she hasn't had an animal companion for a few years. When you have kids, of any sort, you are just naturally a lighter sleeper.

I open the door and Nate is there with two cardboard trays full of breakfast goodies—coffee and donuts to be precise.

"Hi, handsome," I whisper, as I stretch on tiptoe to kiss him over his offerings. He meets my lips half way, and I know this is how I want to spend the rest of my mornings in this life—kissing Nate. I put my finger to my lips to say "be quiet", but Jazzie is now awake, and asking if that fine man at the door has brought breakfast. We laugh, and I let Nate in as I open the curtain to the morning light.

We consume our coffee and donuts in no time and make our plans. First, an early morning drive to visit one of the vortexes. This is Jazzie's idea, though it sounds good to me. I glance at Nate to see if he's rolling his eyes at the woo-woo suggestion, but he isn't. He looks perfectly cool with it, so I say okay, let's do the one on the airport mountain. Then, I say, I can call Karla and make arrangements to pick up the painting, and make sure she's called the vet to okay Sadie's release. I know this may be pushing it for Sadie—they'll want to keep her a day or two. But I'm pretty sure, with insistence, there won't be a problem. When all that's accomplished, we can beat it home.

So we head to the vortex, and sit quietly, each of us using the energy in our own way. We go the rest of the way up the mountain, just for kicks, to experience the awesome view of Sedona and the surrounding areas. From the airport you can see almost forever. Breathtaking. We walk back to the truck and I call Karla. She sounds wide awake and chipper, so apparently I didn't wake her up, which is a good thing.

"Hi, Karla! It's Alli, Don's ex."

"Oh, hi!"

"I hope you had a good time last night," I say. Although I'm not even sure a good time was what was planned.

But Karla enthuses that they had a great time, so I'm glad I took a stab.

"Can we make arrangements for the painting?" I ask.

"Sure," she answers. "Do you know where The Diner is?" she asks.

"Well, I do, but I'd rather meet somewhere more private, if you don't mind," I tell her. "We're kind of here without Don's knowledge, and we'd like to keep it that way," I explain.

"Of course," she says. "Stupid me."

"No, I didn't mean that—" I begin.

She laughs. "Chill," she says. "I didn't really mean it either. Let's see. Do you know where the Sedona Red Rock News is?"

"Yes."

"Well, they have a nice big parking lot, and I don't think anyone would mind if we met there."

"Sounds good to me," I say. "When?"

"How about 5 minutes or so?"

"We'll be there," I tell her, and we disconnect.

"Let's go," I tell my companions. "Uptown to the Red Rock News." I give directions, and at this hour of the morning, since most places aren't open for business yet, the traffic is light. We make it there just as a large, beat-up pickup pulls in. A redhead gets out, about 25 years of age. I roll down my window and call, "Karla?" She waves, so we drive over and get out.

She's reaching into her truck to get something, and for a split second I have a panic attack that she'll pull out a gun—but she doesn't. She has the painting, minus the muslin covering, which she hands over. "Thank you so much, Karla," I say, reaching for my wallet. But she waves her hand.

"Don't bother," she tells me. "I decided since you're going to pay Sadie's bill that that is payment enough," she explains.

"Really?" I ask, although I'm grateful.

"Really," she assures me, then reaches out to give me an impromptu hug—which is difficult because I'm still holding the portrait.

She goes to Jazzie and Nate and hugs them too. Her eyes are filling with tears and she says, "You take good care of that girl, okay?"

"That's a promise," I answer.

"She's such a sweet thing, you know? Always so happy, always a smile. I don't know how that bastard could have done whatever he did to her."

"Kicked her," Jazzie blurts. Karla gives her an inquiring look.

"Well, I don't know how you know that, but I believe it. And I just want you to know, I'd rather starve than ever see that asshole's face again," she finishes with contempt.

"We believe you," I answer. "And we hope to never see the asshole's face again, either," I tell her. And boy, do I ever mean that.

"Well, I'll let you go now, so you can pick up Sadie," she says. "I've already called them and told them to expect you, and that you're paying the bill," she informs us. "Oh, and by the way, I told them the kid's name was Ester, you know, just in case someone thought they recognized her."

"Great," I say. "Take care, Karla. And thank you so much for having such a big heart."

She looks at me thoughtfully for a moment then says, "Well, thank you for saying that, but you shouldn't have to thank people for having a heart, should you? It should just be the natural thing to do, now shouldn't it?" And at that she's in her truck and driving off before we can say a thing. Jazzie looks at me and grins.

"What do you think? An angel, perhaps?" she says.

I smile back. "Perhaps." But then, we should all be angels—just like Karla said.

We stow the painting behind the back seat of the king cab and give directions to Nate. We arrive at the vet clinic in about 7 minutes and pile out of the car. We head inside and a young, pretty receptionist asks our business. I tell her I'm here to pay a bill and pick up Ester.

I almost say Sadie, but catch myself just in time. The receptionist pulls up the bill, and gives me the total. I hand over my credit card, and she swipes it through. As she hands me the slip of paper to sign, someone enters the lobby from the door to my right, and the young woman tells whoever it is that Ester's ride is here.

"I'll tell the doctor," says an all too familiar voice. I finish signing, and hand the slip back to the receptionist, my heart pounding in my chest. Shit.

"Hi, Debra!" I say brightly, as I turn to the woman who used to make my life miserable at this very clinic.

"Hi, Alli," she smirks. "Long time no see."

"It has been awhile," I say nonchalantly. "How've you been?"

"Fine," she replies. "And yourself?"

"Fine," I tell her. She just stands there with that smirk, so I add, "Can you get the doctor? I'd like to get Ester and get going." She waits a beat, then still with that smirk, she leaves the room for the back and, I presume, to get the doctor.

"So," the receptionist asks, "how do you know Debra?" It's just a friendly question, but it brings bile to my throat anyway.

"Used to work here," I tell her.

"Really?" she sounds surprised. "When?" Just another friendly question, but I wish she didn't ask, because I really don't want to even think about it.

"A few years back," I tell her, hoping that's the end of this conversation. I'm saved by the doctor, who enters just then and calls us into an exam room. He's young, also. And cute. But then, in reality, almost everyone in Sedona is attractive. It's been that way for decades. No reason I can think of. It just is.

The doctor goes over the procedure he did, and asks if we could possibly let her stay another day, but I'm firm in my no. So he gives the instructions that go with the care and feeding of a dog with a pin in her leg, and hands over her meds and extra bandages. He tells us we can wait in the lobby and goes to retrieve Sadie — I mean Ester. He brings her back through the exam room to the lobby, and she starts to wag her tail when she sees us. She's walking, well hobbling, but, at least she's doing that, and I'm glad to see her in good spirits. Both Jazzie and I bend to give her kisses and rubs on her head and she does her famous ear to ear smile. The doctor comments that she seems to like us — that he wasn't even sure she knew us, when Karla said she'd be giving her to a new home.

"Yes," I answer. "She knows us." Me, from two personal experiences, and Jazzie telepathically. But of course, I don't tell him that. I just say, "Thank you, doctor, for fixing her up, and taking care of her."

"No problem," he says. "That's what we're here for. Do you need some help getting her into your vehicle?" Jazzie and I look to Nate, who says he thinks he can handle it. But he'll holler if he can't. The doctor seems good with that so we start for the door. As we do, Debra, who has appeared at the exam room door says, "Take good care of Ester," with a sickening emphasis on "Ester". And I know she knows. Crap. Oh well. What can we do? I say a quick silent prayer, as we wait out front for Nate to bring the truck, that all will work out for the highest and best. The highest and best. That's all I want.

Nate pulls up, jumps out, opens the back door and pushes the front seat as far forward as it can go. He gingerly picks up Sadie and gently places her on the back seat. She lolls her tongue off to the side of her mouth and smiles broadly. Looks like we're good to go.

Since we are already at the far west end of town we decide to take the alternate route home, through the Verde Valley. We head out Hwy 89A, toward Cottonwood, through the big flat stretch of land that appears as soon as you clear the last red butte. Up ahead several miles is Mingus Mountain, rising high against the sky. Jerome floats about halfway up—a little artist community that was rescued in the seventies by hippies looking to get away from the city. When the hippie artists moved in, it was a mining ghost town. Now it's a tourist mecca. We drive in silence across the expanse, take Hwy 260 in Cottonwood, and when we approach the turn off for I-17 south I glance in the back seat. Jazzie is gently stroking Sadie's head, a thoughtful look in her eyes. Sadie's eyes are closed, her tongue still lolling out the side of her mouth, her smile still gracing her face.

"We'll find her a really good home," I assure Jazzie. But Jazzie jerks her head up and looks at me like I'm insane. She smiles her apology to me, and goes back to stroking and gazing at Sadie.

"Don't be ridiculous," she says softly. "Sadie's mine, now." I smile, and turn around back in my seat. I steal a glance at Nate. His eyes are tearing. And so are mine.

Life is suddenly very, very good.

As we wind our way home, and clear the confines of the Verde Valley, the vista opens up. In the east thunderheads are towering in a solid line of threat, all the way from the north to the south, as far as the eye can see.

"Looks like we can expect some rain tonight," Nate observes.

I close my eyes and smile broadly. "That would be absolutely fantastic," I say. "Something to wash away any last vestiges of negativity."

From the back Jazzie asks "What negativity? I'd say everything turned out pretty darn well."

I smile, and say she's right. But, in my heart, there's a bit of a nag. And her name is Debra.

However, the best thing I can do, I know, is put her right out of my mind. So I say a quick prayer of gratitude, and I do just that. I swish her right out. All it takes to do that is a good, long look at Nate. He smiles, and takes his right hand off the wheel. With it he holds mine, his fingers softly caressing the top of my hand, exploring my fingers, then tickling my palm. I giggle and take my hand away. He smiles, and places both hands back on the steering wheel. In another hour we will have dropped off Jazzie and Sadie, and we'll be home at my place.

I can't wait. I have a feeling tonight will be very special.

The thunderheads continue their relentless march west.

Chapter 15

Nate and I have just arrived at my house. It took a bit longer than the hour, as Jazzie needed us to go to the pet store and buy some supplies for Sadie. Mutton passed over a couple of years after Alan, so she had nothing in the way of doggie stuff. Not that Mutton's stuff would have been appropriate, anyway—Mutton was a small dog, and Sadie is anything but. We had to get new food bowls, water bowls, toys, and bed. When Jazzie asked what color bed she wanted, Sadie just said for me to use my best judgment. She just wanted it to be soft—and, of course, she wanted to look good in it. I guess it's a girl thing. So Nate and I went to buy Sadie's stuff while Jazzie settled her in and gave her her meds. We returned with several cans of dog food and a bag of dry, a chewy toy and a tug-of-war toy for later, four large stainless bowls, two for water and two for food, and a huge, cushy, doggie bed in scarlet. Sadie should have known that, if she left it up to me, it would be scarlet.

We stayed a bit with Jazzie and Sadie as they settled on a place for her bed and her bowls. When they looked satisfied with all the arrangements Nate and I left.

I'm not sure if I've ever seen two happier gals.

So now we're at my house, and the thunderclouds are about an hour off. Electricity is in the air—or maybe it's just me. I'm not sure. I feel antsy, charged. I unlock the door and turn off the alarm. Rico and Bonnie saunter out to greet me, and I pick each one up and hug and kiss them till they squirm and tell me to cut it out. All the while Nate is just standing quietly and observing. When I'm done with my mommy torture the kids wander over to Nate to check him out. They sniff around his shoes and ankles, then Bonnie says "whatever" and saunters off to her window. Rico plops his butt down and stares up at Nate in adoration. Nate notices this and smiles at him. Rico blinks and starts to purr loudly at Nate, so Nate bends and picks him up, scratching him gently behind his ears. Rico closes his eyes in ecstasy, and starts to drool a little. Nate chuckles. I'm in ecstasy to see that Nate knows cats — and obviously likes them.

I ask Nate if he'd like something to drink and he says he'd love a glass of water, so I leave the men and go to the kitchen. I pick two colorful glasses and fill them with some cold water from the frig. When I return, Rico has joined Bonnie in the window, all happy-faced, and Nate is standing in my front room looking both intrigued and lost. I hand him the water and he takes a long drink. I sip at mine. He hands the glass back and shuffles his feet.

"Well, I guess I better get the painting out of the truck," he says, and turns to go.

My heart leaps, as I realize that I'm losing him — at least for this moment — and I can't stand the thought. I need him here. I need him to stay for at least a while longer. I want him to stay the night. I want him to stay forever! But, at least, I need him to stay for now.

"Would you like a sandwich or something?" I ask. "I could start fixing it while you get the portrait."

"Okay," he says, his eyes brightening. "Sure. That sounds great."

"Roast beef okay?"

"One of my favorites."

"What would you like on it?"

"Whatever you think," he tells me. Then with slight melancholy he adds, "I'm in your hands." And out he goes.

My heart does a dance of delight and trepidation. He's in my hands. Oh, how I wish that were true.

I hurry to the kitchen and drag the makings out of the frig. I use organic mayo and mustard, baby spinach, and thinly sliced organic roast beef I bought at Whole Foods. I place these all on soft 7 grain, sprouted bread slices, and put the sandwiches on two plates. I've made three, just in case Nate is a big eater. I put out a couple of place mats on the wrought iron table and choose party napkins to use. I wonder where Nate is, as he's had plenty of time to retrieve the painting, so I go to look for him. I find him out front talking with Christian.

"Hi, Christian!" I say as I join them.

"Hello, yourself," he replies. "Nate, here, has filled me in on your little adventure."

"Oh," I answer, feeling slightly off balance because Christian seems a bit at odds about something. "Yes, it *was* quite an adventure, I will say that." I look to the ground. What is going on?

"Well, if you don't need anything, Alli, I'll be on my way," Christian adds, his tone flat, his eyes the same.

"No, everything is good here," I tell him, hoping to relay the full implication of what I mean. Because, as far as I'm concerned, everything is way fine here! Then I remember the kids. "Oh! And thank you so much for feeding the kids this morning," I tell him. "I'm so glad I can count on you," I add, hoping to appease whatever is bugging him.

"That you can, Alli, my dear," he answers. "You can always count on me." With a bit of a wave to me and to Nate he turns on his heel and strides to his car. He gets in without another glance our way, and leaves.

"Wow," I say. "That was weird."

Nate looks at me strangely. "How so?" he asks.

"I'm not sure. But Christian was definitely in a strange mood."

"Well, he cares for you, doesn't he?" Nate asks—and I flash on the first night at the restaurant. The night that Christian held my hand, and how Nate had reacted.

"Yes!" I say. "Yes, he absolutely does!" I hesitate a moment. Is it any of Nate's business? Nate's eyes are wary and confused. I decide I must tell him. "Christian is gay."

Nate's eyes register surprise. Then they fade to amusement. Then, finally, they fade to understanding.

"He loves you," he says simply, "as a friend. Like a sister."

"Yes."

"You know," Nate says, taking my hand and leading me back into the house, "I would kill someone who hurt my sister."

"No you wouldn't!" I say, alarmed. Then I reconsider. "Would you?"

Nate smiles. "I really don't know," he admits. "But I would darn well think about it." He stops me in the front room and lifts my hand to his lips. He kisses it tenderly, holding my eyes locked to his. With his lips still brushing my hand he says, "I understand Christian's concern. You, dear Alli, are a treasure to protect."

My heart and stomach flutter in rhythm. A treasure to protect. My god that sounds so wonderful. For the first time in my life I'm being told outright that I'm a treasure. Not an anchor, not a ball and chain, not stupid, not wrong, not any one of the thousand things that I've been told in my life. I'm a treasure.

I am a treasure.

I look into Nate's eyes in awe.

"You are the treasure," I tell him. "You are the treasure, and I'm so glad I found you."

Nate smiles, his eyes soft and knowing. "Let's eat," he whispers, and I'm suddenly confused, flushed. Then I remember the sandwiches and laugh.

"Yes! Let's eat!" I say, taking his hand and leading him to the kitchen "This way."

After lunch Nate helps me load the scant dishes into the dishwasher, and I see I finally have it filled enough to run. I get it going while Nate leans against the countertop and watches. When I'm done he says, "I'd like to see your studio."

I'm a bit taken aback, as I realize I don't know if I'm ready to share this part of my life just yet. As I stand and hesitate, Nate says that it's okay — I don't have to show him.

"I understand if you're not ready," he offers.

"Well, thank you," I answer. Then look away. "I'm not ready — but, I don't know why!"

"Maybe it's because you don't really know me, yet."

"Maybe." I turn away, embarrassed that I'm holding out on this man who has helped me so much in the last day. This man whom I invited into my life — no, *demanded* into my life — by painting his eyes, and calling them my lover's eyes. I made him be here! Why hold back now?

"Come on," I say, taking his hand and pulling him away from the kitchen. We enter my studio, and he looks around appreciatively.

"Very nice," he says.

"Thank you. I bought this house specifically because of this room. The light is perfect, and it's roomy enough to move around in without being cramped." He's studying the portrait of "John Smith", and a look of recognition comes into his eyes.

"I can't be sure, of course, but isn't this the man who was arguing with your ex last night?"

"Yes."

"As is the portrait without the mouth?"

"No."

"No?"

"The portrait of the mouthless man is his twin brother."

"He has a twin brother?"

"Yes."

"How do you know?"

"I met him."

"Really?"

"Yes. Actually, he searched me out. He wanted to tell me something."

"What was that?"

I hesitate. Nate notices. "What did he want to tell you?" Nate asks again. I clear my throat.

"To be careful," is all I say.

Nate turns back to the painting of John Smith. "Of him?" he asks.

"Partly, yes."

"And of Don," he finishes.

"Yes."

Nate lightly rubs his lips with a finger, deep in thought. Then he looks at me directly, his eyes calculating, his mind putting everything together. He tilts his head slightly, his finger still on his lip. He lowers his hand and folds his arms across his chest. He takes a large breath, and lets it out slowly, never removing his eyes from me. He seems to be struggling with the words he wants to say, but I can see into his heart. He already cares for me deeply. He's worried about me. He wants to protect me, but doesn't wish to appear manipulative, smothering.

I love him for that. Yes. I love him. That word just came out—but it's the truth. I love him.

"I plan to take his advice," I tell Nate. "I plan to be very, very careful."

"Thank you," is all he says. Then, without warning, a huge crack of thunder breaks into our thoughts. I jump and shriek. Then I laugh.

"Sorry!" I say. "I don't usually jump at thunder! Guess I was just too involved in our conversation."

He saunters over to me and grabs me, tilting my face up. He kisses me hard this time. His tongue searches for mine, shamelessly, powerfully. I'm caught off guard, breathless. I pull away—not really meaning to—I just do. He considers this a moment, then makes a motion like tipping his hat.

"Good day, Miss Alli," he says. "It's been fun. I think." I stare in disbelief as he strolls out of my studio, and out of my house, closing the door firmly behind him. I run after him and open the door, calling his name, but he doesn't look back. As he climbs into his truck and starts the engine the rain begins a furious beating. I take a few more steps toward the truck, still calling, but stop, and in seconds I'm soaked to the skin by the cool rain. Nate is already half way down my drive when my hand flies to my mouth to cover a choked sob. By the time the sob is released into the fury of the storm he has reached the end of my drive and turned onto the street—and out of my sight. "Oh dear God!" I wail. "Don't let him be out of my life!" I'm crying in huge sobs now, barely able to breathe. The rain streaming down my face enters my wailing mouth and I nearly drown.

What have I done!? What the hell have I done!?

I stand there another five minutes, until I turn and notice Rico and Bonita in the front window, sitting up and staring out at me, with concern all over their precious little faces. So I trudge back to the front door, wipe my feet on the mat, as though it will do any good, and go inside, closing the door softly behind me. I try to smile as I give the kids a little finger wave, but I hiccup a sob, and Rico jumps down to twine between my soaked ankles, water dripping all over him. He doesn't care. His self appointed job is to take my sorrow, or anger, or any lower, negative energies, and transmute them into something higher. He only wishes love and joy for me, and he'll do anything to make that happen. He's my little savior. Without him, I'm sure I'd be a train wreck.

He does make me feel better, and I reach down, still dripping huge drops of water all over him, and give him a scratch on the head.

"Thank you, Rico," I tell him with love. "Thank you very much."

He purrs and gazes up at me with adoration, closing his eyes when a drip hits his face, then opening them again to his look of love. I purr back at him, and he seems satisfied that he's done his job, so he gives me one more leg rub and sashays back to the window where he rejoins Bonita to watch the storm.

I edge to the bathroom with a flatfooted walk, careful to keep from slipping on the tile. Puddles follow in my path. Thank god I didn't go with wood floors.

I strip in the bathroom and press the button for the hot water re-circulation pump. As I wait a minute for the hot water to reach the shower I carefully comb the tangles out of my wet hair. Then I turn on the water, and am met with a hot blast. Wonderful! I adjust the temp and step in. The warm/hot water pounds me all over as I turn slowly in the shower letting it caress every inch before I start to lather. I actually got chilled in the rain, and the hot water feels good, warming me down to the bone. I think, however, some of the chill I feel is the look in Nate's eyes as he left. What an idiot I am, I scold myself. I paint this wonderful man into my life, call him my lover, allow him to enter into an adventure filled with danger and trouble, then rebuff him. Alli, Alli, Alli. You can be such a prude.

After I'm warm and clean I get out of the shower and dry off tho-roughly. When it's hot and dry out I leave myself on the damp side. Right now, however, dry is good. I lotion up and dry my hair, just leaving it long and down. As I finish up my routine I notice a small vial off to the side of my vanity. Forgetting what it is I pick it up to look. It's the scent that Beth gave me a sample of. She had implied that it would have very good results in the romance department, hadn't she? I remove the small cap and inhale. Oh my god! It's wonderful! I immediately feel waves of erotic and loving emotions surge through my body. I take the small, magic vial and move to my bedroom. I'm still naked, so I make my statement to the portrait of Nate's eyes. I stand before the painting and look at him deeply. Then I slowly, erotically apply the scent to all the special parts of my naked body — watching him watching me. I start at my neck, then my breasts, my stomach, between my thighs, the backs of my knees, and the tops of my feet.

"This is my true desire," I tell the painting. "This is how I really feel. This is what I really want." I search the eyes, and they soften. I smooth some of the perfume into my hair, then put the tiny cap back on. I reach toward the painting and stroke it through the air. "Please come back," I whisper. "Please, please come back."

I'm so sure that Nate will return that I crawl into bed. I arrange the covers just so, straightening and smoothing the sheet and silk blanket over my body, folding the upper edge of the sheet down, placing it so that there's just a hint of the mound of my breasts showing. I smooth my hair and flow it out upon my pillow, and I wait. The storm rages around me, and I wait. I close my eyes, and I wait.

But, Nate does not come back. And as the storm strobes and cracks through my consciousness, I fall fast asleep.

I awaken in the dark to an especially loud crack of thunder, and I pull the sheets up to my chest as I sit in the bed and listen. The strobing continues outside, my blinds still wide open. I can see the angry sky in constant motion of pink and white. I suddenly realize I never fed the kids, and I'm surprised they haven't woken me to complain. I stumble out of bed and grab my robe. Pulling it on as I go I feel a draft as I leave the bedroom. I hurry down the short hall and see the front door standing wide open. Oh no! I didn't lock it, or set the alarm! I call for the kids, but I don't immediately see them. I close the door against the storm and move to lock it—but, what if someone is still inside the house? My heart jumps to my throat, causing me to gag with fear. I move to the wall and stand flat against it, arms slightly outstretched along it to feel my way. With the strobing, I have regular flashes of momentary sight, but then it's pitch black again. I begin to tremble, and nausea wells. I inch along the wall, listening, listening. But I can't hear anything except the storm. Suddenly Rico appears before me, calm. I snatch him up and lay my head on him to hear his subtle purr. If he is acting like this, then there is no one in the house. Thank god! I set him down and follow him to the kitchen, where, I presume, he'll be showing me his empty plate with an expression of "what's wrong with this picture?". As I reach the kitchen the strobing halts for several seconds. Not wanting to disappoint Rico I begin to cautiously work my way to the light switch. That is, right until I trip over the body.

I scream. Then I wake up. Rico jumps on the bed, coming to calm me. Oh my god! Oh my god! It was only a dream! I push back my hair, and wipe a trickle of sweat from my brow.

"Hi, Rico," I say as calmly as I can. "Are you hungry for dinner?" He gives me a thrrrpp, so I get up and pull on my robe. We start down the hall, and with dread I strain to notice if there's an unexpected draft. But there is none. I rush to the front door and lock it. And I set the alarm. I pant in relief, wiping sweaty palms on my silk robe. Rico is sitting waiting for me, beaming love and happiness to me. I soak it in as best I can, my heart slows, and I gather my wits. Then I follow my little boy's sashay into the kitchen which is, thankfully, empty of any dead bodies. I switch on the light but turn the dimmer down low, so there is only enough light to barely see.

"I'm so sorry, kids," I say, as Bonnie has shown up, also. "I can't believe I forgot to feed you dinner," I tell them, though I remember why I forgot. But what kind of excuse is that? I almost want to call myself a slut—but I know that would be counterproductive. So I push the accusation from my mind and dish out their food. I place their plates on the floor and they go gratefully at it. I give them some fresh water, then sit down at the little wrought iron table. I trace out with my fingers the place where Nate sat earlier today, and caress my aching heart. I can't believe he didn't come back. But then, what did I expect? I pushed him away. And in the studio no less! The vibes in there are probably rife with sexuality after my dance for him the other day. If he's sensitive at all, which I'm sure he is, he was probably just reacting to the damn strip tease I performed for him. Jeez, you idiot. You do everything you can to get him in lust with you, then you push him away. I put my head down on my hands and shake the images out of my mind. The thunder has abated some, and the storm seems to be passing, so I turn the alarm back off, and open the sliding glass door to the backyard. The breeze is delightfully cool, a welcome change for this time of year. After a few minutes the rain has stopped, and the clouds are thinning enough that the sky is becoming increasingly visible. The thunder still growls, but it growls from a distance. I decide to take a swim.

I open the pool and drop my robe. I dive into the water and come up at the opposite end of the pool. I swim hard to the other side, working off frustration, and anger at myself. I do this for about ten minutes until I am exhausted. Then I get out and put on my robe which, being silk, does little to dry me but, instead, just plasters to my body. I shake out my hair, and go back inside, carefully locking the door and setting the alarm. I say good night to the kids, turn off the light, and carefully wend my way back to the bedroom. I hang my robe up to dry, then crawl into bed, still damp. Pulling the covers up,

I stare at the ceiling. The events of the last 24 hours play themselves out in front of my sightless eyes. Eventually I close them to all I wish to forget, and I fall asleep.

This time, I hope, not to dream.

Chapter 16

I awaken to a day that is refreshed from last night's storm, wishing my heart felt the same. I drag myself up to a sitting position, and dare a glance at Nate's eyes. This morning they are entirely impassive. I lower mine in defeat and get out of bed. I take a quick shower, really just to rewet my hair, since it's a tangle of strings after my swim last night, and then I make myself as presentable as I can. My heart isn't in it, but one has to make an effort, right? I slap on a bit of gloss, pull my hair into a pony tail and fasten it with a purple elastic band. I grab regular blue jeans, and a white tank top, and slip on my turquoise flip flops. I pad into the kitchen and make breakfast for the kids, which they ignore for at least an hour since they had dinner late last night. I fix myself plain oatmeal. I feel absolutely frill-less this morning—which usually mean I'm hating myself. I make some coffee and take it to the studio. I remove the painting of Sadie and place it on my "out" table, after finding a piece of silk to drape it with, and prepare it for delivery to Jazzie. Now that I have an empty easel I go to the front room to get the painting of the mouthless man. I set him on the empty easel and consider him. I really, really want to give him his voice—but I don't know if I'm up to it today. These things, as in all important things, should be done when one is in the proper mood. Meaning one should be in an intuitive state, filled with joy, relaxed, feeling good about oneself and the project. I feel none of those things at this time. What I feel is dead. Dead, and ugly, and useless, and powerless.

I can't work on this portrait in this state, of that I am sure. So I decide to go to Jazzie's. Besides shopping, it's the only thing I can think of to do.

I grab my purse and the painting of Sadie, say goodbye to the kids, set the alarm, lock the door, and head down to Scottsdale.

When I arrive at Jazzie's I find her and Sadie enjoying the backyard. Jazzie has a baby monitor she sets by the front door in order to hear her doorbell when she's outside. Pretty good idea, actually. I should get one for myself. She lets me in, takes the painting from me, and we head out to the shade of one of her huge gazebos. She has a mister going, which is only partially effective this time of year, but the built-in fan provides an additional amount of cooling. Together they make it pleasant enough. Sadie wags her hello and I stroke her lovely head. She looks a bit loopy, and Jazzie confirms that she's still on pain meds. But not for long, she assures me. As we sit in the shade and enjoy the cool, the hummingbirds battle it out around one of the feeders. Jazzie decides we all could use some refreshment, so she goes inside to grab some cold drinks and I stay out with Sadie.

"How's it going, Sadie?" I ask the pretty girl. She smiles broadly, tongue hanging, eyes bright, if loopy. Then just to be sure I understand, she adds a wag of her tail. "Good," I say. "And, Jazzie — she's a pretty good mom, huh?" At this Sadie really wags her tail, hard. Then she gives me a snuffly little "woof", and resumes her smiling. I reach down to pat her head. "Yeah, I agree," I tell her. "Jazzie's the best."

"Did I just hear my name?" Jazzie asks as she lugs out a tray with glasses and pitcher, and a bowl of cool water for Sadie.

"Yes, you did," I answer. "We were just talking about you." Sadie raises her head and gives Jazzie adoring looks. Jazzie laughs.

"And the consensus?" she asks.

"You're all right!"

"Thanks, girls," she blushes. "I can honestly say that I think Don has to be one of the most clueless people on the planet, because here I sit with two of the most lovely women, and he hurt you both." Jazzie shakes her head in disgust, as she pours our drinks and places the bowl near Sadie. "He is an absolute moron."

"And you are an absolute angel," I tell her, "because you rescued us both." Sadie pulls in her tongue, and closes her mouth. She looks intently at Jazzie, her eyes clear and compassionate. "Yes, Sadie," I tell her, "Jazzie rescued me too. She is a gift from God." Sadie considers this and slowly wags her tail. Then she breaks into another broad smile and lets her tongue hang out. Jazzie and I laugh.

"She's a lovely dog," Jazzie says. "I hadn't realized how lonely I was until last night. How empty the house has been. I could say I went too long without someone here, but then I might not have ended up with Sadie, if I already had someone else. So all is well that ends well, right, sweetie?" she asks Sadie. Sadie closes her eyes in complete agreement. Then she lowers her head to her paws and heaves a huge sigh. Eyes closed, she drifts off to sleep as Jazzie and I talk.

"So," Jazzie starts, "now that the underage juvenile is asleep, give me the juicy details about last night. That is what you're here for, right?" she asks, while sipping her drink.

I cough a little, caught off guard by her question. "Well, actually, I'm here with bad news."

"Don't tell me you two didn't do the deed!" Now it's my turn to blush.

"No, we didn't."

"Why the hell not?" Jazzie demands.

"Well," I begin, "it just didn't happen."

"Okay. Why the hell not?" she repeats.

"Because I clammed up, okay?" I snap.

Jazzie sips some more. "Okay. Why the hell did you clam up?" she demands.

I start to laugh, but realize it's a defense mechanism. So I stop. I twirl my straw, and contemplate the question. It's a good one. One I should have already asked myself instead of just letting it dwell on the outskirts of my mind.

"I don't know," I answer simply. "I just really, honestly don't know!"

"Well, girl, we better figure it out so you can move beyond it. Because that is one fine man, and I believe in my heart that he is right for you. Maybe even The One.

I look Jazzie in the eye. "He is The One," I tell her. "I dreamed of him before we even met."

"You're kidding!" Jazzie exclaims.

"No, I'm not. It was after the dream that I painted him. I painted his eyes, and called them my lover's eyes."

"Wow!" Jazzie says. She sips some more, then sets her drink on the table. "So, once again, why the hell did you clam up?" I consider this question for several, long seconds.

"Because I'm still wondering if I have the right to be happy," I conclude.

"And, Alli, you know the answer to that," she growls.

"Yes. Yes I do," I tell her. "I absolutely do! So, why did I react that way?" Now, even I'm baffled!

"I'm thinking it was because it was so close to contact with Don. Maybe you just hadn't gotten the taste of the whole scenario out of your mouth yet."

"That could be," I agree. "Don does have a pretty strong energy," I say. "I should be more cognizant of cleansing my field after any contact with him," I add.

"You got that right!" Jazzie agrees. "So remember that from now on. Don't let a good man get away because your old arch enemy has thrown his evil energy over you."

"You're right. I let Don steal years of my life. I'm not going to let him steal one more day."

"Good! We've got that settled!" Jazzie says triumphantly. "So, when are you going to Roberto's again?"

I thought of my original plans with Nate, before he got roped into our Sedona adventure. "Well, I was supposed to go see Nate tonight," I tell her. "But now I'm not so sure he'd want me there."

"Why? Did it get ugly between you two?"

"No. Well, maybe yes. I don't know," I say in exasperation, "He left in a hurry after I pushed him away."

"You pushed him away?" Jazzie asks, incredulous.

"Yes," I sigh. "He was kissing me in the studio, and I suddenly just put a stop to it!" I whine. "I clammed up! Then he just said 'goodbye, Miss Alli', and left."

"Did you try to stop him?" I thought about myself, standing in the rain, calling out Nate's name, and watching him drive away. I lower my head.

"Yes, Jazzie," I say softly. "Yes, I did try to stop him. But he left anyway."

"Oh. Well, then. I can see your dilemma."

We both sip our drinks for a bit, thinking in silence. I help myself to more from the pitcher, then refresh Jazzie's glass.

"You know what I think?" Jazzie asks.

"No. What do you think?"

"I think you need to get decked out tonight and show up at that restaurant as though nothing happened. Because, it shouldn't have happened. It was Don interfering, and it absolutely should not have happened. So you should just act as though it *didn't* happen—you know, try to erase the incident."

I consider this and, as I do, my heart swells—which means it's in agreement. "Okay," I say. "I believe that's good advice."

"I'd come along for moral support, but I don't think I should leave Sadie alone just yet," she finishes. And as she does, Sadie's tail starts wagging. "Uh-oh," Jazzie laughs. "I think we've just awakened our underage girl!"

We speak of her upcoming consultations, and Brenda's update on her new companion. But as the day warms up we decide we've had enough and we carry everything back inside. Then we help Sadie back into the family room, where she lies down on the nice cool tile and relaxes. I pet Sadie goodbye and give Jazzie a hug. Then I start back up the road to my little hideaway, planning on what to do when I get there. I do believe I am in the proper frame of mind to paint, now, so that's my decision.

I stand before the mouthless man and smile at him. It is so good to have him back, safe and sound. I thank the angels for helping us obtain our goals, and also for the way we were able to achieve the desired outcome without Don's knowledge.

Okay—so I'm knocking on wood here.

As I pull on my smock I load a CD of thunder and waves, and relish the sounds that fill my studio. I close my eyes, and call in my guides. I ask to paint the mouth that is the highest and best for me, for him, and for all concerned. I think of his mouth, as I've seen it. It's a nice mouth. Not lined, like his brother's. Then it dawns on me. What his mouth needs is exactly that! Lines! However, they need to be laugh lines. Excited, I select my paints, brushes, and get to work. In no time at all my friend has a mouth. It is a beautiful mouth, a happy mouth. A wise mouth. I like it, and him, very much. I pull over the portrait of his brother, and place them side by side. They are so much alike, but completely different. I turn their easels in a little, so they are positioned slightly facing each other, though mostly facing me. I talk to them.

"Okay, here's the thing," I begin. "You are brothers. Brothers, for chrissake! You should be each other's best friend, each other's greatest support. I don't know what went down between you two, but, it must be resolved if you," and I point to the once mouthless man, "are to regain your voice. So, you, John Smith," I say, pointing to the other painting, "must now apologize to your brother for whatever it was you did to him." I wait. But truthfully, I feel no apology. In fact, I feel as though John Smith is saying that it is the brother who should apologize. I'm baffled enough by this that I ask him, "Why should your brother apologize? I thought you caused him to lose his voice."

"There's a lot you don't know..." comes floating languidly to my mind.

"Is that true?" I ask the other brother. His eyes cloud for a brief second. Then glisten with a tear.

"Okay," I say. "Then, do you wish to start this reconciliation by apologizing first?" I stare at the portrait, hands on my hips. I feel like a school principal, trying to work out a playground altercation. But I'm aware this has to be a pretty big deal, for a man to lose his voice.

As I'm standing there, waiting, I feel the words float in. "I'm not ready to apologize, yet."

"Ahhh," I say, "but you do agree that there might be an apology owed?"

Only silence meets my question.

"Well, okay then," I say to the two of them. "You can just stay this way until you decide who's going to make the first move. Okay? Okay." I clean up my paints and brushes, remove my smock, turn off the CD, and take a final look at them. Their eyes flicker between hatred and amusement. Yes, I think. These two have quite a history.

Maybe I should stay out of it.

Yeah, right.

Chapter 17

Having some time before needing to get ready for tonight, I decide to make preparations for the evening. You know, just in case. I change the sheets on the bed, putting on my most luxurious and elegant set. I dust, vacuum, and mop. I clean my bathroom, shine the mirror, even semi-wash the windows. I sparkle up my kitchen, and straighten my studio. While I'm in there I shudder at the way I pushed away Nate. I close my eyes, breathe deeply, and send wave after wave of love for Nate out into the studio. I let my heart swell to ecstasy at the thought of him, and I fill every last corner of the room with this love. Then I think, what the heck? And I go around the whole house, filling every corner of it with love for Nate. When I'm finished sending out the love, I sit and rest for a few minutes. I take out my journal and write in it — admonishments and reminders that I deserve very much to be happy. And that anytime I act contrary to that, it's because I'm allowing old beliefs about myself to invade my mind. And that I need to kiss them goodbye. Literally. Kiss them for the way they once reigned in my life, because the experience gave me compassion and insight into others. And kiss them goodbye. So they can live in a past that I no longer dwell in. The feelings need to be honored, but they also, very much, need to be released. So, I do. I release them. I imagine them as balloons that I fill up, then send off to God. God's energy then can do whatever with them. Transmute them, or leave them be. All is love to God. So, they'll probably just be left as is. It will be up to me to do any transmuting. I sigh at this thought.

So much responsibility. So little time.

So I send up some golden balloons to chase after the balloons of my past, and tell them my intent—transmute all to golden love. Make them happy, somehow. Thank you.

There. Now I don't have to feel guilty about leaving feelings like those hanging around in the Universe, where they might invade some other poor woman's psyche. Enough is enough. I wish to help bring a different world into being. I honestly hope the new generation of women being born today never even know such feelings exist. I pray they know only love.

However, immediately on the heels of that thought, another appears—the realization that the pain of having known Don is what makes the knowing of Nate so delightful. I know the pleasure, because I have the pain to weigh it against!

Actually, that thought works for me pretty well. I feel one hundred percent lighter.

As I strip to take a shower and begin my ritual of getting ready to go out I spy Nate's eyes on the wall. Should I remove them I wonder? I decide to make up my mind after my shower, and I do.

Dripping wet and naked, I remove the painting from the wall and hide it in my closet. I feel as though I'm going to telegraph my betrayal if I leave the spot empty, however, so I go to my studio and find a painting I did a year ago—a painting of a spectacular sunset. I could claim that I brought that particular sunset into being by painting it, but the truth is, I don't know if I did or not. Because here in the desert, we are blessed with many, many spectacular sunsets. In any case, it looks good on the wall and I'm surprised I never hung it before.

I finish getting ready, deciding on a pant set instead of a dress. I add lots of chunky jewelry to help dress it up, and slip on my gold sandals. The set is rayon, flowy, roomy without being dumpy, and though it isn't what one would call sexy, the draping of the fabric could conjure "sexy" in the willing mind. I hope it does that for Nate.

I feed the kids, and kiss them goodbye with the promise I won't be out all night, and head to Roberto's.

When I get there it isn't quite as crowded as it has been. Everyone around has now checked it out, and the crowd from now on will probably be a bit smaller. I just pray that it doesn't get too small—but somehow, I believe this restaurant is here to stay. I approach the hostess at her stand and she smiles at me.

"Just one for dinner?" she asks.

"Yes," I reply. "Just one."

"Patio or dining room?" she asks.

"Oh, patio I guess," I answer.

She grabs a menu and says, "Right this way."

She leads me to a table for two toward one corner—a table for lovers who wish to be discreet, I think—and sets the menu down as I pull out a chair and sit.

"Jonas will be right with you," she says, and returns to her post as the busgirl arrives with water and tapas.

"I didn't order anything," I tell her. She smiles shyly.

"I know," she says, then beats a quick exit.

"Okay, then," I murmur under my breath, and help myself to the spicy appetizer. As I munch, Jonas, whom I recognize as my regular server, arrives.

"Good evening," he says with a smile. "It's nice to have you here again."

I laugh and tell him thanks. "It's nice to be here, again," I admit. "I'm going to have to start selling more paintings, however, if I wish to be able to continue all this eating out," I confide.

He brightens. "Oh! So you're an artist, then?"

"Well, that's what I like to believe," I tell him.

"I paint, too," he tells me proudly.

"Really? That's great!" I reply. "What do you paint?"

"Mostly landscapes and horses," he says. "I love to ride my horse out into the desert and one day I just decided to pack an easel and all, and when we stopped for a rest I set up my stuff, and started to paint. It was great!" he says.

"So, you own a horse, do you?"

"Yes," he says with pride. "Her name's Sally, and I've had her since I was ten."

"So, you're kind of a cowboy, then?" I ask, amazed, because this young man is so cosmopolitan I'd have thought he'd be doing the Scottsdale club scene rather than riding horses.

He laughs. "Well, Miss, I wouldn't exactly call myself a cowboy. But I do love to ride — and I do love Sally."

"It's nice to live out here, and to be able to enjoy such a life, isn't it?"

"Yes, Miss."

"Name's Alli," I tell him. He blushes.

"Yes, Alli," he says, emphasizing Alli. "Actually, I wouldn't trade this life for any other life in the world," he finishes.

"Neither would I," I tell him softly. He smiles, a coconspirator in the game of life. I give him my drink order — a chilled herbal tea, this time — and tell him I'll give my dinner order when he returns. He goes off to fulfill my wishes, and I open the menu. A shadow appears from over my shoulder, and my heart races a bit. I turn slowly in my chair, knowing in my gut that it isn't Nate. I look up to see a twin's face. At first I'm not sure which twin. He doesn't speak for several seconds, only looks at me with a strange sadness. But then I notice the lines around his mouth, and while they have softened, they are still recognizable as the lines of smugness. At this moment, however, they aren't active. They are just there, a reminder.

"Hello, 'John Smith,'" I say, with more than a hint of sarcasm.

He sits in the empty chair of my table and appraises me. "Hello, Miss James."

"How are you?" I ask, faking a business-like politeness.

"I'm okay," he answers, with genuine frankness. And I think "okay" meaning he's hanging in there, but not really okay.

"Good," I say, not knowing what else to utter.

"How's the painting coming?" he asks, which greatly surprises me.

"Fine," I answer. "Why?"

"Oh, just curious," he says offhandedly.

"I'll be finished soon," I lie to him. "Just a few more details to include," I tell him. He searches my face as I fidget with my silverware.

"You sure?" he asks.

"Sure about what?"

"Are you sure you aren't already finished?"

I look him straight in the eye. And as I do so, I think of him and his brother, on their easels, facing each other, working to resolve their relationship. I reply that, yes — I'm sure there is more to be done. That way it is only half a lie. Because there is definitely more to be done. It just doesn't have anything to do with paint.

"You really *can* paint something into reality, can't you?" he asks me, with a cock of his head, appraising me, once again.

And, although I'm not sure it's the wisest answer, I tell him, yes. I really can. He nods softly, looks down at the table, then suddenly rises from his chair and says, "Well then. Please call me when you are finished."

"You never gave me your phone number," I tell him. He looks confused for a split second then nods again.

"That's right," he says. "So, I'll call you."

"How will you know when to call?" I ask him, annoyed that he is avoiding giving me his number.

But, he just smiles. "I'll know," he says. "I do believe I'll know." And with that he is gone.

Jonas arrives with my tea, and I tell him I'll need another minute, as I haven't had time to look at the menu yet.

"I know," Jonas says. "I saw Mr. Adams here."

"You know him?" I ask, startled. It had never occurred to me that he was local. I just assumed he was from Sedona, since he was involved with Don.

"Yes, I know him," he answers. "He was my stepfather."

"You're kidding!"

"No, I'm not. But, I wish I were," he adds bitterly.

"What happened?" I ask.

"He's an asshole, with a capital A," Jonas replies, angrily. "He used to hit my mother. And, sometimes, my younger sister."

"God, I'm sorry, Jonas," I say sincerely. "Did he ever hurt you?" I ask.

"No," Jonas answers with a bite. "He was way too much of a coward for that. And he never hit my mother or sister when I was around, either. Probably because he knew if I ever caught him in the act I would've tried to kill him. As it was, I tried anyway."

"You tried to kill him?" I ask, shocked.

"Yes," is all he says. "However, you can see, I did not succeed." He takes a deep breath, and lets it out with a force. Then he clears his throat, straightens, and says, "I'll be back in a few minutes to take your order, Miss. I mean, Alli."

"Thanks, Jonas," I say. And let him walk away. Small world, I think to myself.

I select dinner, and place the menu to the side of the small table. I sip my tea, and study the other patrons. They are a quiet group tonight, maybe because it's a Thursday crowd instead of the weekend. Many of these people will have jobs to go to tomorrow, so perhaps, like me, they are drinking tea. Jonas returns and I give him my order. A breeze picks up, then dies away as quickly as it came. The surrounding area has taken on a pink and orange glow, and I know that sunset is imminent. Unfortunately, the sky that is visible from where I sit contains no clouds, so tonight I'll have to be content with glow.

As I finish my tea I am hit with a feeling—the feeling that it is a mistake to be here tonight. I wrestle with it a minute, unsure as to whether I want to listen. But the feeling persists, so I flag down the busgirl and ask her to tell Jonas that I would like my order boxed to go. She looks surprised, but doesn't offer any argument or inquiry. As she sets off on her assignment, I sip my water, and finish the tapas. Then I set my napkin on the table and retrieve my credit card from my purse, ready to hand it directly to Jonas when he appears. Another minute goes by as the feeling mounts ever stronger in my chest. I'm almost panicked by the time Jonas arrives, which I do my best to cover. I stuff my credit card into the little folder and hand it back to Jonas, asking if I can meet him up front at the hostess stand to sign. He says sure, and takes off to cash me out. I gather my things and fight my way through the now crowded dining room. I arrive at the hostess station just as Jonas does. I add a twenty percent tip, sign, and hand back the merchant copy. Jonas and the hostess wish me good evening, which sentiment I return, and hurry out to my car. From the restaurant the first strains of Nate's guitar float seductively out into the night air. I break into a run, and throw myself inside after beeping open my Ms. Sebring. Panting I raise a shaking hand to my forehead. I'm clammy, and nausea rises to my throat. I will myself to stop shaking, and start the engine. I back out slowly, not trusting my reaction time. I put the car in drive and head unsteadily home. When there I search for the kids, whom I find safe and sound. I strip off my clothes and choose a tee shirt and jeans to take their place. I pad barefoot to the kitchen where I unplug the phone and grab a small plate. Not being certain I can even eat, I dish out just a few spoonfuls of tonight's meal. I turn out all the lights and find my way to the small wrought iron table. There I eat my meager meal in the dark. In the silence. In my fear. In dread.

And I don't even know why.

As the stars brighten with the deeper dark outside, I scrape my plate and put it in the dishwasher. My stomach is holding the food without complaint, so I guess I'll be alright. I take down a blue striped Mexican glass and fill it with water. Taking a few sips I stare out into the night through my kitchen window. I notice a movement past the iron fence of my yard, and my heart quickens. The movement turns into a scramble of immense proportion, and I watch transfixed as a pack of coyotes shout their victory call. Someone has just lost their present life, and gone on to another. I'm just glad I know that souls do not allow themselves to suffer when shedding their bodies. The rabbit, or whoever it was, never knew what hit him. Before the first fang ripped at him he was already outside his body, safe and sound.

Yes, I'm very glad I know that. Or I could find myself, tonight, on the floor in agonizing defeat, wondering if my heart could stand the ripping.

I turn away, grateful that the howling and yipping has ceased. I check on the kids one last time and find them oblivious to the drama. Animals know more than we do. They understand the dance of life and death—and accept fate with grace. Rico heaves a huge sigh and rolls over to present his belly for petting. I stroke the long, silky fur and he purrs loudly. I kiss him gently on that silky belly and he repays me with trills.

"I love you, Rico," I whisper. And he tells me he knows, by offering an ear to ear smile. I smile back, knowing that in the starlight coming through the windows he can see me as though it were practically daylight. He rolls back over on his side and gives a languid stretch. Belly time is finished.

I reluctantly close all the blinds and double check the locks and alarm. We are buttoned up tight, so I lie down on the bed as Bonnie takes her place near the corner. I don't remove my clothes, but just pull the lightweight blanket over my bare feet as I lie upon the sheets. I remember how I was feeling this afternoon, as I cleaned house and changed the bed into those special sheets I now lie upon. I wish I could recapture that feeling, and replace the unease I feel tonight. But it doesn't return, leaving me lost in a grief I can't even name.

I close my eyes and, eventually, drift off to an uneasy slumber.

I dream that Nate is yelling, calling. There is a catch in his voice — not quite panic, but more than concern. He's calling my name, over and over, but I am unable to answer him. Or, am I unwilling? I don't know. I can't tell. I'm somewhere deep down in a well, and confused. My reactions are heavy, sluggish. I open my mouth to say something back to him, but am unable to speak. Or, again I ask — unwilling? Am I unwilling? Why would I be unwilling?

Now the sound of heavy pounding enters my consciousness, alternating with the sound of his calling. Then, I realize — I'm not dreaming. Nate is at my door, pounding and calling my name. I struggle out of the well, now recognizing it to be the well of slumber, and sit up dizzily. I shake my head, willing the cobwebs to flee, and stumble through the dark house to the front door. I disarm the alarm and unlock the door, opening it widely just as Nate lowers the fist that must be red with abuse by now. I stand, still a bit unsteady, still dazed, and blink at him.

"What are you doing here?" I ask in a voice that sounds more accusatory than questioning.

Nate's eyes narrow, and I feel a wave of confusion and hurt. But then, an instant later, his eyes are hooded with a totally different look, and I'm almost knocked over with a wave of love and desire so strong that it rips a gasp from my throat. Nate's tall, lanky frame is now filling my doorway, and his hands are on my shoulders, pushing me inside my house, where he follows. He turns, closes and locks the door. Then in a motion that takes me by utter surprise, he sweeps me off my feet and carries me to the bedroom. He lays me gently upon the bed and slides in beside me. As I lie there, stiff and unsure as a virginal teenager, Nate takes his hand and slowly arranges my hair, fanning it slightly out on the pillow. He runs it through his fingers, as he places each strand, stopping to kiss the final one before gently lowering it to join the rest. His eyes are shining with the starlight coming in through the window above the slider, and I'm so glad that window is there so I can see his adoration. He lowers his face to mine, turning my head toward him and lays the sweetest, softest kiss on my parted lips. I feel the stiffness melt away from my body and we turn in rhythm to face one another. He slides his arm over me and pulls me close, and I feel the hardness of his chest, the strength of his muscles as they flex in the embrace. Age-old waves of desire sweep through me and I push myself further into him, as though to meld with his very being. His next kiss is completely different. Still slow, it is filled with purpose—that purpose being to taste deep into my mouth, to give me a sense of his depth of desire. I shudder involuntarily at the power of that desire, as it becomes my own. Soon we are in a passionate dance of desire, and the kissing obviously is no longer enough. I push Nate to his back and straddle him, eating him up with my eyes. His eyes locked in mine, he reaches his hand up and slides it under my tee shirt, where my naked breasts await him, my nipples already hard. He caresses them with loving tenderness until they want to burst with pleasure. They demand to show themselves, so I remove my tee shirt in a movement both slow and sure, and toss the shirt to the floor. Nate's hands are once again upon my breasts and they strain to become one with those lovely, long, strong fingers. The calluses on their tips stroke my nipples and the roughness of them brings a shudder of pleasure.

I need more.

I slide off Nate and stand beside the bed. I start to unbutton my jeans when Nate springs off the bed and stands before me. He takes my hands in his and raises them to his lips where he kisses each finger. Then he puts them down at my sides and whispers, "Let me. Please." So, I do. I let him unbutton and unzip my jeans and slide them down my legs. I step out of them and he deposits them in the pile with my tee shirt. Then he drops to his knees, and kisses me through my panties. I have a momentary rush of gratitude that, while I chose only a tee shirt and jeans to dress in tonight, I did keep on the lace panties. I guess my subconscious was looking out for me. Nate slides off the panties and adds them to the pile on the floor. I worry for a second that he is going to kiss me again, and I stiffen. I'm not ready, just yet, for such intimacy—at which point I remind myself that I am standing in front of a man stark naked, and one would believe that meant I was ready for anything. But Nate seems to read my mind and rises to his feet, where he draws me into another embrace, sliding his hands over my body with delicacy and appreciation.

I suddenly know, beyond a doubt, that I have to have him now. All of him. So I reach for his jeans, unbutton and unzip them with much less ceremony than he did mine, and start to slide them down. He catches my hands and removes them from their work, and instead, gives me a gentle push to the bed. I sit on it, as Nate slides in beside me. He pushes me down and slips his still jean-clad leg over mine. He kisses my neck, my face, my breasts, my stomach, and unable to stifle it, a moan escapes my lips. I shake my head from side to side, attempting to get a handle on the overpowering lust sweeping over me, but my panting gives away my lack of success.

At this point Nate leaps from bed, and removes his jeans, shorts, and shirt. He stands before me in full masculine glory. The lankiness becomes a statement of the sublime. The angular planes of his body are a play of starlight and shadow, the ripples of his muscles like silken waves. I sigh in appreciation, and he smiles. He approaches the bed and, with a small tilt of his head, pulls an edge of the sheet down a bit. Realizing we have been on top of the sheets all this time I quick raise myself up and help him lower them, to allow us a spot between. Nate climbs in beside me, but tugs them back down low when I start to pull the sheets over us. He gives a small shake of his head, and allows his eyes to travel slowly down my body. Since it is summer, he's right. Who needs sheets? I smile at him, and he matches it. Then, in a bliss I've never before known, we make love. Slow, deliberate, treasured, fantastic love.

I think again, about pain and pleasure. And I realize that this is a pleasure so great, any pain I've previously experienced is a blessing for its contrast. And that no amount of future pain could ever dim the memory of tonight.

Somewhere in the darkened room I can hear my kids purring. And I smile to myself.

That makes it perfect.

Later in the night a lone male mockingbird is singing in the tree outside my bedroom. He's looking for a mate, poor fellow, thinking that by singing in the night his voice will be heard without competition. I always wonder just how successful this tactic is. Not very, is my guess. But he still keeps on, never giving up that love will somehow find him. I snuggle closer to Nate, under the sheets now, and send the mockingbird my love and encouragement. *Never, ever give up*, I tell him with my thoughts. *If I can find love, so can you.* His song strengthens, catching my encouragement on the wind of the ethers, and I smile. If not this year, my little friend, then next.

Nate awakens, and through his haze he notices the bird. "What's he doing, singing in the middle of the night?" he asks.

"Affirming his heart is available," I tell him.

"Oh," Nate says, stroking my hair. He gazes at me, then adds, "A romantic with a mission."

I giggle and say, yes. He has it exactly right.

"I'm thirsty," Nate says. "And, actually, I'm hungry, too. Do you have anything to eat?" I assure him I do, and we slip out of bed. I go for my silk robe as Nate slides into his jeans, commando, I notice, and we head to the kitchen. I take a candle out of one of the cupboards and light it, setting it on the table. It illuminates the kitchen just enough to see what I'm doing, without being intrusive. I take the night's leftovers from the frig and divide them onto two plates, giving Nate the lion's share. I heat his plate first, then set it before him where he's already seated himself at the table. I get out napkins and silverware, then heat my plate. I sit across from Nate and we enjoy the delicious meal in silence. Nate looks lost in thought, so, being a typical woman, I ask him what he's thinking. He finishes his last bite and carefully wipes his lips with his napkin—probably stalling for time, I think. He reaches across the table for my hand, and gently caresses it in his—still stalling for time. Then he says, "I was thinking about how scared I was when I couldn't get hold of you tonight."

"You tried to get hold of me?" I ask, surprised. He narrows his eyes at me.

"Yes! I called and called, and it just kept going to voicemail!" Oops! I'd forgotten about unplugging the phone. "Jonas told me you'd been in, intending to eat at the restaurant, but that you suddenly changed your mind and, it seems, you couldn't get out of there fast enough. He said he even observed you start to run to your car!"

Nate's concern is palpable, and I blush in the candlelight. "Then Jonas told me that you'd had a visit from his ex-stepfather, and that he was worried the two incidents might have been related."

"I'm sorry," I tell Nate sincerely. I withdraw my hand and lean back in my chair. "I actually don't know what came over me," I tell him. "Suddenly, I just had to get out of there. It was a panic attack of some sort. And, I hate to say it, but it was probably more to do with you than with Jonas's stepfather."

"Me?!" Nate replies. "Why?"

"I don't know," I answer truthfully. But then, a thought enters my mind, and it becomes clear. "Let me rephrase that," I tell him. "I didn't know why — but I do now."

"Tell me."

"I was scared that I would see you, and that you would be indifferent — that you would brush me off."

"Why would I do that?" he asks, genuinely confused.

"Because of how I acted yesterday!" I tell him, amazed at how clueless men can be.

"Why? Just because you stopped me from pushing you into something you weren't ready for?" His sincere incredulousness brings a laugh to my lips.

"Yes!" I tell him. "Yes! For stopping you! You must have thought I was a complete ditz!"

"I thought no such thing," Nate answers. "What I thought was that I was being a cad."

"But you didn't come back when I went out to call for you." At this Nate goes quiet. He reaches for my hand again, reclaiming it from my side of the table.

"I don't know why I did that," he admits. "I was confused. And I was also a bit out of control, emotionally — and physically. I didn't want to take any chances, I guess, of going too far, too fast, and ruining, what I felt in my heart, was the start of something beautiful."

"Yet, you show up tonight, and charge right in, taking up where we left off yesterday?" I point out.

"Yeah. Guess that's sort of schizo, huh?" he asks, a little boy look on his handsome face.

At that I lean over the table as far as I can and pucker my lips. He meets me halfway and kisses me with a smack.

"Thank you," I say.

"For what?"

"For loving me," I say, before I realize what just came out. "I mean, for—"

"I know what you mean," he cuts me off. And my heart jumps to my throat. Oh my god, did I just blow it? My heart pounds, pulsing in my neck. "I know what you mean." He repeats.

"What do I mean?" I ask in a voice barely a whisper, afraid of the answer. Nate doesn't reply, so I brave a look at him. His eyes are silky, sexy.

"You mean, thank you. For loving you." My breath catches, and I open my mouth to say something, but I don't know what. So I close it again, and say nothing. My neck still pulses with my racing heart. Nate raises my hand and kisses it, never removing his eyes from mine. "I do, you know."

"You do what?"

"Love you," he answers. "I do love you." I start to drop silent tears onto the table, as he tells me one more time, "I do love you, Alli James. I do."

Chapter 18

When I awaken at seven, Nate is gone. Surprised that the kids didn't wake me I crawl out of bed and pad to the kitchen. There I find that Nate has already fed them—along with cleaning up our dishes from last night. Not only am I amazed at his thoughtfulness, but I'm amazed he did all that so quietly I didn't even wake up! A very special man is he.

Rico comes sauntering into the kitchen and plops his butt unceremoniously onto the floor.

"Morning, Rico," I say to him, at which he smiles sweetly and breaks into a big purr, slowly blinking his eyes at me. "Yeah, I know," I laugh with him. "Mom provided some good entertainment last night, huh?"

Rico gets off his butt and sashays over to rub my legs with his soft head. I bend down to scratch him between the ears, and he moves his head all around to get a full head massage. Satisfied, he saunters off, and I decide to make coffee and oatmeal for breakfast. As I reach for the coffee I find a note.

"I do love you."

And, with those words, I shiver off the last nagging doubt that said, it was only a dream.

I eat my breakfast and shower. I choose the sexiest tee shirt I own, a golden yellow number with gold sequins and cutouts on the shoulders. I slide on white jeans, gold sandals, gold bangles and my huge gold hoops. I twist my hair up and pin it, letting the mandatory wisps fall to soften the look. I slather on the only makeup I need this morning—lip gloss—and admire the natural pink glow of my cheeks.

Love is the best makeup of all.

Singing to myself, I head to the studio. As I turn the corner into the room I'm met with a startling sight. The easels are on the floor, the paintings lying one on top of the other. Oh no! Racing over to them I find that the voiceless twin is under his brother. There is animosity in both their eyes, and I wonder if I've done the right thing by demanding that they work it out. I set the easels back up and place the paintings upon them — but I do not face them to each other. I consider each in turn, looking for any other changes in them, other than the anger in their eyes. I notice nothing else, and turn to Michael.

"What was that all about?!" I demand of him. "Did you attack your brother? What kind of a man are you?" I scold him.

Then I turn to the voiceless twin and ask him if he's alright. The eyes flicker for a moment, and where there was anger a minute ago, there is now sorrow. "What is going on with you two?" I ask him. But the eyes turn guarded, shutting me out. "None of my business, you say?" I state, with hands on hips. "Well, guess again, buddy," I tell the portrait. "It is my business." I point to the other portrait, to include him. "You two twits have made sure of that," I finish, and stomp out of the room, leaving them facing nothing in particular except their own conscience. I grab my purse and start to head to the garage when I hear the front bell. My body flushes with a delicious sensation of butterflies, and I practically skip to the door and fling it wide — expecting Nate. But, it isn't Nate. It's the voiceless twin, and he's got a black eye.

I stare at him mutely, until finally he raises an eyebrow and a hand in question — can he come in? Against my better judgment I step aside and let him enter. He looks around the front room, taking it all in with a curiosity that I find a bit intrusive. I say, "Just a moment, please," and hurry to the studio to close the door. When I return he is carefully regarding the paintings on the walls, then he turns to me and nods his head — giving his approval I guess.

"What can I help you with," I ask, believing that sounds more polite than "what do you want?", which is what I wished to ask.

He removes a notepad from his breast pocket and scribbles something on it. Then he rips off the page and hands it to me.

I want to see Michael's portrait.

I look at him with a scowl. "I can't let you do that," I tell him. "It's a commission, which means it's business. And as far as I'm concerned, it's private, unless I'm told otherwise."

He scribbles another page, rips it off and hands it over. One word.

Please.

"No."

He considers this a moment, then scribbles another page.

Michael can be violent, you know. You must be careful.

He touches his black eye as I read the note, but his eyes aren't as innocent as they once seemed. I'm beginning to wonder if I misjudged him. I hope not, as I'm going to give him the gift of his voice. But at this moment, I'm terribly uneasy.

"What is your name?" I ask him simply. He scribbles, tears, hands it over.

Peter.

"Well, Peter, I thank you for your concern. I really do. But if there's nothing more, I would like you to leave now — because we have nothing more to discuss, as far as I know."

He slowly nods his head, and turns to leave. As I move around him to the door, to open it for him, he suddenly grabs me, and before I know what he's doing he has his lips on mine in a hungry kiss. Shocked, I pull away and slap his face, hard. His eyes register great surprise, and he puts his hand to his face, where the shape of my hand is already beginning to appear. I hurry to the door and open it wide.

"Goodbye, Peter," I tell him. His hand still on his face, he lowers his head. Then he walks out the door, his energy a blend of confusion and desire. It makes me shudder.

I close the door behind him and fall back against it, wondering what the hell just happened. Why in the world would he do that!? The whole thing was so bizarre that I'm totally left in limbo. I feel powerless to move, caught in the floating land of unreality. My energy is shooting off at odd angles, and I feel scattered and drained. Finally, I close my eyes and command my breath. Within a minute I have my energy back under control and centered within me. I check my aura, going around myself, looking for anything amiss, but I seem fine now. I push myself away from the wall and go to my bathroom, to wipe my lips. I'm angry that Peter has done this, because the only lips I want on mine are Nate's. And now, Nate's aren't the last ones to have been there. I confront the mirror with a tissue, and am met with a sight I didn't expect. My lips are flaming, as though they've been bruised. I know he kissed me hard, but he didn't kiss me that hard.

What the hell is going on?

I wipe my lips, tenderly now, just in case they *are* bruised, but I feel nothing abnormal—except for the disgust. I choose a light shade of lipstick and liner, and color away the bruise red, then go over that with lip gloss. Satisfied that I'm back to where I wish to be—except for needing Nate's kiss to replace Peter's—I leave the bathroom and return to the studio. I open the door, and am met by the eyes of the twins, staring straight at me. I stomp over to them and glare.

"You both have pissed me off," I tell them. "As soon as I get what I want from you two, you are both out of my life," I inform them. Angrily I flip both easels around to once again face each other. "Work it out!" I yell, and stomp from the room. I grab my purse and sunglasses, calling a goodbye to the kids.

This time I make it to the garage without incident, and take off to destinations unknown.

Then I wonder—how the hell did Peter know where I live?

Without knowing why I find myself driving to Jazzie's. I pull into her driveway, lock up, and ring her bell. She answers immediately, swinging the door open wide, a huge smile on her face.

"Welcome, *amiga*!" she says.

"Hi, Jazzie. I hope I'm not interrupting anything," I tell her.

"Not at all! Come sit with me in the kitchen. That's where Sadie and I are hanging out this morning."

I follow her to her beautiful, gourmet kitchen and pull up a stool at the island. Sadie wags her tail and I blow her a big kiss. She smiles her famous smile, then puts her head down on her paws.

"Everything okay with her?" I ask Jazzie.

"Everything's just fine. She had a pain pill a little while ago, so she's just relaxing, if you know what I mean."

"Good," I reply.

"Soooooo—tell me all about it."

"About what?"

"You obviously did the deed. Last night?"

I laugh. "How did you know? Did Rico and Bonita tell you?"

"No," she answers, "though it might be fun to get any details from them that you might be inclined to leave out."

"They better *not* tell on me!" I say, mocking shock.

"So, spare them the effort. Come clean."

"I still want to know how you knew," I say.

"The way you're dressed," she says. "Now stop stalling, and give mama the details."

"Okay, okay!" I laugh. "Well, it *was* last night."

"You went to the restaurant, and..."

"Well, actually, I went to the restaurant—then left with a to-go box before Nate started his gig."

"You left? Why!?"

"I just had a panic attack I guess."

"Because of Nate?"

"Yes. I wasn't sure at the time what was going on—but yes, it was because of Nate. I think I was worried that he was going to brush me off. And I didn't want to go through that."

"Makes sense."

"So I went home with my food, unplugged my phone, ate dinner in the dark, and went to bed. Well, actually, I fell asleep with my clothes on—which came in handy, because after he was through playing, Nate came over to my house and woke me up. So, at least when I answered the door, I was dressed."

"And, that's a good thing—why?"

"Well, because he had the fun of removing my clothes a short time later!" I laugh.

"Ahhhh! That *is* a good thing," she agrees, with chuckles.

"Oh, Jazzie. It was wonderful. He was wonderful! So gentle, but..."

"Mmmmm. That perfect combination of soft, yet hard. Gentle, yet commanding. Dripping with desire, yet controlled."

"Oh stop it!" I blush down to my toes. "You're embarrassing me!"

"Why? A good man is nothing to be ashamed of!"

"I know," I say. "But it's still all so new. I've never had a man like Nate before."

"You deserve to have a good man. A man who loves you proper."

"He does, you know." I say softly.

"Love you proper?"

"Love me," I reply. "He's already said he loves me."

"Alli! I'm so happy for you!"

"Of course, it was right after I let slip, like a dodo, 'thank you for loving me.'"

"Who cares? He would've just made his goodbyes and ran, if that had made him uncomfortable. Men don't feel compelled to play along if they don't really feel it. Especially not after the first fuck."

"Jazzie!"

"Sorry!" she says. "I know it wasn't like that."

"No, it wasn't! It was lovemaking—good and proper. It was no fuck," I finish, with a prim and proper smirk.

Jazzie is smiling ear to ear. "I am so, so, so happy for you, Alli. Really I am."

"Thank you," I tell her. "Now, maybe we should work on getting a good man for you," I tell her.

"Oh, don't bother," she says. "I'm not ready."

"Why not?"

She hesitates. "I'm not sure," she admits. "I just don't think about it, I guess. I consider my life pretty full. Good, actually. I don't know if I want a man complicating it."

"I understand that. But you are still young and beautiful, and you have such a huge heart. If there was a man out there good enough for you, you could bless him so much. And any added happiness, on anyone's part, is good for the whole, you know."

Jazzie laughs. "Yes, I know. I'm the one who's always telling *you* that, remember?"

"Yes—so don't *you* forget it."

She smiles bittersweetly. "I won't forget it, *amiga*."

"Good."

"Now," Jazzie continues, "why did Nate feel compelled to come get you out of bed last night?"

"Oh!" I start. "Yes, I guess there is more to the story."

"Of course there is—though we've already covered the really good part."

"Yes, well." I clear my throat. "Okay, here's the rest of the story. While I was deciding what to order for dinner, I had a visitor."

"Who!?"

"John Smith—better known as Michael Adams," I tell her.

"He was there? And you found out his last name?"

"Yes and yes."

"What did he want?"

"He wanted to know if I'd finished the painting yet."

"What did you tell him?"

"I inferred that I hadn't. Which is a lie—and it's a lie that he seemed to know I was telling."

"What did he do?"

"He went with it, though he said to let him know when it was finished. Then I reminded him I don't have his phone number, to which he replied, oh, right. So, then, he'd contact me."

"How would he make the determination of the proper time?"

"I asked him the same thing," I tell her. "And he just said, he'd know."

"Wow."

"Yeah."

"So, apparently he's feeling the difference in himself, from your portrait."

"I would say so, yes."

"So, why aren't you ready to give it to him?"

"Because I finished the portrait of his brother, whose name is Peter, by the way, and—"

"How did you find that out?"

"Let me finish this story first."

"Okay. Sorry. Go on."

"Well, anyway, I feel those two need to work some things out, so I have their portraits face to face, so they can figure it out."

"Cool! So, anything happen yet?"

"Well, this morning I found them on the floor, easels knocked over, Michael's portrait on top of Peter's."

"What?! How in the world? You don't think Nate did it, do you?"

"Not at all," I reply. "I think it was a result of one reality affecting the other. Peter stopped by this morning, sporting a black eye, and warning me that Michael is violent."

"He stopped by?! Holy crap! I don't know if I like that," Jazzie says, concern on her face.

"I don't particularly like it either," I tell her. "Especially after he had the nerve to grab me and kiss me."

"He what!?" Jazzie yells loud enough that Sadie raises her head in foggy concern. "Oh, sorry, sweetie," Jazzie tells her. "Mommy just had a momentary lapse. Go back to sleep, punkin." Sadie sighs and puts her head back down on her paws. In seconds she's drifted back off to sleep. Jazzie looks at me and says, "Okay. As you were saying—he kissed you?"

"Yes. Quite forcefully, actually. It was weird. It was almost like he couldn't help himself. And when I slapped him—"

"You slapped him!?"

"Yes, quite hard. And when I did, he seemed very surprised."

"That *is* weird," Jazzie agrees. "So why did he come to see you in the first place?"

"He wanted me to show him Michael's portrait."

"So he knows there's a portrait."

"Apparently."

"Very, very strange."

"I agree," I tell her. "Also, I'm wondering how he got my address."

Jazzie is looking at me with a look dawning upon her. She comes around the island and leans on it, close to me. "I would like to try something, if you wouldn't mind," she says.

"Try what?"

"I want to see if I can intuit any information about the three of you."

"The three of who?"

"You and the twins."

"You think I have something to do with them?"

"I don't know," she answers. "But, it did occur to me just now that you might."

I sit a moment and stare out her window. It hadn't occurred to me that I might actually be a part of this. I thought I was just kind of pulled in by accident. Maybe it would be good to know if there was more to it.

"Okay," I tell her. "Let's try."

"Good," she says. "Come. Let's go to my consultation room."

We leave the kitchen for her "reading" room. It's a beautiful room she has designed to give her the most help possible, when she's doing psychic work. She has her crystals, incense, and meditation CD's in there, plus comfortable chairs that one can sink into, and enter the space of total relaxation. She sits me down in one of the chairs, and puts on a CD she's selected after searching through about a dozen. She lights a stick of incense, then sits in the other chair, facing me.

"Just relax," she instructs. "Close your eyes, and clear your head, if possible."

"Okay."

We sit for a few minutes, listening to the CD, which is extremely soothing. Then she has me think of Michael—not anything in particular—just hold the vision of him as he is. After a few minutes she gives the same instructions for Peter. Then, even though we hadn't discussed it, she gives me the same instructions for Nate. Then Don. After about twenty minutes she says, "You can open your eyes now. I think I've got it."

I open my eyes, and ask, "Really? You know something?"

"I do believe so." She rises out of her chair and paces the room slowly, arms crossed over her chest. Then she stops and looks at me hard. "You, my dear friend, are involved with those two up to your neck."

"You're kidding!" I say. "I've never felt it!"

"Nonetheless, you three have a very strong history. You're quite entangled, and this meeting you're having now was something that was agreed to, before you came here, this life."

"Wow."

"Yes. Wow."

"What am I supposed to be doing?" I ask.

"Pretty much what you're already doing," she answers. "Helping them to work it out."

"Should I be doing anything more? You know, to help?"

"I have a suggestion..."

"What?"

"Paint a portrait of yourself, and add it to the mix."

"You mean, make it a threesome?"

She laughs. "Yes, make it a threesome. You have to work it out with them."

"Okay," I say. "I'll do that." Then I add, "What about Nate and Don? How do they fit in?"

"Well, Don isn't a part of the whole thing. But Nate is."

"How so?" I ask, fascinated.

"I'm not completely sure," she answers, "but he was a part of the original mix. He wasn't as heavily involved as you and the twins, but he was there. And he is supposed to be here with you, now, in this life. That was also agreed upon before you came."

I sit a moment, soaking it all in when she adds, "And one more thing — Rico, Bonita, and Sadie are all in the mix as well."

"Really?"

"Most certainly," Jazzie finishes. One thing she didn't mention, however, which I was to find out later — Jazzie was part of the mix, too. And the part about Don not being involved — was a bold-faced lie. I guess she just didn't want me to know.

We return to Jazzie's kitchen, and catch up on Sadie's progress, which is better than wonderful. Then I decide I'd better go home and paint my portrait. I want all this weirdness cleared up ASAP — and that means getting to work. I thank Jazzie for a most interesting morning, and drive back up the road. When I get home I grab a mirror, and get out my desk easel. I set the mirror and easel up side by side, and paint my portrait. As I do, just because I can, I paint myself with a huge smile on my face.

Can't hurt.

When it dries I'll make a "threesome" as Jazzie says.

Being that it's Friday, I make a reservation at Roberto's to insure a table, then head to the art supply store to buy another easel. I've always made do with two, but maybe I'll find good reason in the future to use three — besides being able to look Michael and Peter in the face. When I arrive I find there are only two easels of my preferred style left in stock. Something tells me to buy both, so I do. Why I feel I need four easels is beyond me, but I try to follow my gut feelings, whenever possible. I add a few new canvases, and pay for the booty. As I'm leaving, Jonas walks in.

"Hi, Alli!" he says jovially. "Are you coming in tonight?"

"Yes," I reply. "I just made a reservation a bit ago."

"Good thinking," he says. "I believe we're going to be very busy tonight. Nate and the dancers are really bringing in the business," he offers. "Don't know if it would be so good without them." I think of the money I've spent there because of Nate—and I agree with his surmise. Then a thought occurs to me.

"Jonas," I start, "what was your stepdad's brother like when you knew him?"

Jonas looks confused. "Brother?"

Now I'm confused. "Yes, his twin brother, Peter."

"Miss Alli, I didn't know he had a brother."

"Oh," I say. "Well, then. I guess that means you can't tell me what he was like, now can you?"

"Guess not," he answers. "So, Michael had a twin brother?"

"Has a twin brother," I correct him. "And yes, they are almost identical, except for some differing lines in their faces." I didn't bother with the information of Peter being mute.

"Wow. That's fricking amazing," Jonas says. "He always said he had no siblings. He specifically told us he had no living family at all!"

"Well, it would seem there's some animosity between them—so, maybe he was being philosophical in his denial."

"Could be. Though I don't think philosophy was his strong suit."

"No, I suppose not. Well, I better get going. See you tonight?"

"You bet! Later, Alli!"

By the time I arrive home my portrait is dry, so I set up one of the new easels, forming a triangle, and put my portrait upon it.

"There!" I tell Michael and Peter. "Now we can all work it out together."

And, with that, I march out of the studio, change into my swimsuit, and hit the pool. I do hard, hard laps, churning up the water, splashing the deck with my exuberant kicks. Then I grab a floatie and pull myself atop. I float for a few minutes, admiring the picture perfect sky, and the sway of the trees. A Red-tailed Hawk circles by, lazy upon the hot air currents, and as silent as the spotty clouds. Finally I realize I'd better get out, seeing as how I didn't put on sunscreen, and so I do. Reluctant to go inside just yet, I select a chair under an umbrella, and plop myself down. As I drip on the deck I recall the events of the day.

There's much to think about.

Back inside I towel dry my hair and slip back into my jeans and tee shirt. It is still hours before my reservation so I put on a whale song CD and make some lunch as I think about what I want to do for the afternoon. As I finish my salad I decide I'm in the mood for a painting of the sea. I've never lived by the sea, but my heart is definitely into it. I love the desert, and I love the sea. I dig out some old photos I took years back of a vacation by the Sea of Cortez—desert by the sea, perfect—and pick one. The water is brilliant turquoise blue, almost indistinguishable from the sky. The shoreline is a mix of rugged brown-gray rocks and blinding white sand. A pelican sits atop one of the rocks. What one doesn't see in the photo is the teeming life underwater. Sea turtles, fish of a hundred descriptions, and, in certain seasons, dolphins and whales breaking the surface, having babies, plying magic.

Glad, now, that I bought two new easels, I take the last one and set it up by the window. I glance at the triangle of portraits and call out, "Worked it out, yet?" No answer. So, I guess not.

I pull on my smock and set up my palette, water, and paints. Grabbing the CD from the kitchen player I put it on in my studio and push the repeat button. I stand for a few minutes, just breathing with my eyes closed, reaching into my creative brain. When I open my eyes I set aside the photo. I won't be using it—but the reminder of the fantastic blue of the water and sky was worth the look. I squirt massive amounts of four different blues onto my palette and begin to apply them with abandon. The sky takes shape over the sea, subtle currents and miniature waves breaking into the glass of the water. The sky is cloudless. I suppose, in the back of my brain, that clouds would add interest—but, this isn't about creating an interesting painting. This is something else. This is about painting what I see in my mind—and there are no clouds today.

Suddenly I see a snatch of shore—just a few grains of pure white sand. There is, perhaps, a man there. I'm not sure. I'll leave him out for now.

However, there are dolphins. Lots of dolphins. A large, happy pod of sleek, beautiful, riotous dolphins. Three, in particular, are amazing. They leap out of the water together, their joy palpable. They trail splashes of water that glint like diamonds. I add a few touches of gold to the glints. Just a few. The glisten on their muscular bodies get a few touches of gold, too. There are sea birds in the sky. They are too far away to tell what they are, but they are winging over the sea.

Yes, there is a man there. I know nothing of him except for windblown hair and gauzy clothes. That and his love. He watches the dolphins, and he feels love. Great love. I wish I could see his eyes, to bask in that love, but his back is to me, so I'll have to be content to know that it is there. I remove my smock and pull up a chair. I sit before the painting and rejoice in the joy that I feel there—the dolphins and the man. I send a wave of blessings and love to the painting, then shower myself with those same feelings.

Revived, I go to the kitchen for a glass of water, and notice that the afternoon has passed in the blink of an eye. I return to the studio and hurriedly wash up the brushes, and secure the paint tubes. I ignore the threesome, enrapt with the sea. "See you all, later," I whisper. And the dolphins answer with a chattering laugh.

Chapter 19

I sprint down the short hall to my bedroom and strip off my clothes. I shower quickly, but take the required time to lotion every square inch of me. I apply minimal makeup, then add some mascara. Okay, maybe I'll squeeze in a little eyeliner, too. Not as easy to do when the mascara is already on, but not impossible. I note that with the bit of sun I got today, while floating, that I don't need blush.

Now, what to wear. I search through my closet, flicking aside every item of clothing I have. Shit! I don't have anything in there I want for tonight! I've already worn everything that's suitable, and the restaurant has only been open a week. I can't rewear something so soon!

Okay, what I need is an attitude adjustment. Pulling on my robe I head to the kitchen. Not that wine is truly an adjuster, but I don't know what else to do! As I reach for a glass I notice the light on my phone is blinking. I check my voicemail, and it's from Jazzie. I can hear the air conditioning in her car blasting like a wind tunnel through the recording.

"Hi, Alli! Jazzie, here. Was just at your house, but got no answer. Maybe you were in the shower. Anyway, I left you a present at your front door. Hope you like it! Have a very special night, tonight, with that very special man. Bye!"

I hurry to the door, thankful I live away from a busy street and that packages are generally safe out front. I find a large garment box which I bring in and set on the countertop. I carefully open it. Inside is a dress the color of the Sea of Cortez. And on the only shoulder, is a dolphin made of crystals. I gasp in delight and awe. It has to be one of

Evie's. But how did she and Jazzie know? They are ahead of me, that's for sure. I get goose bumps at the "coincidence", and rub them away with brisk moves up and down my arms. I hold the dress up to me and I feel magic.

I hurry back down the hall, strip off my robe and fling it on the bed. Standing before the mirror, I hold the dress in front of me, The color makes me look like a bronzed goddess — queen of the sea. Mermaid queen, perhaps. I choose a strapless bra and matching lace panties and slide them on. I ease the dress on over them, closing my eyes while turning to the mirror. When I open them I almost faint from wonder. The dress fits like a glove, and I've never been more beautiful. I move to the bathroom and look at my hair. I decide to remove the dress to do my hair, but I know the perfect way to wear it. After carefully laying out the dress on my bed, I take my hair, and comb and brush it until it gleams like water. I pull it up and away from my right shoulder, the one that will display the dolphin, and twist it and pin it. I pull only a portion of the other side up and away, leaving a long thick strand of silk to fall over the other shoulder. I push in some crystal ornaments, here and there, like water diamonds in my hair, and appraise the effort. It's perfect. I go back in and slide into the dress. I look in the mirror, and I am definitely a queen. I choose the shoes I bought for my first Evie dress, and put on diamond stud earrings. I grab my small gold clutch, load what few things will fit, then remember I haven't put on any lipstick. I hurry to the bath and apply an apricot gloss, with a touch of bronze mixed in. I trot to the kitchen and make dinner for the kids in haste. They stroll in and give me approving looks, for which I thank them. Then as they chow down, I tell them goodbye and lock up, setting the alarm.

I'm off to Roberto's. And not a minute too soon. I'll barely make my reservation. But then, I suppose, they would hold the table for me anyway, being as how I'm sort of a VIP. I laugh out loud at this, and sail into the parking lot on a cloud of joy.

I lock up the car and hurry up the steps. As I enter the lobby the hostess says, "There you are! By the way, my name is Belinda," she offers, holding out her hand. I shake it warmly, say nice to meet you, and thank her for holding a table. "No problem," she says. "And may I add that you look beautiful tonight. That dress is spectacular!"

"Thank you," I blush. "Do you know of Evie?"

"Oh, yes!" she nods. "I had her make my wedding dress! It was extraordinary!"

"That's our Evie," I answer, as though I, too, have had a long relationship with her. I'm probably one of the few women in town who hasn't long been a customer of hers, I scold myself. Oh well.

Belinda leads me to a table in the corner of the dining room, and for tonight I'm content to eat indoors. It's still pretty hot out, and the humidity is high enough to discourage the misters. She sits me, hands me a menu and takes my drink order. I see her give it to a server I haven't yet had, but Jonas quickly appears and I observe him talking to the other young man. They look in my direction, Jonas waves, I wave back, then with a nod to each other the other young man departs and Jonas fills my order at the bar. He strolls over to deposit it on the table before me.

"Good evening, Alli," he says warmly.

"Hi, Jonas. How're things tonight?"

"Great! We'll be full tonight. Good for my tips."

"That's great," I tell him. "So, did you steal me from that other young man?" I ask him.

His cheeks flush as he fumbles with the tray. "Well, I have something I may wish to share with you, tonight," He answers. "So, yes, I stole you from Mark."

I laugh and tell him I'm glad he did. "You are going to make it up to him, though—aren't you?"

"Yes," he answers with conviction. "I'm going to give him a table of four! So, you see, you're worth quite a bit!"

Now it's my turn to blush. I murmur a thank you and give him my appetizer order. He hurries away, and as I sip my wine I wonder what it is he wants to share with me. Guess I'll find out later.

I gaze around the dining room, basking in the warm glow of the golden lighting that now is bringing magic to everyone's complexion. The laughter reminds me of the dolphins I painted today, and I smile at the memory. I close my eyes, momentarily, and take a deep breath. When I open them, some of the other patrons have turned into dolphins! They are smiling and chattering in their chairs, love emanating from their glossy bodies. I chuckle and look down at my wine glass. I soak in the magic of second sight, something that occurs with me only so often, and for only so long. When I raise my eyes, everyone is human again. But I remember which ones were dolphins, and I gaze at them in wonder. The woman with the golden silk dress, her eyes sparkling with amusement and love, as her lover sits, rapt, before her—the gentleman in the drapey gray shirt, sleek and muscular, his eyes kind and loving as he talks with the lovely woman across the table from him—the young girl radiating zeal for life as her parents dote on her. And the two men, across the room, facing each other at a table for two.... Oh my God! As I focus in I see it's Michael and Peter. Sitting together! One of them is talking, and I hope for a second that it's Peter, but then I see the other scribble something on a pad before him, and I realize that he is still without his voice. But they are sitting together! I say a silent prayer that they are working out whatever needs working out but, as I am in the middle of the prayer, Michael suddenly stands and throws back the note that Peter has given him. His body language says "disgust", and I'm taken aback.

He glares at Peter for a several seconds, then turns on his heel and strides from the restaurant. I see Peter lower his head, then slowly shake it. He throws a wad of cash on the table, and he also leaves.

They were dolphins. I touch the dolphin on my shoulder, and it slowly dawns on me that we were all dolphins in our life together. We weren't human—we were dolphins. We were dolphins! I'm still considering this when Jonas appears.

"Did you see them?" he asks excitedly.

"If you mean Michael and his brother, then, yes, I saw them," I answer him.

"Wow!" he says. "You're right! They look just like each other! Amazing."

"Yes, they most certainly do," I agree. Especially now. Now that one seems to be taking on a slightly more sinister note, and the original seems to be—what? Evolving? I shake my head.

They are confusing, that's for sure.

"Wait until I tell you what I found out from my mom," Jonas says, "but it will have to wait until later, after the crowd thins a bit. You are staying awhile, aren't you? To watch the show?"

"That was my intention, yes."

"Good. Then I'll have the time. By the way, are you ready to order?"

I laugh and tell him to please just order what I had the last time, and he says no problem. He takes my menu and heads off. I look at the others in the room who were dolphins, and wonder if we all knew each other. Could be. But then, there are a lot of dolphins in the world. It could just be coincidence. However, whether or not I knew them before, I feel a kinship now, so I send them a wave of love. The woman turns and smiles at me, and I return the smile. Then she returns her attention to her rapt lover.

For good measure I send everyone else in the room a wave of love. No need to be stingy.

Jonas returns with my appetizer and says he'll wait a bit before turning in my dinner order, to give me plenty of time to enjoy it, and I thank him. I pick at the spicy deliciousness, savoring each and every bite, giving thanks for the complex marriage of flavors. As I work my way through, suddenly the chair across from me fills. I look up to see Nate smiling at me. I smile back, my body afire with desire for him. He slides a hand across the table and I reach for it, delighting in the strength and love I feel there. He raises it to his lips and slowly kisses it, his eyes never leaving mine. The rush I feel is almost too much to bear. I decide to make the glass of wine I'm having the *only* glass. No way do I want to dull the feelings I'm having right now. Nate returns our hands to the table top and looks me over.

"You are so beautiful, Alli," he says softly.

I blush from head to toe, and lower my face, to hide it. But, I can't help grinning like a school girl.

"The dress—one of Evie's?" he asks.

"How do you know about Evie?" I laugh.

"Everyone knows about Evie," he scolds.

"Uh-huh," I raise an eyebrow. "Is there something you'd like to tell me?"

Nate laughs. "Okay. If you must know..."

"Yes?"

"She makes my sister's flamenco dresses," he finishes.

"Whew! I'm glad that's all it is!" I tease.

He smiles, his eyes twinkling. God I love those eyes. Suddenly they look dreamy—thoughtful. He gently squeezes my hand, which he is still holding.

"The dolphin queen," he whispers, and a chill goes up my spine. "I love you, my queen," he says. Then he gently rests my hand upon the table and quietly rises from his chair. He bows slightly, and leaves me, my emotions in total disarray.

I stare at the half-eaten appetizer and feel my insides shaking, part fright, part love. Raising my eyes, I see the dolphin-girl observing me. She smiles with delight when I see her, and blows me a big, smacking kiss from where she sits. I laugh—almost a sob—then blow her a gentle kiss back. She squeals lightly, reminding me of the dolphin she was, and turns her adoration back to her handsome parents. Tears fill my eyes, and I'm not sure why. I blink a few times to put the tears back in place, and finish my wine. Jonas appears.

"Would you like another?" he asks, taking my empty glass.

"No thanks," I tell him. "Please just bring me a glass of water with a slice of lemon."

"You got it!" he answers cheerfully. Then he pauses, sobering. "My mom knew," he says quietly.

"Knew what?"

"About Michael's brother, Peter."

"She did?"

He nods slowly. "She had an affair with him," he whispers. Not because he was afraid of anyone overhearing, but because of the shock. "She loved him," he adds, matter-of-factly, and I wonder if those are her words or something Jonas wants to believe. I nod in agreement, for his sake.

"I'm sure she did," I tell him.

"I'll tell you more, later," he says, whisking off, wine glass in hand. The shaking subsides a bit, and I finish my appetizer. Jonas arrives a few minutes later with water and dinner in hand, and serves me with a flourish, no more mention of the strange turn of events. I set upon my meal, and the magnificence of it shreds away any lingering quiver. I sip the water, and look around the room, hoping to see something magical, but the only magic is of the normal variety. Soft lighting, charming décor, and beautiful people. As I savor every morsel of my meal I turn my awareness fully upon myself. I chew, taste, swallow, feel the progress of the nourishment to my stomach. Repeat. After awhile, my plate is empty—something that rarely happens at a restaurant. Now I'll have to cook something for tomorrow's dinner, instead of heating up leftovers. I dab at my mouth with the linen napkin, and dream of making dinner for Nate and myself. Unfortunately, he won't be off until Tuesday, I remind myself. And as if to bring me out of my reverie, the lights dim, the piped music fades, and the magic of Nate's guitar weaves its way from the back of the restaurant. It is slow, mournful, heart wrenching—like the song of a whale. The dancers appear, and start a slow twirl in each other's arms. Instead of flamenco, they are ballroom dancing. They glide and twirl in the slowest of motions. They are like the fluid motion of a lazy wave. A twirl, a gaze, a pause, then a rush back to the sea of the dance. Ebb in, ebb out. Mesmerized, I watch them in all their beauty. Finally, after twirling Maribela slowly in a complete circle around him, the male dancer captures her in his arms, holding her gaze. Then as the music comes to a quiet close, he dips her low, and places a soft kiss upon her chest. I shudder at the strength of him. As he raises her upright, in total silence, he spins her out, catching her hand at the last moment. They gaze at one another for a second, then, still hand in hand, they face the room and slowly bow. The patrons applaud with fervor, and I dab tears from my eyes. Nate also bows, guitar held away from him to his side, and it flashes in the light, sending the blinding glow into my eyes. For a second I'm blinded, but when my sight returns I am looking at the underwater sea. The room is filled with deep blue water, tranquil, warm. I feel as though I'm in the womb. Serenity and comfort surround me. I am at total peace.

Then, in an instant, I'm back.

Nate begins another song—this one fiery and driving. The dancers push their passion to the limit, providing heart stopping beauty to the music falling from Nate's guitar. When the dance is over, they bow quickly to the applause and disappear to the back. It's break time.

I expect to see Nate during the break, but he doesn't show. I'm disappointed, but I understand. The break turns out to be a short one, just long enough for the dancers to change their clothes. When the music starts up again, however, there are two guitars. The limo driver, Maribela's husband, has joined Nate. The dancing takes on a slightly different flavor, in tune with the guitars. Since there are two guitars, flamenco becomes more difficult. Flamenco is too free-flow, too ad-lib. Only one guitar can really keep up with dancers who are making it up as they go along. So instead, there are now rumbas and tangos. Gorgeous displays of passionate dance. The music falls from both guitars with a fluidity that signals these two men have played together for a long, long time. Jonas sneaks over quietly and asks if I'd like more water and lemon slices. I tell him, yes. But to please just have the busgirl refill my present glass, and for him to bring me some lemon slices. While he's away the second set comes to an end, and the troupe disappears into the back. The busgirl refills my water glass and Jonas appears. He's carrying a small dish with lemon slices and a piece of cheesecake, topped with cherries.

"Thanks for the lemons, Jonas," I tell him, "but I didn't order the cheesecake."

"I know," he replies. "Someone ordered it for you."

Thinking it was Nate, I blush slightly. "Well, then thanks!" I tell him. "Please tell the gentleman I said so."

"What makes you think it was a gentleman?" Jonas asks, straight-faced. I start to stutter something inane, but Jonas laughs. "Don't worry," he says. "You're right. It was a gentleman." He grins and walks away, leaving me to a decadent slice of cake that I'm not even sure I can eat. But when I take the first bite, it melts in my mouth in such a burst of velvety richness that I realize it is just the thing I need right now. Comfort dessert—that's it. I drink my water and finish the cheesecake, marveling at the cherry sauce, and wash it down with fresh, un-lemoned water. As I do, the third set starts, but with just one guitar this time. However, it's Carl, not Nate, and within seconds Nate is at my table, sliding into the empty chair with a grace that momentarily stops my heart.

"Hi again, beautiful," he whispers, giving my hand a quick squeeze. "I see you've had dessert," he says, with a nod to my empty plate.

"Yes, thank you," I reply, smiling at the thoughtfulness of this wonderful man. But Nate looks confused.

"What do you mean, 'thank you'?" he asks.

"For the cheesecake!" I say, surprised at the question. "Obviously," I add, almost annoyed with him. But he just gives me a funny look, silent for several seconds.

"I didn't order any cheesecake for you," he says quietly. "I wouldn't even know that you liked cheesecake."

A wave of dread washes over me, and I look quickly around the restaurant. I catch the back of the head of a man just passing out through the front door. I believe it is Don.

Not sure. But I think so.

The blood drains from my face and I feel faint. Nate notices the change, and quickly scoots his chair next to mine and puts an arm around me, to steady me. Not a minute too soon. I almost topple over from the dizziness, and Nate quickly dips my napkin into the water glass and holds it to my face. The coolness revives me instantly.

"Thanks," I tell him gratefully. "Wow! I'm sorry!" I say, not sure what else to say. Nate rubs my arm, still holding on to me.

"Want to tell me about it?" he asks, concerned.

"I think I just saw Don leave the restaurant," I reply. "He must've bought me the cheesecake," I add. "He knows I love it, and he knows just the way I love it. With cherries on top. 'Just the way you like your life', he used to say. 'With cherries on top.'" I stifle a sob of horror — horror at the present, horror at the past. Horror of the future.

Where does love go? What happens to life? When does the pain stop? And for god sake, why, oh, why do beautiful things turn ugly? I fight tears that overwhelm my eyes. But they win, and flood down my face. I dig in my purse for a handkerchief, and pull out the beautiful laced one that belonged to my grandmother. I dab at my eyes until they are reasonably dry.

"Do I have mascara running down my cheeks?" I ask Nate, regretful, now, that I ever applied it tonight.

He studies my face, carefully. "Don't see a single sign," he says.

"Thanks," I say with a nervous laugh.

He removes his arm from around me and gently strokes my hair. "No problem," he answers with a smile. We turn our attention back to the dancers. Carl's doing a beautiful job in Nate's place. Not quite as good as Nate, I think. But then, I'm probably prejudiced. When they are finished with the set, they head to the back to prepare for one more. Nate takes my chin and guides my face towards his.

"Would you like to go home, now?" he asks. "I'm off for the night."

"Really?" I ask, my mood rising.

"Yep! I just wanted to make sure Carl was okay on his own before leaving." He smiles. "What do you think — is he okay on his own?"

I laugh. "Well, not quite as good as you," I say, "but, good enough, I suppose." Nate raises an eyebrow. "Okay, he's good enough," I laugh again. Nate motions for Jonas to bring the check, and I realize that Jonas has never told me the rest of what he wanted to. But, since it was all in the past, I guess that's okay. I can find out soon enough. Nate pays my bill, over my protests, but Jonas whispers in my ear that they all get a substantial discount for friends and relatives, so I should just shut up about it. So I shut up about it! It feels fun, anyway. Like a real date. We head out to the dark parking lot and are met with the sight of thousands of sparkling stars. The air is silky warm, so perfect that you don't even feel it until a breeze brushes over you. It is quiet except for the sounds of laughter escaping the restaurant and a chorus of crickets.

"Ahhhhh," I say, smiling in Nate's arms, because he has taken hold of me tightly, possessively. "Listen to those stars!"

"*Listen* to those stars?" he laughs.

"Yes!" I say in mocked seriousness. "Listen to those twinkling stars! Can't you hear them?" I frown at him.

The poor man just stands there in disbelief, so I laugh and give in to telling him the joke.

"When I was little, around three, I think, I used to lie out in my grandmother's yard on summer evenings and listen to the stars. I would eat blades of grass to make my eyes greener, watch for falling stars, and listen to the rest of them twinkle."

"Okay..." Nate says.

"Then, one day, my grandmother broke my heart."

"Okay..."

"She told me that I wasn't listening to the song of the beautiful stars. No. I was listening to the lowly crickets," I explain.

Most people laugh at this point, but Nate actually looks sad, and strokes my hair. "I'm sorry," he says, in all sincerity. No one has ever said that before, when I've told them the story.

"Thank you," I whisper.

"For what?" he whispers back.

"For understanding," I say simply. He tilts my head and kisses me lightly, at first. Then, with more hunger. Then he tightens his arms around me and kisses me until I think my toes are going to fall off. When he releases me I'm panting. I fan myself with my hand, trying to make light of how I feel. But Nate knows.

"Would you like to see *my* home, tonight?" he asks. I'm surprised, but strangely pleased.

"I would love that," I say. "However, I would like to stop by my place first — just to check on the kids, if that's okay."

"Of course it's okay," Nate says. "I'll follow you, then we can either drop off your car, or you can follow me to my house. Whichever you would prefer." I nod, smiling, glad that he has left that decision to me, without pressure. We head for our separate vehicles, and drive to my house. When we arrive, we go in and check on the kids. They are perfectly fine, grumpy, almost, at having been woken up to be "checked on". So I set the alarm, lock up, and as I had decided on the way home, I follow Nate to his house.

It's surprisingly far out. A couple miles further north than my house. It sits right in the middle of ten acres, and there isn't another house that is close enough to see at night. As our headlights sweep across the front area, I see a forest of palo verdes with a few mesquites mixed in. Close to the house there's a landscaped area that includes a fountain, two man-made watering holes, a small wrought iron table set, and copper torches. The entrance is decorated with huge pots sporting small yuccas, and smaller pots with a large variety of succulents. The house itself is very Spanish Territorial, and looks quite old, as though it was one of the original homes out here. Nate pulls into a double wide carport, and motions me to park beside him. Good sign! No one else must live here.

We get out of our vehicles and Nate takes my hand. He leads me to the front door, as there's no door from the carport. I'm glad. There's something very grand about being at the front door. He unlocks it and switches on a wall lamp inside. Then he swings the door open and gives a slight bow with a sweep of his hand, to usher me in. I step past the old, massive door into a wonderland of vigas, flagstone, and floor to ceiling, wood clad windows that stare off into the vacant desert. The stars shine through them, visible even with the small wall lamp glowing like candlelight. I walk through the sparsely furnished room to the huge windows and breathe in the sight. Nate turns out the lamp, then joins me, silent. We gaze upon the desert in the starlight, and a meteor streaks across the sky.

"Make a wish," Nate whispers. But he's too late. I've made my wish already. As if he knows that, Nate takes my hand and leads me to a long wide hall. He reaches into his pocket and flicks a lighter, which he then uses to ignite a huge candle resting in a niche in the wall. The hallway glows in the illumination. The walls are painted much the same color as my bedroom walls, the glow of love-light. The color of dawn, and the color of candlelight. He continues to lead me down the hall. We arrive at the last door on the right, and Nate stops and turns to me.

"Wait here," he whispers. Then he disappears inside. Soon the room is illuminated with candlelight from a votive resting on a mesquite wood table near the door. The candle isn't very bright but I catch my breath as I notice the deep brilliant blue of the walls. Around the light of the candle it is the bright, almost electric blue of sea water reflecting turquoise skies — sea water washing over shallow white sand. Tropical blue. In the corners away from the light, the blue is deeper. Darker. Sea water reflecting turquoise skies over great depth. Over great mystery. Nate moves to the other side of the room, and suddenly there is more light. Another votive, this one on a mesquite night table. The heavy, rustic table sits next to a huge four poster bed made of the same rustic mesquite as the night table. The posters rise seven feet into the air, the headboard swells gracefully in the middle to the same height. I feel dwarfed by the bed. It's an exciting feeling. Nate has now moved to a corner where he puts a small fountain into play. The water trickles soothingly over rocks and patinaed copper, splashing quietly into a slate basin. Then Nate lights a small stick of wood in a smudge bowl and the scent of juniper fills the air. The spicy aroma is intoxicating. Very sensual, very masculine. Nate turns on a CD, and music falls gently from the small speakers, filling the room with floating guitar music.

"You may come in, now," he says. I enter the large room, and feel the quiet power of it. The sturdiness. The steadiness. I am instantly in love with this room. As I stand just inside the door, unsure what to do, Nate comes to me, takes my hand and leads me to the middle of the large woven rug at the foot of the bed. It is done in the colors of deepest sunset, when the sky is still on fire, but the fire has turned to embers. A Native American flute has now joined the guitar, and the haunting tune wraps itself around me, igniting every cell with magic. I've barely noticed that Nate has already taken the clips out of my hair, which now falls around my shoulders and down my back. He runs his hands through it with focused appreciation, then lightly kisses my mouth. He takes my earrings out, then kisses me again. I smile. There could be a lot of kisses between now and "then". He turns and goes to a table against the wall opposite the bed and places the clips and earrings upon it, as though placing items on an altar. He then returns and leads me into a slow rumba. I think of Evie, and realize that I'm finally dancing in my shoes. As we dance Nate unzips my dress. As the first song finishes he slides the one shoulder off, and the dress immediately falls to the floor, due to the weight of the crystal dolphin. I step out of the dress and Nate picks it up and rests it carefully on a chair. He returns and deftly removes my bra, which he simply flings at the chair. I stifle a giggle, but Nate catches it and smiles broadly at me, giving a lazy wink. He grabs me, catching me completely by surprise, and lifts me to the bed where he deposits me with a mixture of gentleness and impatience.

The bed is tremendous. It's soft, but supportive. The sheets are cool, inviting. There is no blanket. The pillows are plush. And scented with the same juniper aroma that fills the room, although, underneath, I detect the faint scent of lavender. I succumb to the headiness of the atmosphere, and close my eyes. I feel Nate remove my shoes. When I reopen my eyes, he has already undressed, and stands beside me in complete beauty. The candlelight flickers and moves over the smooth planes of his body, and I find myself hoping, really hoping, that I am as beautiful as he is. He leans over me and slowly pulls my panties down and off. I feel a momentary flush of embarrassment, but Nate's eyes are moving over my body and his appreciation is apparent, so the embarrassment dissolves. He moves to the other side of the bed and scoots in beside me. As his hands move reverently over my skin, I realize that, after my initial flush of fear at seeing Don, I have felt perfectly safe. With Nate I feel safe. I hadn't even given Don a second thought until just now. And the thought now is just that—a thought. Not a feeling, not an obsession, not a loss of freedom. Just a thought. And I flash on my dream—the blue dream, with the net of music that supported me and made me safe.

This is it. This is the dream. This is the blue, and the golden candlelight, and the music falling from the beautiful guitar—which I now recognize as Nate's—and I float and swim in this sea of love and safety. Nate makes love to me, and it is absolutely wonderful. But he has already made love to my heart and soul. And that is even better.

As I fall asleep in his arms, the music has ended, but the water keeps trickling. The candles still burn, and the blue still occupies the depths of my mind. Soon I am swimming in warm water. The blue of the sea surrounds me, and the sun glows above, soft and yellow. As the water rushes past my ears it sounds like trickling. I am playing with the feel of the silky salt water. I swim fast, then slow, as the current I just created catches up with me and provides a caress. I laugh at the joy of it. I swim on, twisting and turning, until I rush to the surface for a breath. I leap high out of the water and chatter my welcome to the air. Then I splash down into the water again, and continue my play. Soon I'm swimming with another dolphin. He's a handsome male. He loves me, I can tell. But then soon after that, another male appears. He seems to love me, too. These two males are respectful, and join me with reservation and regard. Soon we are leaping from the water together, all three of us, classic Beings of love and light. Or, are we?

Suddenly I feel a bit of menace from one of them. Not toward me, toward the other male. Animosity? Why? Jealousy? No one has the right. We swim on together, circling the small bay. Our swimming becomes faster and faster, and I begin erratic movements trying to shake off my admirers, but they keep up with me, mirroring what I do like we are all one. As I leap out of the water this time, I spy the man at the shore's edge. He is tall and lean, his hair longish and blowing freely in the wind sweeping from the sea. He waves to me, and I feel a rush of love from him.

He loves me. The human man loves me. I become enthralled by this realization. I don't really love him back—I don't know him! But he is handsome. And he is human. I've been interested, lately, in this other race. They are quite a dichotomy. Intelligent, but incredibly stupid. Beautiful, yet incredibly ugly. A life of love and hate, sadness and joy, dark and light.

As I said, they are very interesting. I start to show off for him and the males with me attempt to steer me away. We become totally involved in this game of wits, of domination. Each time I leap from the water I see the man, his eyes shining with adoration. We are so enrapt in our game that all else falls away. All awareness diminishes except for the four of us.

Then, as I next leap out of the water, I see the man wave at me in desperation. His eyes are full of panic, his voice shouting. I leap again and see him waving in the direction to the north of the bay. I leap and turn my attention there only to see a vessel bearing down upon us. There's a man at the front, one boot resting up on the rim of the fast moving boat, a rifle in his hand. I scream to my two companions, but only one seems to hear me. I swim with all my might away from the impending doom, and dive.

What I don't see is the male, the one who heard my warning, open, then shut, his mouth. Right before he dived. Right before he left his companion—confused, unguarded, oblivious to the approaching danger—to die in the next instant at the hands of the man with the rifle.

And, as he swims from the danger, and from the blood of his friend spreading quickly through the once beautiful water, he realizes he will not be speaking again. Ever again, as far as he is concerned. He is ashamed, confused, lost. As he swims off, forever to leave the pod, he swims past three ancient sea turtles. They watch him with the knowledge of what he has just done. But they don't judge him. They feel compassion for what he is going through. They know he is only an actor in this game of life, and that we all must play our parts, even though it can bring the most distraught of endings.

They know that no one is suffering more than he.

We never see him again. And I always feel that, somehow, it is all my fault. Mine, and the man on the shore. The one who so distracted me. It is our fault.

I awaken in the first bare glow of dawn, quietly gather my clothes and move to another room to dress. I find a pad of paper in the glorious kitchen, which I hadn't had the pleasure of seeing last night, and draw just one big heart on the top paper. I leave it on the countertop and quietly slip out the front door, closing it as softly as I can. I pull out of the carport, head down the long drive, and wind my way, hopefully, back home.

I arrive about seven minutes later, and find everything safe and well. Except that half the lower kitchen cabinets are opened, and Rico and Bonnie are sitting on the floor with concerned looks on their faces.

"Hey," I tell them. "I'm not that late!"

They give me a pouty look that says, "How were we to know if you'd come home at all?"

"Oh, come on!" I say. "You guys don't believe for a second that I wouldn't be here to take care of breakfast. Or, if I wasn't, then Christian would be." I bring out a can of food and begin the process of dishing it out. "Besides, you have to know that your food is in the top cupboards, not the bottom," I finish, with a large degree of smugness.

But then, I swear, I do believe I hear Rico snicker. Or maybe it was just a slurp as he goes to town on his meal. In any case, I realize I'm just the victim of cat humor.

I head down the hall to my bedroom and strip off the dress I had only put on a short time earlier. I step into the shower and, almost reluctantly, wash — sending all physical traces of last night down the drain. I cleanse and condition my hair, then end with a good scrub. I towel off, lotion up, dry my hair haphazardly, apply a bit of gloss, then select a white pair of jeans and an ocean blue tee shirt. I add pearl earrings and shelled sandals. No reason, really. I'm not going anywhere. I just feel like it.

Then I remember the dream. All of it. And I realize the reason for Michael's cruel, smug lines. He is hurting. And Peter, who has lost his voice. Did he ever have it, this life, I wonder? Was he born mute? I feel much compassion for both of them.

I eat a light breakfast of cherries, berries, and toast, then head to the studio. When I confront the trio of paintings, we all have tears on our cheeks. Tears rise to my own eyes.

"Everything will be okay," I whisper to the three of us. "It will all work out. Trust me," I say with a confidence I do not possess. I leave us still in a triangle, still confronting, still working it out. Because, after all, it isn't over, yet.

Of that, I am sure.

I spend the day in mundane tasks such as laundry and shopping. I tidy the house, rearrange the pantry, dust and mop the floors, polish the countertops, then sit to think about dinner. As I realize I'm a bit bummed that Nate hasn't called, the phone rings. I recognize his number and answer with more anticipation than I care to admit.

"Hello!"

"Hi, beautiful," Nate's voice silks through the receiver. I tingle at the feel of it.

"Hi, beautiful, yourself," I sweet talk back to him. He laughs.

"As long as you mean that in the right way, thank you," he chuckles.

"Oh, I mean it in the right way," I assure him. Strength and power can be very beautiful — as long as it's wielded with love. Nate is the perfect experience of that.

"So," he begins. "I was wondering if you would like to get together tonight," he says.

"Tonight? Really?" I ask. "I thought you had to work — or, do you mean after your gig?"

"No," he answers. "I mean all night. Carl has agreed to cover the show tonight. He's still jazzed by his success last night, and wants a little more limelight time. So, I'm free if you are," he finishes.

"Yes!" I practically shout. "I'd love to see you tonight! How about you come over around six-thirty or seven, and I'll feed you something wonderful."

"Is that bragging I hear?" Nate teases.

"Maybe," I reply. "Or, maybe it's just delusion," I finish.

"Either way, sweetheart," Nate chuckles, "I don't care. A fabulous dinner would be terrific—don't get me wrong! But it's you that I want," he explains. "I just want to be with you. And I mean, just be with you. To talk, to cuddle—to eat spectacular food." He pauses. "And, you know, if anything else comes up, that's good too."

"Okay, Romeo," I tell him. "See you in a few."

We disconnect and I set about designing dinner. As I'm moving through the kitchen I glance out the window and notice that the wall of thunderheads that had started forming earlier are clearly marching this way. And rather quickly, too. I do suspect that we are in for a storm tonight. One hell of a one, if the size of those thunderheads are any indication. Just then the wind picks up, and I begin the process of dinner preparation.

Chapter 20

Nate arrives at six forty-five, carrying two bottles of wine, one red and one white. I have prepared salmon, so I open the white. He pushes himself up to sit on the countertop near where I'm finishing the last of the salad prep.

"I missed you this morning," he says.

"I woke up early, and thought I should get back to the kids."

"I understand. Still, you didn't even put coffee on, or anything," he tells me, seriousness written across his brow. I slug him on his arm and he grins. "I could get used to that, you know."

"What? Getting slugged on the arm?"

"No," he chuckles. "Actually, you have quite punch!" I shake my head as I place the last of the tomatoes. "What I meant was, I could get used to you being with me. Waking up with you. Although I didn't exactly do that this morning, did I?" I laugh. "Maybe I was just too exhausted from all the hard work I had to do last night." Now it's my turn to act serious.

"Excuse me? You call last night 'hard work'?"

"Well, it was! You wouldn't let me stop! You are such a slave driver, I can't believe it!"

"Ahh. So, you're my slave, are you?"

At that Nate jumps off the countertop and grabs me for a kiss. "You bet," he says, when he finally lets me go. "I am definitely your slave. Your willing slave, I might add."

"Well then," I say. "Put these salad bowls on the table while I check the pilaf." Nate bows with a flourish, and as I go to punch him again he agilely steps aside, grinning.

I check the pilaf and all looks well, so we sit and enjoy the salads.

"Great spinach," Nate says. "And these tomatoes! Delicious."

"All from my neighbor, Beth," I say. And I notice that we're both talking with our mouth full. I like that. It means we're already that comfortable with one another.

"She can grow spinach this time of year?" he asks, amazed.

"Well, she does use a special strain that is heat tolerant," I explain. "But by the way you asked the question, I guess you realize how difficult it is to grow summer spinach here."

"I've never been any good at it," Nate confesses.

"You like to grow veggies?" I ask, loving the sound of that.

"Yep," he answers. "But I usually do a winter crop."

"Well, Beth has an advantage that most of us don't. She has greenhouses that she cools with swamp coolers."

"Ahhh! She must live down the road from here! That big house that's surrounded with all those greenhouses!"

"That's her. Good stuff, huh."

"Can anyone stop by and buy from her?"

"I believe so," I tell him. "She also sells at the Carefree Farmers Market on Friday mornings. I'll call her, though, and give a formal introduction. You know — that way you'll get special treatment."

"Fantastic," Nate says, finishing his salad. Just then there's a crack of thunder that sends both of us an inch off our chairs.

"Wow! That was close!" I say, calming my heart. "I hadn't realized that the storm had moved in so fast."

"Guess I was distracting you."

I smile at my distraction. "I guess you were," I answer, honestly. I rise and take both bowls and place them on the counter. Nate rises and looks out the window.

"Do we have time to take our wine out and watch a few minutes?" he asks.

"I don't see why not," I answer, grabbing the glasses and handing his to him. We step out onto the patio and the wind has cooled considerably. The sky is dark and angry above us, swollen with the weight of water. A few drops hit the pool and I excuse myself, handing my glass to Nate, and go to close the pool cover.

"Nice touch," he says. "An electric pool cover. I wish I had one."

"Well, sell some more of that wonderful CD you played last night, and you'll soon have the dough to get one," I tell him.

"Actually, I haven't sold any of that CD," he says.

"Why not?" I ask, surprised.

"I don't know. Haven't even tried. There's just the one copy."

"You're kidding!"

"No. I'm not."

"Well, it's absolutely beautiful!" I tell him. "You should reproduce it and get it on the market!" He just shrugs. "I'm serious," I tell him. "I bet it would be very successful."

"Really?" he asks, doubtfully

"Yes! Really! I can't believe you even have to ask that. It's really, really, good, Nate."

"Okay, then. Guess I'll try to market it."

"No try. Do." I scold him.

"I guess I'll market it."

"No guess — do."

"I'll market it — and sell a billion, trillion copies."

"That's the spirit," I say, as lightning bursts above us, followed in a split second by another crack of thunder. We stand our ground, and within thirty seconds the sky opens and begins the torrential dump of monsoon rain. In less than ten seconds we are thoroughly soaked, yet neither of us moves a muscle, except to cover our wine glasses with a hand. I look to Nate, who is staring at me with an intensity that sends shudders up my spine. As rain runs down my face, making me gratefully aware that tonight I did forego mascara, he reaches over and strokes my wet cheek. I grab him behind his neck and pull his face down to mine. I kiss him hard — very hard. Then after taking his breath away, I say that, perhaps, we should go in now. He smiles a small little smile and holds his hand out. I take it and we slosh back into the kitchen, slipping off our sandals by the door. As we drip into huge puddles, forming where we stand, I tell him to strip.

"Excuse me?" he says. "Strip?"

"Yes," I scold. "Take your clothes off."

"We're going to eat au naturel?"

"You'll see," I say, taking off to the bedroom.

When I get there I remove my own clothes and slip into a dry rayon dress, and a dry pair of panties. Then I grab the bag off the bed that contains the swim trunks I bought for him today while out shopping. I head back to the kitchen to find him butt naked, and beautiful in the waning light.

"Here," I say, smiling as I hand over the trunks.

"You bought me swim trunks?" he asks, incredulous.

"Sure. Why not?" I ask.

"I don't know," he answers. "It's just really nice of you," he says with a shrug. He steps into them and ties the little cord thing, cinching it around his waist. I admit, he looks sexier in jeans, but he looks good even in these silly, baggy swim trunks that are the style today.

"There, now you can be dry and comfortable."

He pulls me close and gives me a light kiss. "Thank you," he says, "seriously."

"It's no big deal," I tell him, amazed that he's apparently so touched by my gesture. "They weren't expensive," I add.

"I don't care about the expense. I care that you care. Thank you. I mean it."

"My pleasure," I tell him. "And I mean it." We look at each other for several moments, the love growing between us even as we stand there. I feel my heart opening, aching a bit. Stretching to include this wonderful man I've found. "Let's eat dinner," I say, to break the hold of the moment. Nate nods, and sits at the little wrought iron table as I make him a plate, then place it in front of him.

"Wow. It's looks terrific," he says.

"Thanks. Hopefully it will taste as good as it looks."

Nate waits for me to sit then shovels in a forkful. "Mmmmmmm," is all he says. I smile and shovel in my own forkful. He's right. It is mmmmm. We eat in silence, savoring, enjoying, me giving my gratitude to the fish and the rice and all the herbs, spices, people, and God, who worked to bring this delicious meal to me. I keep this to myself, though I suspect Nate wouldn't think it as weird as some people do. We sip our wine, finish our meal, and listen to the pounding rain. The room grows dark so I turn on one light, dimming it to barely there. It is enough.

I sit back down and bask in the wonder of it all. The beauty of the rain, the wine—the man sitting across from me. I feel a glow, an aliveness that has been missing all my life. I feel complete, happy, as though all the puzzle pieces have fallen into place.

What I don't know at that moment—at that moment that everything seems so wonderful, so right—is that, in seconds, my life will never be the same again. It will be good—wonderful, even. But it will never be the same.

The phone rings.

I let it ring.

It stops.

I smile at Nate, and raise my glass. We clink, in silence, no toast being necessary.

The phone rings again.

I let it.

It stops, but I'm a bit disconcerted.

My cell phone rings. I can barely hear it in the front room, tucked away in my purse, and if it had been my heavy hobo purse, I would never have heard it at all.

"Get it," is all Nate says. So I hurry to the front room and dig it out just before it would have gone to voice mail.

"Hello?" I ask, because I didn't have time to check caller ID.

"Alli!" I hear Jazzie's relieved voice. "I'm so glad I got hold of you." My heart grows cold.

"What's the matter?" I ask. "Is something wrong?"

"Don's on his way over to your house," she tells me, without preamble. "He's after the portrait again. Wrong painting, of course, but he doesn't know that."

"How did he find out we have the portrait?" I practically scream. "I thought he thought it was destroyed!" By now Nate has wandered in to the front room, so I wave him back to the kitchen, where I follow, and throw myself into the chair.

"I believe it was Debra who alerted him," she says, voice dripping with acid.

"Debra? Shit! I had an awful feeling she wouldn't let this drop. She knew Sadie was Don's dog," I spit. "She knew, and she told the bastard."

"That's how I see it," Jazzie replies. "When Don realized that Karla hadn't done Sadie in, and that we had her, he probably figured we had the painting, too."

"Damn! God, I hope Karla's all right," I say.

"She's fine," Jazzie answers. "Pissed, but fine. I checked in on her."

"Thank God," I say. "But how do you know that Don's coming over?"

"Sadie told me," was all she says in answer. "I'll be right over to help. But for now, I'd say you get to that portrait and hide it best you can." And at that, the line goes dead.

I quickly fill Nate in as we trot to the studio. I push the easels apart and grab both Michael's and Peter's portrait. I scan the room quickly, but don't see any place that could actually hide something that someone was going to search for. I consider all that's at stake, about what Don might be capable of, and about what might happen if the portraits were to be destroyed — and I panic.

"The pool cover," Nate says.

"What?"

"We'll tape them to the underside of the pool cover."

"That's brilliant," I tell him. "Even if they get wet I can remove them from their mounts, and have them redone. The portraits themselves should be fine."

I hand the paintings to Nate and run for the duct tape. We run out to the pool and as I move the cover back a few feet Nate jumps in. Amazing how I thought to buy trunks for him today. It seemed a bit off the wall when I thought of it — but, something said it was just the right thing to do. Not that a lack of trunks would have stood in the way. It's just a point of serendipity I think. I hand Nate the tape and he blindly tapes Michael's portrait to the underside of the cover. He reaches and I hand him Peter's painting, which he tapes next to Michael's.

He jumps out and I quickly close the cover.

It had stopped raining as we came out to hide the portraits, but now the rain starts up again. Nate gives me a knowing look, and we beat it back inside.

"May I use the towel in your bathroom to dry off?" he asks.

"Help yourself," I answer. Running to the front to set the alarm, I notice Rico and Bonita watching me intently. They seem extremely interested, but calm, as though they know what's going on, but are only here for the show. I blow them a quick kiss.

"Please stay out of the way, should it get nasty," I admonish. They smile and blink slowly. "I love you, too," I tell them. But, in my heart, I also know that they will probably not stay out of the way. Especially Rico. He will be a pacifist, but he will also be in the middle of it.

Shit.

As I trot back to the bedroom I strip off my wet dress and reach for yet the third thing I will wear tonight.

Something tells me to put on the dolphin dress. I hesitate. "It seems rather fancy, don't you think?" I say out loud, to no one in particular.

"Excuse me?" Nate says from the bath.

"Nothing," I answer, and I put on the dolphin dress.

Nate comes out of the bath and looks at me with a raised eyebrow. "Don't ask," I tell him. "It's just a hunch," I add, and trot out of the bedroom, leaving him to stand and wonder. I return to the studio and find two other paintings to set upon the empty easels. I arrange them, then decide to stick the painting of myself in the closet. I grab Nate's eyes, and put them in its place. I turn the easels this way and that, trying to make it look as natural as possible. Not like I had just thrown them together to hide something. Satisfied, I turn out the studio light and return to the kitchen, where I find Nate sitting with his wine, looking as cool and calm as possible. I plop in the chair opposite and just stare at him.

"I love you," he says, and I find that very comforting. After all, it seems I've done very little except drag Nate into the middle of things that are none of his concern.

The doorbell rings. We sit, unsure.

"It could be Jazzie," I say, but I don't really believe it. It usually takes her longer to get here—unless she called me on her cell phone. I remember now that I hadn't seen the number. I grab the phone and check the CID. She called from home. It isn't her.

Suddenly there's an explosion of pounding on the door, and I jump in my seat. I hear Don's voice through the beating of the door and the beating of the rain. He's yelling at me to open the door, or he'll break a window. I hesitate, knowing that if he broke a window it would alert the alarm company, and they would call the police. But I paid a lot for those windows, and the one in front is particularly large and expensive. And I have this wonderful, strong man here, dressed in ridiculous swim trunks with large tropical flowers on them, and — oh, crap.

"What do you think?" I ask Nate.

"I think we should open the door," he answers, lips tight, jaw set, eyes blazing.

"Okay," I say. I move to the front, and, on impulse, disable the alarm with the silent "call-for-help" code. I swing open the door and Don pushes in past me, furious.

"Where is it, bitch," he says.

"Where is what, bastard?" I counter.

"You know what," he replies, already charging toward the studio. "And tell that creep of a boyfriend of yours to stay out of my way," he calls over his shoulder as I run behind him.

He slams the light on and surveys the room. He moves to the stack of paintings in the corner and rifles through them, flinging them back against the wall when he doesn't find the portrait. He glares at me for a second then moves to the closet. He spends a few seconds in there, realizing quickly that what he seeks is not in there. He grabs me by the shoulders and screams at me.

"Where is it?! Where the fuck is it?!"

A hand rips Don's hands from me, and a voice growls with a ferocity I'd never heard from that throat, "Keep your hands off her, bastard, or I will kill you." I move to Nate, thankful for his protection. Now, when I consider the two of them, I realize that they may be evenly matched. Nate is definitely younger and stronger, but Don has several pounds on him. And, for his age, although he has let himself go to a degree, he is still in better shape than most.

That thought does not comfort me.

Don pushes past both of us and heads to my bedroom, stomping through the hall like he owns the place. I view Rico and Bonita still perched on the front room table, calmly watching the events as though they mean nothing but good entertainment.

What is it about those two? Are they nuts?

I rush down the hall, Nate behind me, to find Don tearing my room apart. At this point I understand that I might as well let him. The cops will soon be here, and I don't want anyone to get hurt for nothing. There's nothing he can break, or ruin, that can't be replaced. Nothing except Nate, the kids, and I. We might as well just stay out of the way.

I turn to Nate and take his hand, pulling him from the room. He shakes his head and gives me a questioning look. I just nod, shrug, and walk on back to the kitchen without him. He follows a few seconds later. We stand in the dim light and Nate takes me into his arms, rocking me slightly.

"I'm sorry," he says.

"Me too," I answer. "I'm sorry for both of us," I tell him, into his chest. "I'm sorry for me, and I'm sorry for you, and I'm also sorry for Michael and Peter."

"Why are you sorry for us?" I hear, and jerk away from Nate, to find the twins standing in the kitchen.

"My god!" I say. "How did you get in here?"

"The front door is wide open," Michael answers. Crap, that's right.

"Okay, but what are you doing here?"

"My portrait is finished," Michael answers. "Isn't it?"

"Actually," I start, "it is. But there's a problem at this moment."

"A problem?"

Just then Don bellows, half scream, half demand, "Where the hell is that goddam painting, you cunt? WHERE IS IT?!" I turn back to Michael.

"Yes. A problem."

"I see," he answers, coolly.

Just then Don charges into the kitchen, but pulls up short when he sees Michael and Peter. He looks shocked for a second, to see them together, I imagine, and I wonder if he can even tell them apart. He recovers quickly, however, and faces Michael, unerringly.

"Hello, Michael," he says calmly.

"Hello, Don," Michael answers. "What's up?" he asks him, simply, quietly.

"Oh, there's been a development—a glitch, actually—that I'm trying to remedy."

"A glitch? In what?" Michael asks coolly.

"In our partnership, you asshole," Don sneers. "In our little plan to snag our piece of the pie."

"And what is the glitch?" Michael asks, simply.

Don grabs him by the shirt collar and jerks him. "The glitch is, my partner has turned pansy on me," Don snarls. "He's turned coat and run. He's left me without the help he promised me." Don releases Michael's collar and gives him a shove backward. "He's turned into someone I don't recognize, nor do I want to."

Michael adjusts his shirt with a couple of shrugs, and stares evenly at Don. "What we were doing was wrong," he says.

"I don't fucking care!" Don screams at him. "I don't fucking, fucking care! Jeez, man! What the hell happened to you?!" Don has started pacing, pulling at his hair. I've never seen him so agitated, and it scares the shit out of me. I look to Michael and he is still cool as a cucumber. Don suddenly stops pacing and glares at Michael again.

"You are such a frigging idiot," he tells him. "You just had to go and commission a portrait from Alli," he says, almost sadly. He runs his hands through his hair, standing it up on end. He looks on the point of breaking, his eyes glazing over. I can see it even in this light. Suddenly I'm aware of Bonnie and Rico in the room. They are sitting side by side, calmly watching the horrid scene playing out in front of them. Still calm. Still just there for the show.

What I don't see is Jazzie and Sadie, standing in the shadow just outside of the kitchen.

Don resumes pacing, mumbling to himself. He starts to talk to himself as though he is an interested third party.

"What do you think I should do? Huh? What do you think?" He paces and paces, around and around in his corner. He goes and leans on the countertop a moment, surveying the faces in front of him. He pulls at his hair again, and Michael turns to leave. He's taken three steps when out of the corner of my eye I see Don reach into his pocket. Everything goes into slow motion. I see Don slowly pulling a revolver out—first I see the butt, then I see the barrel. I see Don's arm start to raise, slowly, slowly, taking aim at Michael who is oblivious to what's happening. He is slowly, slowly striding away, head high, the swing in his arms confident, final. Then I hear the voice—the voice. It's Peter.

"Michael!" the voice calls, in slow motion. "Watch out!" Michael turns as Don starts to squeeze the trigger, but there is a black blur, and in an instant it is upon Don. In an instant Don is falling under the weight of the mighty Sadie, arms flailing. In an instant Don's head hits the edge of the countertop as he falls hard, the whack sending his head off at an odd angle to his shoulders. And as he falls to the floor, the gun goes off.

And I fall to the floor, the dolphin on my shoulder in pieces, which fall to the floor with me. I sit, dazed, my hand to my shoulder which is now being covered in blood. Slowly I see Nate, Peter, and Michael racing to me. Slowly I see Don try to get up, crawl a few feet, and collapse in a heap in the middle of the kitchen floor, blood spreading out around him.

The last thing I remember thinking is, "The bastard. He's going to ruin my grout."

Then I pass out.

When I come to I am standing in an amazing crystal room which glows of light that seems not of this world. It has no point of origin. It just is. As I watch, the light changes colors, slowly pulsing from all the choices of the rainbow. I feel total peace. A Being enters from somewhere and, smiling broadly, approaches me. He appears male, but he is glowing, angelic.

"Hello, Alli," he says warmly, taking my hands into his. The love I feel in his hands surges through me, and I feel wonderful. I take my gaze from my hands and I turn it to the face of the angelic being in front of me. He looks vaguely familiar. Then I realize it's Don.

"Hello, Don," I reply, amazed that I feel no animosity for him. On the contrary, I feel at complete ease.

"That was quite a show we put on, wasn't it?"

"Yes," I answer, though I'm not sure why.

"Peter has found his voice," Don continues.

"Yes."

"And Michael has found his peace."

"Yes."

"Would you like to know the whole story?" he asks.

"Yes," I say. "Yes, I would." He leads me to a golden bench, and I sit down next to him. He takes the hand nearest him and holds it tenderly.

"I am the man in the painting," he tells me. "The man in the dolphin painting, the one on shore."

"Oh."

"I am the man who loved you, my dolphin queen." I blush and lower my gaze. He takes his fingers and gently lifts my chin. "I did love you, too. I always have — for as many lifetimes as I have known you. In whatever forms we took." I blink at him several times, and he smiles. "I want you to know that this was the hardest life I've ever lived," he states.

"Why?" I ask, curious.

"Because I had to hurt you, in order to play my part."

"Oh."

"I also want you to know that I would do it again. I would do whatever I had to do, be whoever I had to be, or suffer whatever I had to suffer to help you reach your goals, your purpose."

I swallow the sob which rises to my throat, in remembering our life together.

"Why did you hurt things? Kill things?" I ask him.

"It set the stage for what you needed, Alli. For what Peter and Michael needed. But I will tell you, no one and nothing ever suffered without their consent, from anything I did. They were all part of it, for you — along with for themselves. And their angels were always there, to keep them from unnecessary pain. Everything still lives on — exalted, even, for their gifts to you this life."

"I see." Then I remember Michael confronting Don about the young girl he hit. I ask him about her.

"When Francis shot Michael —" he begins.

"Who is Francis?"

"Well, Francis is the man who shot Michael when he was a dolphin, and Frances is also the woman Michael was married to. It was why she put up with his abuse. She knew, or I should say her higher self knew, that she was part of the cause of Michael's problems. She very much regrets what she did that day, to Michael the dolphin, and wanted to experience the other shoe, so to speak."

"I see."

"However, when Francis went out to shoot a dolphin, he did so because another man put him up to it. This other man inferred he was having an affair with Francis's wife, even though it wasn't true. But he knew the belief would drive Francis crazy. He goaded Francis, and told him he was a pansy, and that he doubted he was even man enough to kill a dolphin. He used that particular taunt because he knew how much Francis's wife loved dolphins, and he was angry with her for her rejection. The little girl I slapped—she was that man. The man who goaded Francis into it." I nod. "And Michael's stepdaughter, she was the one who manned the boat that enabled Francis to kill Michael."

Tears come to my eyes. Don wraps his arms around me and gives me a squeeze.

"I never saw you again, that life. After that day." I look up at him and I feel his sorrow. "You and the rest of the pod disappeared from our bay, and we never saw any of you again." I lay my head on his chest, sad to my depths. "The village was never the same, either. Something died that day. In a few years the town itself was dead. Today you would never even know it had been there, if you were to visit the bay." I nod, feeling the truth of it.

Don strokes my hair, gently, like I'm a small child. Which is pretty much how I feel at the moment.

"There's something else you should know," he continues. "There was someone else who loved you, probably as much as I."

"Who?" I ask, my head still on his chest.

"My brother. The man you now call Nate."

I raise my head and consider this Being before me. "Nate was your brother?"

"Yes. And a fine man he was," Don continues. "Charitable, loving, musical..."

"Did he play the guitar?" I ask.

"No. He played the flute," Don answers. I nod. That seems right. Don smoothes the hair from my face and looks me deep in my eyes. "Stay with him, Alli," he says. "He's the one you're meant to be with this life. He was the last one to leave our doomed little village, you know. Because he was sure you would come back. He was so sure you would come back, and he couldn't stand the thought of missing it."

I consider this a moment, then decide. "I didn't go back," I say, feeling it to be true. "My heart was too broken. I didn't go back."

"I would guess not. You were all so betrayed that day. We had always loved you, honored you. Why would any of you *ever* believe we could have betrayed you that way?" Tears start in my eyes again, and Don wipes them with a gentle finger.

"One last thing you must know, my love," he says. My heart breaks at the feeling I'm getting from him. I'm about to lose some-thing — something precious. I feel it. And I'm scared.

"What?" I ask quietly, dreading.

"Jazzie is not just your best friend."

I look at him, confused.

"She's your guardian angel, my love. She's your angel. Always has been, and always will be." At that Don rises from the bench and helps me up, also. "Time for you to go," he states simply. "And, time for me to go." He squeezes my hands gently. "I love you, Alli," he says with a smile. "Until next time...."

He turns and disappears into the violet mist, and a part of my heart goes with him. I close my eyes against the tears. I keep my eyes closed until the pain has turned to acceptance, and the tears have dried in the truth. Then I open them.

When I do, I'm in a hospital room, and Nate's loving face is mere inches from mine.

"Welcome back, my love," he says. And the relief in his eyes draws tears quickly back into mine.

"Thank you," I say.

"For what?"

"For loving me," I tell him. "For always loving me."

Epilogue

I was released from the hospital the following morning, and reunited with Rico and Bonnie, who, I must admit, warmed my heart with their enthusiastic purrs and tail hugs.

My grout had been replaced.

Nate had moved some of his things in, setting himself up as nurse and caretaker. He told me that Carl was taking his place at Roberto's, at least for now. He also said that, in his despair at the thought I might not return to him, from wherever I was for the day I wouldn't awaken, he had made a promise to me—one that he had already begun to move on. And that was to make a go of his CD—with many more to follow, of course.

My first day home I learned that the police had shown up seconds after I blanked, and that everyone had been questioned. Since Don was the only one with a gun, however, the account of what had transpired was taken at face value, and all were released without further trouble. The only question, as far as everyone was concerned, was why Don had taken his sudden, fatal fall? The one that caused the killing wound on his head. I thought that a bit weird, because it obviously had been Sadie's doing—but I was still on pain meds, so I didn't argue at the time.

I learned Michael and Peter were fully reconciled, happy to be true brothers, apparently for the first time in their lives. Peter had used his new found voice to apologize to Michael about the affair with his then wife, Frances, and Michael had forgiven him—thinking that, for some reason, it was easier to do than he had thought it would be.

On this second day of being home I'm feeling exceedingly better. The wound on my shoulder is not really that severe. The crystal dolphin had deflected most of the bullet's damage, and I am already healing at a rapid rate. I was warned that a few small pieces of crystal might still be imbedded, forever, in my shoulder, and I laughed at the thought. What better shrapnel than beautiful, natural, powerful crystals?

Being antsy I tell Nate I need to go out for a while—to visit Jazzie. He gives me a small questioning look, then says okay. We load ourselves into Ms. Sebring and Nate asks me for directions. I laugh and say, oh you know where—jeez. He tells me to humor him, so I roll my eyes, but give him directions. He smiles and starts the car.

We arrive at Jazzie's, and somehow the house looks a little different. I think maybe it's the pain meds, which I'm still taking. Nate helps me out of the car and assists me to the front walk, but since I seem to be doing okay he lets go, and returns to wait by the car. I ring the bell, and several seconds later the door swings open. A petite brunette with twinkling blue eyes the color of the sea, stands where I expect Jazzie.

"Oh," I say, momentarily caught off guard. "Is Jazzie home?" She looks at me quizzically.

"Jazzie?"

"The woman who lives here," I say, dread rising in my chest.

"I'm sorry," she answers. "I'm the woman who lives here. You must have the wrong address." Her eyes are kind, and concerned, as she views my sling, and the bandages bulging under my tee shirt.

I am taken aback, but the light has begun to dawn.

"How long have you lived here?" I ask, as friendly and noncommittally as I can manage.

"Oh, let's see," she thinks a moment. "Around five years or so."

"I see," I manage, with a choke.

"I bought the house from the estate of an Alan Solzberg," she explains. "He had no immediate heirs, just some distant family in New York. I got a really good deal on it," she adds. "It's quite a beautiful home. Surprising that he had no one to share it with, a home of this size and grace." I smile, knowing how untrue that was. He'd had a home filled with some of the highest love of all. An angel's love. He'd shared this home with an angel. I now know my final encounter with Don was real. It wasn't a dream. And Jazzie was truly an angel.

"Wait a moment," Emma says. "I'll grab one of my cards. I'd love to have you over some time. We can talk more then," she calls over her shoulder as she grabs her purse in the foyer. When she returns she hands me a card that reads *Emma Foley, Animal Communicator and Intuitive.* Her phone number and address are across the bottom. "I would talk now, but I have an appointment soon. I hope you understand."

"Of course I understand," I tell her. "Well, I'll be going," I add, my emotions in turmoil. Just then a bouncing being of joy and energy shows up at the door, tail wagging, tongue lolling—and without a hint of a broken leg. I almost call out Sadie's name, but stop myself just in time.

"What a gorgeous dog!" I tell Emma.

"Yes, isn't she?" Emma fondly scratches behind her ears as Sadie fixes her loving, knowing eyes on me, still smiling her silly broad grin. "It was the strangest thing," Emma continues. "Three days ago I was out plucking the newspaper from the walk when she appeared, seemingly from nowhere! I hadn't seen her coming up the sidewalk when I came out, and she is a rather large dog. But all of a sudden, there she was! It seemed as though she was listening to someone—she was so focused. But then she just whipped her head in my direction, and bounded right up to me, plopping her butt down and staring up at me. I looked all around, and as far as I could see up and down the street, but no one was in sight. So I knelt and read her tags." Emma's eyes tear up, and she stifles a small sob. "They said 'My name is Sadie, and I now belong to you, Emma.'"

Emma looks at me with wonder. "Isn't that something?" she asks simply.

I reach out and touch her shoulder. "Yes, that is really something."

"And I've tried several times, in the past three days, to get her to tell me her story—but she's not talking," Emma says with a sigh. Sadie grins and gives me a sly wink. I return her smile.

"Maybe, someday, she'll share with you," I offer.

"Maybe," Emma whispers, with a slight nod.

I hesitate a moment then say, "Well I best be going," and I turn to leave.

"Oh, wait!" Emma cries. "I'm getting something from Sadie." She closes her eyes, listening, then nods. "She says to tell you that she, and two magnificent cats that you know, spent a wonderful life together as sea turtles." Emma hesitates. "Does that mean anything to you?" I smile broadly.

"Yes," I answer. "Indeed it does. Hope to see you soon, Emma."

"I look forward to it," Emma says, smiling. Sadie gives a small woof, then scrambles back inside as Emma closes the door.

I stand a moment on the walkway, touched. And saddened. Sad that I might never again see Jazzie in this dimension. Sad to lose the most beautiful friend a woman could have. And so very, *very* sad that no one but I will even know she's gone.

I return to the car, and allow Nate to help me in. He trots to the driver's side and slides in behind the wheel. He takes my hand, concern in his eyes at the expression on my face.

"Everything okay?" he asks. I turn to meet his eyes.

What I'm thinking is, the road to enlightenment is bittersweet indeed.

"Let's go home. There's much I need to think about," is all I say.

A Final Note from Jazzie

Please know, we are always with you, we guardian angels.
You are our joy, our purpose, and our pleasure.
We can never leave you, nor would we ever wish to.
And no matter from which dimension we work, you are
protected and cared for.
All you need to do is ask — ask anything — and we will assist you
with all the power of Heaven.
Also know, we love you. Deeply and unconditionally.

You are so very, *very* loved.

About the Author

Sharon Teresa is a rebel and a dissenter, as evidenced by her firm refusal to honor grammatically correct usage of quotation mark, comma, and period dynamics. (She apologizes for any distress this may have caused English Majors and proof-reader types.)

She lives in Arizona with her patient, long-suffering husband, and two beautiful, if bossy, cats.

She spends her time writing, reading, painting, swimming, floating, gardening, pretending to take care of her family — and dreaming of a better world.

Please visit her website at SharonTeresa.com.